PATRIOTS—VOLUME II
REBEL GUNS

DANIEL REED—After Lexington and Concord the British have marked the young Virginia aristocrat as an insurrectionist, forcing him to flee from Boston, and into trouble. That trouble is a prickly Tory beauty named Cordelia who's not only in terrible danger . . . but is dangerous to Daniel's heart.

ROXANNE DARRAGH—The fire in her lovely eyes is fueled by patriotism, and by Daniel Reed. As one of America's first spies, she's flirting with death to stop a British shipment of guns . . . but will she end up sleeping with the enemy?

ELLIOT MARKHAM—Heir to a Boston shipping empire, he's supposed to be a Tory sympathizer. Only Roxanne knows he's a Revolutionary spy who is having dinner with the British—and passing her secrets for dessert.

CORDELIA FAULKNER—This spoiled blonde is running away from a marriage made in hell, and straight into Daniel Reed's arms. Her ruthless husband wants her dead, and Daniel will be torn between fighting for his country . . . or for her life.

ETHAN ALLEN—A daring woodsman who leads the famous Green Mountain Boys, he's come out of the Vermont hills to strike at the British stronghold of Fort Ticonderoga with a courage that is a clarion call to freedom.

PATRIOTS by Adam Rutledge
Ask your bookseller for the books you have missed

SONS OF LIBERTY
REBEL GUNS

PATRIOTS — *Volume II*

REBEL GUNS

Adam Rutledge

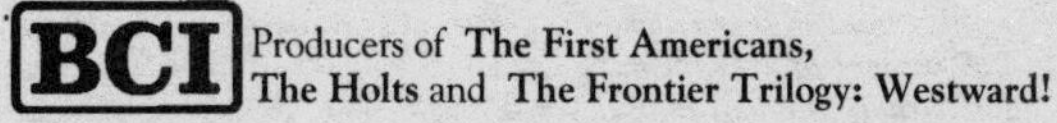

Producers of The First Americans, The Holts and The Frontier Trilogy: Westward!

Book Creations Inc., Canaan, NY • Lyle Kenyon Engel, Founder

BANTAM BOOKS

NEW YORK • TORONTO • LONDON • SYDNEY • AUCKLAND

REBEL GUNS

A Bantam Domain Book / published by arrangement with Book Creations Inc.

Bantam edition / October 1992

Produced by Book Creations Inc.
Lyle Kenyon Engel, Founder

DOMAIN and the portrayal of a boxed "d" are trademarks of Bantam Books, a division of Bantam Doubleday Dell Publishing Group, Inc.

ISBN 0-553-29200-5

Published simultaneously in the United States and Canada

Bantam Books are published by Bantam Books, a division of Bantam Doubleday Dell Publishing Group, Inc. Its trademark, consisting of the words "Bantam Books" and the portrayal of a rooster, is Registered in U.S. Patent and Trademark Office and in other countries. Marca Registrada. Bantam Books, 666 Fifth Avenue, New York, New York 10103.

PRINTED IN THE UNITED STATES OF AMERICA

OPM 0 9 8 7 6 5 4 3 2 1

REBEL GUNS

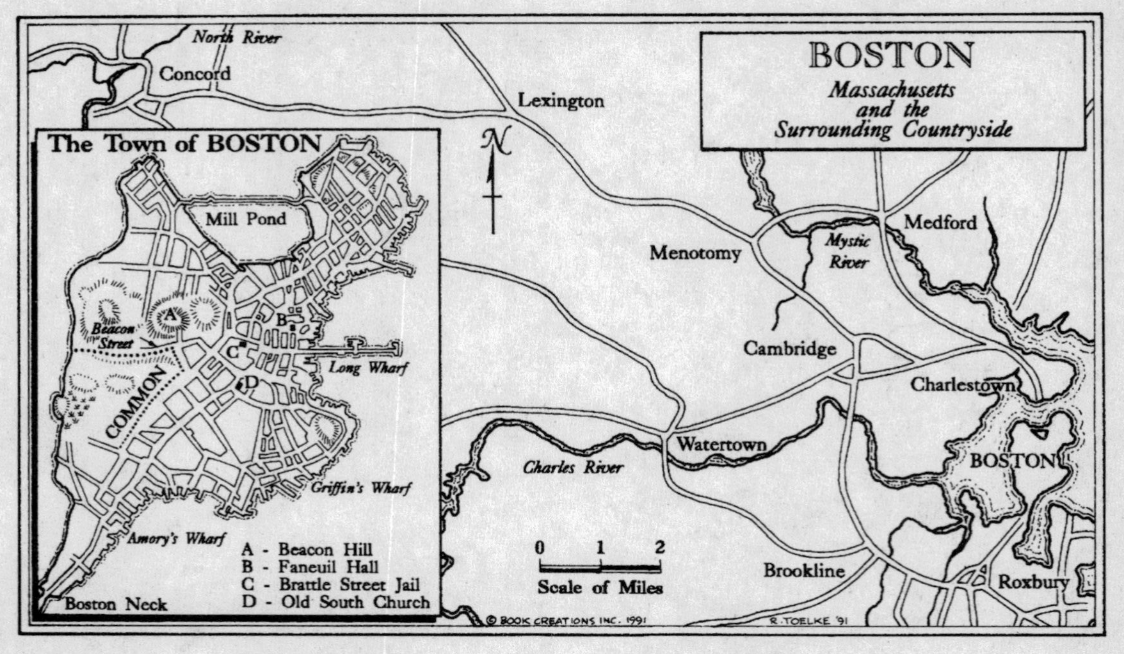
BOSTON
Massachusetts
and the
Surrounding Countryside
North River
Concord
Lexington
N
Menotomy
Medford
Mystic
River
Cambridge
Charlestown
Watertown
Charles River
BOSTON
Brookline
Roxbury
0 1 2
Scale of Miles
© BOOK CREATIONS INC. 1991
R. TOELKE '91
The Town of BOSTON
Mill Pond
Beacon
Street
COMMON
Long Wharf
Griffin's Wharf
Amory's Wharf
Boston Neck
A - Beacon Hill
B - Faneuil Hall
C - Brattle Street Jail
D - Old South Church

Chapter One

Thick dew sparkled on the grass in the early morning sunshine as Daniel Reed, his younger brother, Quincy, and Murdoch Buchanan led their horses out of the barn.

"We've picked a splendid morning t' be riding," Murdoch said. He drew in a deep breath of the warm, fragrant air. " 'Tis a beautiful day."

"Yes, it is," Daniel said quietly. *At least it's true as far as the weather is concerned,* he added silently. Despite the blue sky overhead, the scent of wildflowers, and the songs of the birds in the trees behind the farmhouse near Concord, Massachusetts, it was as gloomy a day as he had known in a long time.

He took his time checking the cinches on his saddle. Quincy might be in a hurry to leave the Parsons's farm, where they had been hiding from the redcoats ever since Murdoch and his cousin Roxanne Darragh had broken them out of Boston's Brattle Street jail. Daniel, however, was not eager to leave, for it meant that he would be separated from the young woman he had come to love. But the saddlebags were well stocked with provisions, and their long rifles, muskets, and flintlock pistols were primed and loaded. There was nothing left to do on this warm, late April day of 1775 but to ride away.

"So, you're ready to go, eh?" Lemuel Parsons called as he walked around the corner of the house and strolled toward the barn. He was the lanky, middle-aged owner of the farm where Daniel, Quincy, Murdoch, and Roxanne had been staying ever since the trouble that had forced them to leave Boston. Lemuel had his arm around his wife, Lottie's, waist, and the couple's five children followed close by. In the past weeks the youngsters had grown fond of their guests—especially of big Murdoch, who, despite his intimidating presence, was surprisingly gentle with children.

"Aye," Murdoch said as he knelt and swept the littlest ones into a hug. "We wanted t' make an early start of it."

"The three of you certainly look handsome this morning," said Lottie Parsons, smiling. "We're going to miss you around here."

"Wife!" Lemuel exclaimed. "Is that any way for a married woman to talk?"

Lottie smiled good-naturedly at her husband's teasing.

She was right: Daniel, twenty-two, and Quincy, sixteen, were both fine-looking young men, with a strong resemblance. Daniel's brown hair was a shade darker and not as curly as Quincy's, but they had the same warm brown eyes. Quincy had shot up in height and was almost as tall as Daniel, though not as muscular. Both wore brown whipcord breeches, butternut shirts of linsey-woolsey, high-topped black boots, and black tricorn hats. Daniel also wore a black vest.

Murdoch Buchanan's face, while not handsome, had a compelling quality to it. The frontiersman was dressed in buckskins, with fringe along the sleeves and across the broad chest of his hunting shirt as well as down the sides of his leggings. A wide black belt cinched his waist, and jammed down on his rumpled red hair was a raccoon-pelt cap, with the ringed tail of the animal dangling down the back of Murdoch's neck. One huge hand held the reins, and the other rested next to the brace of flintlock pistols tucked away under his belt. His hands, covered with hair, could move with great speed and ease when drawing the pistols or reaching for the long, heavy-bladed hunting knives sheathed in his boot-topped moccasins.

Murdoch reached over and tousled the heads of the older Parsons children while Daniel shook hands with Lemuel and Quincy tolerated a hug from Lottie.

"Will we be seeing you again when you come back this way?" asked Lemuel.

"Perhaps," Daniel replied. Lemuel did not know the exact nature of the mission that was taking his three visitors away, but he was aware that they were involved with the Committee of Safety, the inner circle of patriot leaders who were working for the cause of freedom in the revolution that had been born at nearby Lexington and Concord about a week earlier, on April 19, 1775.

"Well, we'll be here," Lemuel said. "Crops still got to be tended, war or no war."

"Tha' be one o' the reasons I never made much of a farmer," Murdoch said. "Too many things tha' be more exciting than working the soil."

"It has its own rewards," Lemuel said and smiled affectionately at his wife and children.

"Are we going or not?" Quincy asked impatiently.

"We're going," Daniel said heavily. "Come on. Mount up."

Gripping the reins too tightly, he swung up into the saddle. If nobody was going to say anything about Murdoch's cousin Roxanne, he would be damned if he was going to. He had thought she would come out of the house to say good-bye to them—to him—but if she didn't want to, that was fine with him. He wasn't going to wait around all day.

There had been no argument between Daniel and Roxanne Darragh about his departure; he had direct orders from the Committee of Safety to meet up with Ethan Allen's Green Mountain Boys and join the expedition to take Fort Ticonderoga, on the southern shore of Lake Champlain. Roxanne understood because she was as passionately devoted as Daniel to the cause of liberty and had risked her life more than once in pursuit of freedom for the colonies. But that morning Daniel—the young man she professed to love—was leaving, and the future was too uncertain.

With bittersweet melancholy flooding through him, Daniel heeled his big bay into motion and slowly rode away from the barn and around the farmhouse toward the lane that led to Concord. Murdoch Buchanan and Quincy Reed rode right behind him.

Daniel was less than ten yards past the house when the front door banged open and a voice called, "Wait!"

Reining in sharply, he turned in the saddle to watch Roxanne hesitantly step onto the porch and down the steps to the ground. She stood there, her beautiful green eyes focused on him. The morning breeze plucked idly at her long red hair.

Murdoch stopped his horse next to Daniel's, and Quincy reined in on the other side.

"We need to go, Daniel," he said impatiently.

"Hush, lad," Murdoch said. "Your brother has something else t' do tha's just as important." He paused for a moment, then said to Daniel, "Dinna just sit there. Go tell th' lass good-bye."

Daniel handed the reins to Quincy, who opened his

mouth to say something else but was silenced by a glower from Murdoch. He slid down from his horse and walked toward Roxanne.

"Come on, children. Leave them alone," Lemuel said. "There's eggs in the chicken house that need gathering."

"Would ye look there, my boy?" Murdoch said sharply to Quincy. " 'Tis a crow in tha' tree."

"I've seen crows before," Quincy said.

"Aye, but no' like this one. Come along, and we'll take a look at it." Murdoch nudged his horse forward, and Quincy followed reluctantly, with Daniel's horse trailing.

Daniel stepped up to Roxanne and looked deep into her eyes before he gently put his hands on her shoulders. She leaned into him, and his mouth pressed against hers in a soft, warm kiss that quickly became more demanding. He dropped his hands to her waist, and their bodies came together with a wanting that so far had been denied.

After ending the kiss, Roxanne rested her head on Daniel's chest. He stroked her hair, his senses full of its fragrance and feel. The warmth of her breath on his throat made him shiver.

"I'll be back," he whispered in her ear.

"I know." Her husky voice was strong and firm.

"Will you be here?"

"I don't know, Daniel. I'll be wherever the revolution needs me."

"I was afraid you weren't going to say good-bye," he said quietly.

She licked her lips. "I didn't know whether to say anything or not. I didn't—didn't want to make things more difficult for you."

He bent his head and kissed her again.

She broke the kiss and trembled in his embrace. "It's not

fair!" she whispered angrily. "I never expected to fall in love!"

"The day's going t' be getting warm and heavy with blackflies in a bit, once the sun's up good an' high," Murdoch said loudly, hinting that they needed to get started. He and Quincy were walking their horses back to where Roxanne and Daniel stood.

Daniel embraced her fiercely one more time, released her, turned, and without a final look returned to his horse. He took the reins from Quincy, climbed into the saddle, and urged the animal into a trot. Quincy matched the pace. Only Murdoch hung back a little to turn and wave a big hand at those who were left behind.

Roxanne stood in the farmyard, watching until the men had disappeared down the lane.

The story about Samuel Adams had already made the rounds, and only the man himself could say whether or not it was true. The unimpressive-looking Adams, a firebrand when the subject of liberty for the colonies came up, had been in hiding from the British at a farmhouse within earshot of Lexington green. When the gunfire that had signaled the start of the fight for freedom had rung out a week earlier, it was said that the sound made him look up with one of his infrequent smiles and exclaim excitedly, "What a glorious morning!"

Not everyone in the colonies shared that feeling, Daniel Reed thought as he cantered his horse down the road with Murdoch and Quincy. Most of the people on either side of this conflict had probably been as confused and dismayed as he was when the news of the fighting at Lexington reached him. Later that day, he and Murdoch had been in the battle at the North Bridge over the Concord River.

British troops, sent out from Boston by the colony's military governor, General Thomas Gage, had located and destroyed several stores of patriot munitions and supplies but had been routed and sent back to the city with heavy losses. A feeling of pride had swept through the colonies, along with stories such as the one about Sam Adams. The British giant had been defied. The colonists had spit in the eye of John Bull.

Daniel also felt that pride. The need for the colonies' freedom was just; he believed that with all his heart. But he could not forget the blood and death he had seen that day, the fear that had gone through him. He had fought in spite of the fear, but he did not consider himself a hero.

Several hours had passed since they had left the Parsons's farm, riding west. As Murdoch had predicted, the air had grown warmer as the sun climbed in the sky. The spring had been unseasonably warm.

"You think there'll be as big a battle at Fort Ticonderoga as there was at Concord?" Quincy asked.

Daniel lifted a hand and wiped a sheen of sweat from his forehead. "We don't even know if there'll *be* a battle."

"You don't expect the British just to hand the fort over to us, do you?"

Daniel shrugged. "I don't know how strong the British garrison is, nor how many men Colonel Allen can muster. That's why we're on our way to New York, so we can let the committee know how things stand."

"Well, if there is a lot of fighting, I hope it's not over with before we get there."

Daniel told himself not to lose his temper with his brother. Clearly he could not fault the lad's courage. Quincy had knowingly charged into a British trap in Boston to save a group of patriots. He had turned a debacle into a success and had taken a musket ball from a British Brown Bess in the leg for his trouble. For the past several weeks, he had been recuperating from the wound and had a scar on his thigh and a slight limp as reminders of what had happened. But the incident had not dampened his enthusiasm.

"I would'na count on the Green Mountain Boys o' Colonel Allen's waiting around very long, lad," said Murdoch, riding easily on a sturdy black gelding. "From what I hear, they like their fighting just about as much as any highlander. By the time we get there, they may have run all the Englishers back across the sea."

"I hope not," Quincy said emphatically.

Murdoch and Quincy kept talking, but Daniel concentrated on the information that his cousin Elliot Markham had brought him. Elliot, a year younger than Daniel and the son of one of Boston's most prominent Tory families, was working as an agent for the committee. Despite the support his father, Benjamin Markham, gave to the Crown, Elliot had been won over to the patriot cause. On the surface he was an indolent young man whose chief interests in life were a mug of good ale and a pretty serving wench in his lap. Daniel suspected that was still true, but Elliot was coming around. It was he who had ridden out to the Parsons's farm in Concord to bring the news that they had been assigned work to do elsewhere.

Colonel Ethan Allen, the leader of a band of militiamen known as the Green Mountain Boys, was planning to take control of Fort Ticonderoga, on the southern shore of Lake Champlain in the upper reaches of New York Colony. The lake was important, Elliot had explained, because it was the quickest, easiest route from Canada into the colonies, and Canada was firmly in British hands. If the rebels could control this waterway, they could prevent a British strike from the north that would split the colonies and isolate them from one another.

From the sound of Elliot's voice, Daniel had known that

he was reciting the information from memory. Although both Daniel and Quincy had had some exposure to military science at the academy they had attended in Virginia, Elliot was not familiar with military tactics and was only repeating what the committee had instructed him to.

Ticonderoga . . . Lake Champlain . . . They were just names to Daniel. Murdoch, however, had been to Lake Champlain and swore he could find the place again.

"You won't have to find it by yourselves," Elliot had told them. "Colonel Allen is putting his party together in Bennington, in the New Hampshire Grants. You can rendezvous with him there—if you get there in time."

Four days after the three riders left the farm near Concord, they had ridden nearly the length of Massachusetts Colony and were angling northwest toward the New Hampshire Grants. The ownership of this rugged, isolated area was disputed by New Yorkers to the west and New Hampshire's citizens to the east. Men such as Ethan Allen had fought hard and often, albeit thus far unsuccessfully, to make the territory independent and known by the name the French had given it long ago: Vermont.

The road that Daniel, Quincy, and Murdoch followed was little more than a trail through the thick forest of pine, ash, and birch. The newly budded leaves, the calls of the bobwhites and phoebes, and the fresh scent of spring reminded Daniel of the Virginia woods he had played in as a boy. But the mission he was on allowed no time for the woodland games he had enjoyed then.

"Are you glad to be out of the city?" Daniel asked Murdoch.

"I be telling ye, there were times I thought I was going t' suffocate in Boston," he said. "I needed t' get back in the wild, t' breathe some fresh air again."

Daniel admitted that the wooded hills were pretty, and from the heights he could gaze across the wide valley of the Connecticut River and see the rounded gray upthrust of the Berkshire Mountains. But he could not fully appreciate the beauty of his surroundings because of his preoccupation with the mission they were on—and with the young woman he had left at the Parsons farm.

He let his mind wander. What would it be like if the war were over and he and Roxanne were together? He could see the two of them moving to a place like this to begin a life of their own: clearing the land, building a cabin, tilling the soil, raising a family. . . . An ironic smile plucked at his mouth. It was an appealing fantasy, but that was all it was.

Roxanne had lived her whole life in Boston. She was the daughter of a printer, and unlike many people who could not even read, she had been exposed to a wide variety of subject matter. Her curiosity was insatiable, and during her childhood she had read everything she could. In many ways, Daniel thought, she was better educated and more sophisticated than he was, though he had graduated from a prestigious academy in Virginia, attended Yale, and read for the law at Harvard. She would never be happy to be a simple farmer's wife.

"What the devil!" he exclaimed when the sound of gunshots suddenly yanked his thoughts back to the present.

The three riders reined in, and Murdoch lifted an arm and pointed. "Coming from over there. Are we going t' see what's up?"

"Come on, Daniel," Quincy urged. "Somebody's in trouble!"

"Wha' do we do, Dan'l?"

Damn it, why are they asking me? Daniel thought. *I'm no leader.*

The decision was taken out of his hands when a rider

rounded the bend and thundered toward them. A dark cloak flowed out behind the figure bending far forward in the saddle.

"Get out of the way!" Daniel snapped to his companions when the rider urged the horse to greater speed.

Suddenly the advancing horse stumbled. Its front legs tangled with each other, and the animal went down hard. As it fell, the rider was thrown from the saddle, landed heavily in the road, and rolled over several times before coming to a stop at the feet of Daniel's horse.

The rider's tricorn hat had been knocked off in the fall, and blond curls tumbled around the pale face. Daniel and Murdoch gaped as Quincy exclaimed, "It's a girl!"

And a beautiful one at that, Daniel thought as he stared down at her. But someone was chasing her, as the sound of rapidly approaching hoofbeats proved.

Daniel glanced at the young woman's mount and saw that it was on its feet, moving around skittishly.

"Get rid of her horse, Quincy," Daniel rapped, sliding off his big bay. "Murdoch, give me a hand with her." As he bent to grasp the woman's shoulders he saw the rise and fall of her breasts underneath her white shirt and knew she was still alive.

Murdoch lifted a leg over the back of his horse, jumped quickly to the ground, and strode to Daniel.

"I'll take her," he said. One arm went under the woman's shoulders, the other under her knees, and he lifted her as if she weighed no more than a kitten. "Ye can get her hat."

"All right," Daniel said. "Hide her in the thicket over there."

Then the sound of hoofbeats was louder, although the gunshots had stopped. Down the road, Quincy caught the reins of the woman's horse, pulled it into a fast trot, then slapped his hat against the animal's rump. The riderless horse leapt forward and galloped out of sight along the trail.

Murdoch emerged from the thicket where he had deposited the woman, then turned to make sure there was no sign of his passage through the brush. Satisfied, he joined Daniel and Quincy. The younger Reed was still mounted, and Daniel and Murdoch hurriedly got up into their saddles and rode leisurely toward the ridge.

Out of the corner of his mouth, Murdoch growled, "I hope ye ken what ye be doing."

"Me, too," said Daniel.

Less than thirty seconds later eight men rode around the bend in the trail. All of them were brandishing pistols. The leader slowed his horse and waved the others forward. They surrounded Daniel, Quincy, and Murdoch.

"Take it easy, Murdoch. We don't know what's going on here yet," Daniel said quietly.

They were rough-looking, burly men with beard stubble on their faces and patches on their clothes. Their weapons appeared well cared for, however.

The leader was dressed in expensive though dust-covered clothes. He was well built and handsome, but Daniel did not like the way he held his gun with such casual ease.

"Have you seen anything of a blond wench on a chestnut pony?" the man asked.

Daniel pointed to the south, the direction in which Quincy had chased off the young woman's horse, and said, "Aye. She gave us quite a start, racing past us that way. Nearly trampled right over us. She's going to break her fool neck if she keeps on riding that fast."

The stranger laughed, but it was a harsh, humorless sound. "Fool neck is right, my friend. A fool is exactly what the lady is."

One of the pistol-wielding riders sullenly asked the leader, "You believe 'im, guv'nor?"

"No reason not to." The man turned to Daniel. "You are telling the truth, aren't you?"

"You can look at the tracks in the road if you don't believe me," Daniel said, silently praying his bluff would work. "They'll show that a single horse rode off to the south."

The man gestured sharply with his pistol. "Let's go. We've wasted enough time here." He kicked his horse into a run and headed down the road; the others followed closely at his heels.

Daniel heaved a deep sigh of relief, echoed by Quincy. "I thought sure he wasn't going to believe you," the lad said.

"What do ye suppose that was all about?" Murdoch asked.

"I don't know," Daniel said, hoping that his impulsive actions had not gotten them into trouble. "But I intend to find out."

He turned his horse, rode a few yards down the trail, dismounted, and stalked to the thicket where the young woman was hidden. Murdoch and Quincy hung back to see what Daniel planned to do.

After that hard fall she's probably still unconscious, Daniel thought. Thrusting the underbrush aside, he found himself staring down the barrel of a pistol.

The woman held the weapon unwaveringly in her hands and said sharply, "I don't know who you are, sir, but if you come one step closer, I'll blow your bloody head off!"

For a long moment, Daniel said nothing as he looked at the gun pointed at him. His right hand was hanging at his side, and with his leg concealing the movement, he gestured to Murdoch, hoping he would catch his meaning. Slowly Daniel straightened and said, "You have nothing to fear from me, miss. I mean you no harm."

She watched him intently, her pistol still menacing him. "You're working for him, aren't you?" she demanded.

"Working for whom?"

"For Perry." Her voice caught slightly, as if the name choked her. "For Perry Faulkner."

"I've never heard of Perry Faulkner," Daniel replied honestly.

His heart gave a little leap when her finger twitched on the trigger, but she eased the pressure before the weapon fired.

"Prove it," she snapped.

Daniel had no idea how he could prove he was not working for Perry Faulkner. But the need for proof suddenly vanished when Murdoch lunged into the thicket, reached out, closed his fingers over the flintlock of the pistol, and wrenched it away from her, unfired.

Abruptly unarmed, the young woman let out a frightened cry and flung herself away from Murdoch's looming figure. She rolled over agilely, sprang to her feet, and plunged into the woods.

Daniel went after her. Branches tore at his clothes and clawed at his hands and face. Finally he caught her arm, and they jerked to a stop.

With an angry cry, the woman twisted around and struck at him with her free hand, but Daniel grabbed her wrist and held on tightly, pulling her against him.

"Stop it!" he said.

"Let me go, damn you! You've no right—"

"We're the ones who saved you from those men, young lady," Daniel grated, well aware of the warmth of her body as she squirmed in his grasp. "I think that gives us the right to an explanation."

She struggled for a few seconds, then looked at him in bewilderment. "You—you saved me?"

"That's right. Don't you remember falling off your horse?"

"I—I remember the horse stumbling. But after that—I don't know."

"There were three riders in the road ahead of you. That was us. Your horse fell and threw you. You were knocked out."

"I was?"

Daniel led her out of the trees, encountering Murdoch and Quincy on the way. The young woman cast a dubious, frightened glance at Murdoch and looked curiously at Quincy. The four emerged from the brush and stood in a clearing beside the road.

Daniel let go of her wrists and said, "I'm Daniel Reed. This is my brother, Quincy, and this big fellow is Murdoch Buchanan."

"Hello," Quincy said shyly, keeping his eyes on the ground. He was almost overwhelmed by the young woman's beauty.

" 'Tis pleased I be t' meet ye, missy," Murdoch greeted her in a booming voice. "Even if ye did go waving a gun about."

"I—I was afraid." Her chin lifted defiantly. "I didn't know who you were. I still don't, for that matter. For all I know, you intended to harm me and perhaps still do."

"If we had meant you any harm, we would have turned you over to that bunch of roughnecks who were chasing you," Daniel pointed out. "The one leading them was the man you mentioned, wasn't he? Perry Faulkner?"

She shuddered. "I don't even like to hear his name. But yes, that was Faulkner. He's been after me for several days now, and he almost caught me."

"Why is he pursuing you?"

She shook her head stubbornly. "That's none of your

business. It's enough for you to know that he's an evil man and wants to hurt me. If the three of you are gentlemen, you won't press me for details."

"I would appreciate it if you would at least tell us your name."

For a moment she did not answer, and Daniel thought she was going to be stubborn about that, too. But then she said quietly, "Cordelia Howard."

"Well, Miss Cordelia Howard . . . It is *Miss Howard,* isn't it?"

"Of course!" she exclaimed.

"I'm wondering what we're going to do with you."

"Why should you have to do anything with me?" She sniffed. "Just let me get on my horse, and I'll be on my way and no more trouble to you." She looked around, dismayed. "My horse! Where is my horse?"

Quincy answered her. "We ran it off."

"Ran it off! For God's sake, why?"

"As a decoy to mislead Faulkner and his men," Daniel said. "And it worked, too."

"I thought you said you didn't know Faulkner."

"We didn't—then. But I don't think any of us liked him, even without knowing his name or what he was up to. And we certainly didn't want him getting his hands on you until we found out what this was all about." Daniel sighed. "Something we still don't seem to have accomplished."

"But my horse is gone, that's the important thing."

"Your horse is gone," Daniel agreed. "Although we might be able to locate him again with some searching."

Her bottom lip quivered. "How will I get to Saratoga now?"

"Saratoga? That's where you're going?"

She nodded, and her eyes shone with moisture.

"You don't have to cry," Daniel said. "We'll take you with us."

Quincy grinned, but Murdoch just threw his big hands in the air and turned away, muttering to himself.

"Get the horses, Murdoch," Daniel said. "We've already lost enough time." He looked at the young woman. "We're going to Bennington, Miss Howard. That's just north of here in the New Hampshire Grants."

"I know where it is," she said petulantly.

"There'll be plenty of people around once we get there, and I'm sure you'll be safe. You can make arrangements to travel from there to Saratoga."

"Thank you, I suppose."

"You're welcome," Daniel said curtly. She would slow them down, he knew, but there was nothing else they could do but take her with them. "You'll ride with Quincy. We don't have time to go looking for your horse."

"What?" The exclamation came from Quincy, who could hardly believe his good fortune but immediately blushed crimson.

"All right," Cordelia said brusquely. She looked at Quincy. "Go ahead, mount up."

As his face flushed even more, Quincy swung up into his saddle, then took his left foot out of the stirrup. Cordelia placed her foot in it, grasped Quincy's arm, and lifted herself up behind him, swinging her right leg over the horse's back. Under her long cloak she wore boots, gray twill pants, and a man's white shirt—efficient riding attire, even if the outfit was a bit scandalous.

Cordelia slipped her arms around Quincy's waist. Her body was pressed against his, and he gulped as he felt the softness of her breasts against his back. The look he shot Daniel was a mixture of fear, excitement, and desperation.

Murdoch mounted up and took the lead. Quincy and

Cordelia followed, and Daniel brought up the rear. He kept an eye on the trail behind them, just in case Perry Faulkner and his men doubled back.

When night fell, the travelers made camp in a clearing screened from the main trail by a thick stand of pine. Murdoch built a small fire, and Quincy heated salt pork and cooked corn cakes over its flame.

Cordelia ate in silence and did not look at her three companions. Finally, after they had finished and Murdoch had put out the fire, she said angrily, "I'd roll up in my blankets and go to sleep—if I still had any blankets. But they were on my horse, along with everything else I had."

Daniel smiled wearily as he stood up and went to where he had piled the gear. The three horses had been unsaddled, watered, and staked out nearby to graze for the night. "I'll give you a blanket," he said.

"Don't trouble yourself, sir. I shall be fine."

Ignoring her caustic tone, Daniel bent to take a blanket from his pack.

"Here," he said, tossing a rolled-up blanket to Cordelia. The moonlight was bright enough for him to see that she caught it easily. However, in the shadows under the trees on the other side of the camp, Murdoch and Quincy were merely dark shapes in the gloom. The rays of moonlight seemed to find their way through the trees just to illuminate Cordelia.

"Thank you," the young woman said, the words mumbled so softly that Daniel could barely make them out. She spread the blanket on a bed of pine needles, then lay down and wrapped it around her.

Something prodded him to settle himself on the ground beside her. Still she did not look at him.

"It seems to me that since you're under our protection, we have a right to know what kind of trouble you're in,"

Daniel said. He was determined to get some information from her. "Otherwise we won't know how to help you."

"I'm hardly under your protection. We simply happen to be traveling together because of an unfortunate turn of events."

"Unfortunate?" he repeated. "I'd call it very fortunate, if I were you. If we hadn't been there, Faulkner would have found you unconscious in the road. You'd be in his hands now, instead of safe with us."

Cordelia sat up. "You call being in the middle of the wilderness safe?" she said loudly. "Why, there could be a hundred Indians out there in the darkness, just waiting to murder us!"

"No hostiles 'round here, lass," Murdoch called. " 'Tis farther west they are."

"Well—there could be a few of them around," she insisted.

"That's not the point," Daniel said. "You've admitted that Faulkner is after you. Were his men shooting at you, or merely trying to frighten you?"

"I'm sure I wouldn't know. I had my back turned and was riding away from them."

"Is Faulkner a constable, or some other authority?" he asked abruptly.

"What?" Cordelia sounded shocked. "A constable? You think I'm a criminal, is that it? That's the furthest thing from the truth!"

"Then Faulkner is a criminal."

"I didn't say that, either."

"Ye'll no' be getting a straight answer from this one, Dan'l," Murdoch said from his side of the camp.

"You claim you want to go to Saratoga," Daniel pressed on, "yet you were riding in the opposite direction."

"I was riding in any direction I could to get away from

those men," Cordelia snapped. "If I had escaped from them, I could have circled around and gone back toward Saratoga."

Daniel frowned. He found himself believing Cordelia, even though she had not told him much.

"All I want to do is get some sleep," she said. She lay down again and pulled the blanket snugly around her. "It's been a dreadful day."

"Yes, it certainly has."

Daniel rolled up in his own blanket, but he did not fall asleep easily. Quincy had agreed to stand guard first, and as his brother leaned against a tree trunk, Daniel shifted around restlessly and felt a stirring deep within. Cordelia was beautiful, but he had left behind an equally beautiful young woman who was intelligent, passionate, and in love with him.

Roxanne . . . He would have given anything to have her beside him right now so that he could draw her into his embrace, cradle her in his arms, and feel the strength that she gave him once more. He had argued with her in the past, but they had been arguments of principle, not petty squabblings with an ill-tempered shrew like Cordelia. Tonight, more than ever, he missed Roxanne.

Chapter Two

In a small house in Cambridge, across the Charles River from Boston, two young men sat smoking pipes and talking solemnly. The house belonged to a storekeeper sympathetic to the patriot cause, and the two men occupying it now were nothing else if not patriots. Both had given up their professions—that of schoolteacher and shopkeeper—to devote all their time to the cause of liberty.

Robert Townsend leaned forward in his chair, his gaze intent on his companion, Benjamin Tallmadge. The single lamp in the room had been turned low, so that it cast only a small circle of light.

His voice firm, Townsend said, "We're agreed, then."

Tallmadge, lean and more sullen than his friend, said, "I don't think there's any doubt. If we're going to have a chance against the British, we're going to need a better source of intelligence than we have now—especially if there's a traitor in the Committee of Safety, as we suspect."

"Our friend Hale is going to be disappointed that he's not here for the launching of our espionage ring."

"Well, you can't blame him for not wanting to leave his students. He takes his job as a teacher quite seriously." Tallmadge puffed on his pipe. "At any rate, I'm sure there will be plenty of chances for Nathan to serve his country."

Townsend put his hands on his knees. "I suppose we should get down to details. We'll have no official contact with the committee, correct?"

"Correct," Tallmadge said briskly. "The less the Committee of Safety knows about our efforts, the better. In fact, that holds true for everyone. You and I, Robert, will be the only ones to hold all the strands of the web in our hands. The less our agents know about anything other than what concerns them directly, the better off we'll be."

"You're thinking of torture, of course, and what might be revealed."

"You don't believe the British are incapable of such acts of inhumanity, do you?"

"Not at all," Townsend replied grimly. "You're absolutely right, Ben."

"How shall we identify ourselves, though?" mused Tallmadge. "False names, perhaps? Or by means of a code or password?"

"Numbers," Townsend suggested, smiling suddenly. "You and I should be Operatives One and Two, Hale will be Three, and any agents we recruit will be known only by numbers as well. But before we take someone into our confidence, he will have to prove his allegiance to the cause in some verifiable manner."

"An excellent idea!" Tallmadge's voice revealed his excitement.

The game they were about to begin would be the most dangerous ever played, Tallmadge knew. He refused to contemplate failure, not with everything that was depending on their success.

The two young men talked long into the night, planning the steps that would take them down the road to victory—or to death.

Roxanne Darragh was nearly packed. By the time Elliot Markham arrived, she would be ready to go back to Boston with him. He had wanted her to go with him the day he came to the Parsons's farm to inform Daniel, Quincy, and Murdoch of their mission at Fort Ticonderoga. But Roxanne had refused to go until after Daniel and the others left.

Now Daniel was gone, and she had nothing to keep her there. She missed him terribly and prayed he would return safely from New York.

Roxanne closed the small bag that contained her belongings. She was nervous about returning to the city for fear that one of the British soldiers would recognize her as the woman who had helped the Reed brothers escape. She had pointed a gun at one of the guards at the Brattle Street jail and threatened to kill him if he did not take her to the cell where Daniel was being held. The same night, after she had rescued Daniel, they had freed Quincy, who had been wounded and was in British custody. Shots had been fired, although no one else had been hurt as far as she knew. The British sense of dignity had been deeply offended, however, and General Gage had forbidden his officers to speak of the incident.

But as Elliot had pointed out, after what had happened at Lexington and Concord almost two weeks earlier, the redcoats had more on their minds than a simple jailbreak. He had assured her she would be safe.

When she heard the thudding of hooves and the squeaking of wheels outside the farmhouse, she picked up her bag and carried it out of the small bedchamber. Through the front door of the house, she saw Lemuel Parsons talking to a man on the front porch.

She stopped short, surprised to see Dr. Benjamin Church. The physician was a tall, sleekly handsome man who wore a powdered wig, even on a warm day like that one. He was well dressed in white breeches and a frilled shirt, with a blue swallowtail jacket over it. He held a black tricorn in his hands as he talked to Lemuel.

"Ah, there you are, dear," Lemuel said. "This gentleman's come calling for you."

Roxanne tightened her grip on the valise and stepped onto the porch. "Hello, Doctor," she said. "I didn't expect to see you here."

"Yes, well, young Mr. Markham asked me if I might substitute for him today," Dr. Church answered without hesitation. "It seems there was some sort of business meeting his father insisted he attend. I was happy to accommodate him, of course. He sends his regards."

"Thank you."

"You look a bit disappointed, my dear." Church smiled. "I know I'm not as young and handsome as Mr. Markham, but perhaps you can tolerate my company for the hour or so it takes to reach Boston."

"I'm not disappointed at all, Doctor," Roxanne said quickly. "True, I was expecting Elliot, but I appreciate your going to so much trouble for me, and I'm sure I'll enjoy the ride in your luxurious open carriage."

"No trouble at all on this nice day," Church assured her. He reached for her bag. "If you're ready to go . . . ?"

"Yes." She handed him the valise, then turned to Lemuel and hugged the startled farmer. "Thank you for everything."

"Well—well, you're certainly welcome, Miss Roxanne. We've been glad to have you and your friends here."

Lottie Parsons appeared from the rear of the house,

bringing the children with her. "Roxanne, are you leaving?" she asked.

"Yes, I really must go."

Lottie threw her arms around the younger woman and patted her on the back. "You take good care of yourself and come back to see us, all right? The children and I are going to miss you every bit as much as we miss your young men."

"Don't worry. I'm sure I'll be back." Roxanne looked at the carriage and saw that Dr. Church had stowed her bag away behind the seat. "I have to be going now."

The children clustered around her to say their goodbyes, and Roxanne hugged each of them. Then, with a hand from Dr. Church, she climbed into the carriage, and the physician stepped up to take his seat. A flick of the lines got the two well-trained horses moving, and the carriage made a wide turn as Church swung it toward the lane. Roxanne leaned from the vehicle and waved at the Parsons family before settling back in the seat.

"They seem like friendly people," Church commented as he steered the team down the lane.

"Yes, they're wonderful," Roxanne replied. "I don't know what we would have done without their help."

"Fine peasant stock, I suppose."

She glared at him, but he was concentrating on the road. Dr. Church was an aristocrat, at least to his way of thinking, but he was also one of Boston's leading physicians and a trusted member of the committee's inner circle. He had contacts with British officers and accepted medical work from the British army, which had led Daniel to be suspicious of him until Church explained that such contacts enabled him to get his hands on information that could be of value to the patriots. The British army hardly made a move without Church's knowing about it first.

"Did Elliot have any message for me?" Roxanne asked after a moment.

"Indeed he did. He wanted me to tell you that he would meet you at the Salutation Tavern this evening. He indicated it was important he speak to you."

Roxanne frowned. "Did he say what about?"

"No," Church replied. "Affairs of the heart, perhaps? Young Markham seems rather impressed with you, my dear, but I had an idea that you and Daniel Reed were—how shall we say—?"

"I think we've said quite enough," Roxanne broke in, flushed with embarrassment. "Elliot and I are fellow patriots and nothing more. The same holds true for Mr. Daniel Reed."

Really, she thought, *such things are none of Dr. Church's business.* Some things were personal, even in time of war.

"Of course, my dear Miss Darragh, of course. Doubtless young Markham wants to speak to you about some sort of espionage assignment, but I wouldn't know the particulars of that."

To change the subject, Roxanne said, "I hope I don't encounter any of the guards who were on duty the night we rescued Daniel and Quincy from the Brattle Street jail."

Dr. Church laughed. "I doubt very seriously that will happen. You see, I have it on good authority that those men have been reposted to the frontier as punishment for their laxity that night."

"Really?" Roxanne leaned back in the seat. The news made her feel better.

"I don't believe you have a thing to worry about, my dear."

The Salutation was a friendly tavern on a small side street of Boston. It was run by a man named Pheeters, who was built like a bear, but his formidable figure and gruff exterior concealed a gentle soul. He always spoke in a growl, and the expression on his bulldoglike face varied only in the degree of its forbidding gloominess.

But Pheeters was utterly trustworthy and believed that the colonies should be free from the heavy-handed rule of the Crown. So he let the Committee of Safety use his tavern's back room for their meetings. The committee had moved around quite a bit, meeting for a time at the Rose and Crown, then at the Red Lion, and finally at the Green Dragon Inn, before settling on the Salutation. In times like this, it never hurt to be careful.

Roxanne had been to the Salutation many times, and every time she entered, she felt as if she were coming home. Pheeters ran a very respectable establishment, where a young woman alone didn't worry about being accosted. This evening, as she headed for an empty table in a rear corner, Pheeters stepped out from behind the bar and walked over to her.

"Good evening, Miss Darragh," he said. "Haven't seen you in a while."

"I've been out of town, Mr. Pheeters."

The burly tavern keeper wiped his hands on his apron. "What can I bring you?"

"A mug of cider would do nicely."

"Put a little cinnamon in it for you?"

Roxanne smiled. "Thank you. That sounds fine."

"I'll get it for you right away."

He hurried away, and Roxanne sat back to wait for Elliot.

Her father and mother had objected when she told them she was coming to the tavern tonight. It had been only a few weeks since they learned of her involvement in the insurrectionist activities around Boston. Roxanne had managed to send a letter to them from the Parsons's farm. In it she had explained her absence and promised to return home as soon as it was safe.

Now that she was back, William Darragh did not want her going off to some grog shop, as he put it, even though he knew the Salutation Tavern was not the unsavory place he made it out to be.

Pheeters brought the mug of cider to her table. As Roxanne sipped the hot, spiced brew she reflected that a cup of tea would have been nice, but since the Boston Tea Party a year and a half earlier, when tons of East India Company tea had been tossed into the harbor, the scarcity of it was felt by everyone. She had suffered from a dreadful headache for days after the incident, but giving up tea was a small price to pay for freedom.

She saw Elliot come in the door. He was tall, with blond hair, blue eyes, and handsome features that were usually set in a cocky smile. He wore an expensive brown coat, matching breeches that met the top of his snow white stockings, a frilly white shirt with a silk cravat, and shoes with shiny brass buckles.

His gaze locked with hers across the room. Then he sauntered casually along the bar and greeted some of his cronies, pausing to listen solemnly as two of them argued drunkenly. After a moment Elliot clapped each man on the back and moved to where Roxanne was waiting.

He sat down, then reached across the table and clasped her hand. "It's good to see you again," he said.

"You saw me at the farm only a few days ago, Elliot."

"Yes, but no one else in here knows that. We should give the appearance of two good friends greeting each other, shouldn't we?"

"Perhaps you're right." She tightened her fingers on his. It *was* good to see him again. They had attended quite a few Tory parties and balls together, she with Daniel and Elliot with his fiancée, Sarah Cummings, and had moved easily through Tory society to gather information they could pass on to the committee. Sarah had known nothing about that, of course, and had been shocked when Daniel was exposed as a patriot spy.

"I'm sorry I couldn't bring you into town," Elliot said quietly. "My father is still convinced I'm a good little Tory and I'm going to take over his shipping line someday."

"Don't apologize for that. It's exactly what we want him to think, isn't it?"

"I suppose so. It's rather difficult to keep up the pose, though." Elliot signaled for Pheeters to bring him a mug of ale, then turned his attention back to Roxanne. "Did Dr. Church have any trouble finding the Parsons's place?"

"None so far as I know. We had a good talk on the way in about how the rebellion is going."

"Church would know. He's about the most well-informed man I've ever met. Seems to know just about everything."

"I wish he knew how all of this is going to turn out."

A bold grin broke across Elliot's face. "We're going to win, of course. The colonies will be free of Britain, and we'll take our rightful place among the nations of the world."

"You've been listening to Samuel Adams again."

Elliot shrugged. "I've been reading his pamphlets, as well as those of Mr. Thomas Paine."

"Surely they're not the reason you want to talk to me tonight, Elliot."

Before he could respond, Pheeters arrived with his ale. Elliot flipped a coin to the tavern keeper and took a long, thirsty swallow. He licked the foam from his lips. "Much better," he said. "My father is giving a party for General Gage and his staff tomorrow night. Sarah and I will be there, of course, and I thought you might like to come."

"No, I don't think so."

"Why not? Sarah likes you; I'm sure she'd be glad to see you again." Elliot lowered his voice. "Besides, who knows what we might find out if we keep our eyes and ears open?"

"I just don't think it would be a good idea—not after what happened at the Wallingford's ball." She thought back to that night when British soldiers had appeared at the Wallingford mansion, arrested Daniel for treason, and carted him off to the Brattle Street jail. "After all, I'm sure my association with Daniel has done little for my credibility."

"I was afraid you might feel that way. That's why I have another idea." He clasped his hands together on the table and leaned forward. "Some of the officers might remember that you were involved with Daniel, and they could be less inclined to talk if you are around. But I want you there anyway, in the garden."

"I don't understand."

"If I discover anything important, I'll want to pass it on to the committee right away. Who knows? I might learn something that would require immediate action on our part. If you're hiding in the garden, I can slip out anytime during the evening, tell you what I've heard, and you can carry the information to the committee."

"And if you don't hear anything?"

"I'll admit in that case you'll have wasted an evening. But I don't think it will be too unpleasant. You can sit in our gazebo and enjoy the night air."

"All right, I'll do it," Roxanne said.

"Good! I'll make certain the garden's back gate is unlocked so you can get in. Any time after dark will be fine."

"How will I know it's you? Anyone could wander into the garden from the house."

Elliot thought for a moment, then said, "I'll whistle a

tune, and I'll be by myself, of course. If anyone goes into the garden who's not whistling or who's with someone else, you'll need to stay out of sight. Can you do that?"

"Yes, Elliot, I can do that." Roxanne could not prevent a slightly exasperated tone from creeping into her voice.

"I'm sure you can," Elliot said quickly. He drained the rest of the ale from his mug. "Well, I suppose that covers everything."

"I suppose so."

He rested his hand on hers again. "I'm glad we're going to be working together, Roxanne. I think we're going to do great things for the cause."

Aware of the warmth of his touch, she said, "I'm sure we will."

The way Roxanne and Elliot were leaning close together and talking in low voices, their hands touching, anyone watching might have thought they were having a romantic rendezvous.

After dark on the appointed evening, Roxanne approached the Markhams' three-story, red brick estate on Beacon Hill. She left her horse tied to a post at the end of the narrow alley behind the mansion. The gardens were closed off by high brick walls, but there were gates so the tradesmen could come and go. If Elliot had kept his part of the bargain, the gate would be unlocked.

Roxanne tested the latch and found it unfastened. Slowly she pushed the gate open and slipped through, then pulled it shut behind her. The hinges, newly greased, were silent.

She had decided to wear a plain, dark brown dress so she would easily blend into the shadows of the garden. A scarf of the same shade was wrapped around her red hair, and a light woven wrap kept away the early May evening chill.

Her eyes had already adjusted to the darkness of the alley, and as she peered around the garden, she discerned the bulky shape of the gazebo in the center of a flower garden surrounded by a square of knee-high boxwood hedge. A flagstone path led up to the small building. She darted through the opening in the low wooden wall that enclosed the airy circular structure and sat down on the whitewashed plank floor. In this position, her head was just above the gazebo wall, and while most of her body was concealed, she could easily see the house due to the soft glow spreading over the garden from the candlelit windows.

She settled down to wait, listening to the music from the string quartet, which played the most popular minuet of the day. Roxanne smelled the fragrant odor of snowdrops, crocuses, and hyacinths that had bloomed and lingered in the garden. From where she sat she could see the shoots of daffodils and peonies that, when in flower, made the Markhams' grounds a local showplace. And as she sat there her thoughts turned inevitably to the questions that haunted her every waking hour since she had returned to Boston: Where was Daniel Reed? Was he safe? What was he doing?

In the elegant ballroom of the Markham home, crystal chandeliers from Europe shone with the light of hundreds of candles and reflected the colors of the dancers' silks and satins in the mirrored walls, the French doors, and the gleaming parquet floors. The delicate fragrances of the women's perfumes as well as the strong smells of the mulled cider, punch, and wines that were served gave the room an intoxicating atmosphere.

Elliot Markham stood by the doors that opened onto the terrace and held a delicate crystal goblet of brandy in one hand and the smooth, cool fingers of Sarah Cummings in the other. There was a smile on his lips, but not in his eyes.

He listened to a minor British army functionary drone on about his home in England and how barbaric the colonies were. Elliot's father, Benjamin Markham, and Sarah's father, Theophilus Cummings, were standing close by, nodding in solemn agreement with the officer. Elliot would have preferred to be across the room, near General Gage and his senior staff officers, but it was a bit early in the evening for him to attach himself to the general. He did not want to do anything that would look suspicious.

"Excuse me," Sarah murmured, tightening her grip on Elliot's hand. "I hate to interrupt you, sir, but I seem to be out of punch."

"Oh! Well, I'd be happy to replenish that for you, my dear—" the British officer began.

"Don't trouble yourself," Elliot said quickly, glad to get away from this conversation. "Come, Sarah. I'll get you some more punch."

He led her aside, and the Englishman resumed his conversation with Benjamin and Cummings.

"I thought we'd never get away from that dreadful man," she said quietly. "I don't really want any more punch right now."

"All right. What do you want?"

She linked her arm with his. "I want to dance." Sarah wore a powder blue satin ballgown with white lace ruffles around the low-cut neckline and elbow-length sleeves. Her tiny waist was accentuated by a wide, white satin sash, tied in the back with streamers that hung down to the hem of her full skirt. The dress perfectly matched her blue eyes and set off her upswept blond hair.

"That can be arranged," Elliot said grandly, then whispered in her ear, "especially when you look utterly irresistible." He drank the last of his brandy, took her glass, then set it with his on a sideboard. The string quartet was seated at the other end of the ballroom, and the polished hardwood floor on that side of the chamber was filled with gracefully swirling couples. Elliot and Sarah moved to join them.

I am a lucky man, Elliot thought as he took Sarah by the hand and led her to the center of the dance floor. With her cool, blond beauty, she was the loveliest woman in the room. Yet coupled with her classical elegance was a surging passion that could drive Elliot mad. Even now the urge to pull the streamers that hung from the sash around her waist, open her dress, and touch her skin was almost overwhelming. He would have made love to Sarah before now if she had allowed it; after all, they were engaged to be married. But she was adamant in her virtue, leaving him to satisfy his needs with a variety of tavern wenches who were more than willing to romp with him.

As they danced Elliot noticed a knot of redcoated officers drinking and laughing in a corner of the room. If he could ingratiate himself with them, their unguarded talk might prove very illuminating.

When the musicians ended the minuet, Elliot said to Sarah, "I'll get you that punch now."

"I'd rather dance some more." She pouted prettily.

"Perhaps in a few minutes. I have to mix with the guests, you know. My father would be unhappy if I devoted my entire evening to you and ignored everyone else—much as I'd like to."

His smooth words mollified her, and she waved to several young women friends. She would drift over to them, Elliot knew, and be kept busy for a while.

He sauntered up to the officers. "Good evening, gentlemen. I trust you're enjoying yourselves."

"Yes, indeed," the heaviest officer said. He was shorter than Elliot and had a ruddy complexion and dark hair that formed a wreath around his balding head. "You're young Markham, aren't you?"

"That's right, Elliot Markham."

"Major Philip Dorn here."

He introduced the other men, and Elliot carefully filed their names away in his memory. Dorn was the friendliest of the bunch, as well as the most talkative.

His smile verged on a leer as he said, "I saw that bit of fluff you were dancing with. Quite a beautiful girl, old chap, quite beautiful indeed."

"Yes, she is," Elliot agreed. "Her name is Miss Sarah Cummings. We're betrothed."

"Ah! Any relation to Mr. Theophilus Cummings?"

"His daughter," Elliot confirmed.

"Then your marriage will be something in the nature of a business merger, what?" Dorn brayed with laughter.

Elliot did not find the major's comment humorous. "I suppose you could say that."

The other officers were wandering away, and Elliot grew worried that he had attached himself to the most obnoxious of the group. Major Dorn was drinking heavily, and Elliot realized that the other men were grateful to him for taking Dorn off their hands. Well, he would have to make the best of it. Just because Dorn was a boor did not mean he didn't have some useful information in his bewigged head.

"Markham and Cummings," mused Dorn. "Quite a successful partnership, eh?"

"Are you speaking about my father and Sarah's?"

"Of course."

"They have done fairly well."

Dorn took a sip of brandy from the snifter he was holding.

"More than that, from what I hear. These past few years have been difficult. All this dreadful turmoil with the insurrectionists. But through it all, Markham and Cummings's ships have sailed regularly."

"We're strong supporters of the Crown," Elliot pointed out.

"So I've heard. I work in the customs office, you know. See a lot of ships' manifests from Markham and Cummings. Don't know where we'd be without the supplies they deliver." Dorn drained the rest of his brandy and licked his lips appreciatively. His voice was becoming thicker. "Good man, your father. Willing to do anything he can to help the Crown."

"Of course," Elliot said.

Dorn leaned closer to him. The major's breath was sour from smoking and drinking. He gave a lopsided grin and whispered, "Pretty soon he's really going to help us out. Soon as those guns get here, we'll show those bloody traitors what for."

"Guns?" Elliot asked quietly, adopting the same conspiratorial tone.

"Remember when those colonial bastards blew up the warehouse down by Avery's Wharf? They don't know how badly they hurt us. All our extra munitions went up in that explosion." Dorn squinted at him. "But that's all about to change, old boy. There's a Markham and Cummings ship on the way from England right now, loaded right to the gunwales with powder and shot, muskets and cannon. Things'll be back to normal as soon as that ship gets here." The major lifted his hand to stifle a belch. " 'Scuse me."

Elliot's heart was pounding. "Ah, yes, my father did tell me about the shipment, though I don't recollect the name of the ship," he lied, trying to make his voice sound casual.

"The *Carolingian,* that's what she's called," Dorn said.

"Oh, yes, of course." Elliot did indeed remember seeing the name on some of the paperwork he had grudgingly scanned on one of his infrequent visits to the shipping offices. As far as he could recall, though, the *Carolingian* was returning from England with a cargo of trade goods.

He glanced across the room at his father, who was smiling blandly as he spoke with General Gage. There was more to the old boy than Elliot had thought, if he was actually involved in the scheme.

"Got to keep it secret, you know," Major Dorn was saying. "The general was quite firm about that. No point in adding any more fuel to the fires of unrest, he says. Quite agree with him, myself. Say, perhaps I shouldn't be mentioning this to you, old boy."

"Oh, no, don't worry about that," Elliot said quickly. "My father doesn't have any secrets from me. You forget, I work closely with him."

"Of course, of course." Dorn looked relieved. "Still, might be best if you don't speak of this to anyone, eh?"

"Certainly. I'll keep it in the strictest confidence."

He had to get away from this drunken fool and find Roxanne. The *Carolingian* was due to arrive in less than a week, and it would take time to work out a plan that would put those British guns in rebel hands.

Chapter Three

Roxanne felt as though she had waited in the Markhams' gazebo for days, brushing away mosquitoes as they whined near her ears. The pests' shrill song stretched her nerves. She hoped the party in the Markham mansion would soon be over.

The music stopped, and she heard carriages departing from the side of the house. Not everyone was leaving yet, but the festivities were definitely drawing to a close.

Suddenly the French doors at the rear of the house opened, and a single figure stepped out onto the terrace, then silently closed the doors behind him. The man strode swiftly toward the gazebo, whistling a tuneless melody.

"It's me, Roxanne."

"I know," she told him, her whisper matching his own. "Is the party over?"

"Almost." He stepped close to her and raised a hand to massage his temple. "I was forced to spend hours listening to the most boring people I've ever encountered, especially one

Major Philip Dorn. He's gone now, though, and I was able to slip away." He put his hands on Roxanne's shoulders, surprising her a little. Unable to keep the excitement out of his voice, he went on, "Dorn may have been a crashing bore, but I learned something very important from him."

"What?"

"One of my father's ships is on its way from England with a cargo of munitions intended for the British forces here."

"A Markham and Cummings ship? Why aren't they using a Royal Navy vessel?"

"I asked Dorn about that," Elliot said. "They're interested in secrecy right now. They don't want the citizens here knowing that so many guns and so much powder are on their way to replace what Quincy and his friends blew up."

"If we could just get our hands on those guns and that ammunition," Roxanne muttered.

"The patriot cause would be much better armed than it is now," Elliot concluded. "We could help ourselves, while at the same time dealing a blow to the British."

"This is wonderful, Elliot!" Roxanne raised her hands to rest on his chest. "Uncovering this information is a real stroke of luck. We'll need to know the name of the ship and its schedule, so I can pass all of this along to the committee."

She broke off her statement as a shaft of light from a bull's-eye lantern fell on them as they stood close together in the center of the gazebo, Elliot's hands resting on her shoulders, her hands on his chest and her head tilted back to look up at him. Roxanne tried to pull away, but he tightened his grip and held her firmly. She was even more shocked when he drew her to him and kissed her.

His lips were warm, urgent, and demanding. A second after their mouths touched, though, Elliot whispered, "Play along!"

Roxanne let her body flow into his embrace as if they

were lovers. The kiss, for appearance's sake, was very passionate. She slipped her arms around Elliot's waist and pressed herself tightly against him.

It was impossible not to hear the choked cry from behind the light. They turned to see Sarah Cummings holding the lantern.

"My God!" she said in a quivering voice. "My God, Elliot, what are you doing?"

"I . . . I'm sorry you had to see that, Sarah," Elliot replied.

Roxanne looked up at him and saw a terribly embarrassed expression on his face. His shame was genuine.

"Sorry?" Sarah repeated bitterly. "Is that all you have to say for yourself, Elliot Markham?" Her voice strengthened, and anger replaced the pitiful surprise that had been there a moment earlier. "You'll be sorry you ever trifled with my affections, I can promise you that!" She swung toward Roxanne. "And you! I thought you were my friend! Don't just stand there, Roxanne. Say something!"

"I'm sorry, too, Sarah," Roxanne offered. "Neither one of us meant for you to be hurt." That much, at least, was the truth.

"Well, I *am* hurt. My God, I see the man I plan to marry slipping out into the garden, so I go after him to surprise him with a kiss, and what do I find? He doesn't need my kisses! He already has a redheaded hussy to paw as if she were some sort of whore!"

Roxanne stiffened, her own anger growing.

"Please, Sarah, there's no call for that kind of talk," Elliot said sharply. He walked toward her. "We can talk about this later, like three civilized adults—"

"There's nothing to talk about," Sarah screamed. "I don't want to see you or talk to you ever again, Elliot

Markham, you or your trollop! I'll leave you to your animal lusts!"

With that, she stormed into the house, taking the lantern with her.

Elliot watched Sarah walk away, then returned to Roxanne. They both spoke at once, saying the other's name. Elliot held up his hands and went on, "Please, Roxanne, hear me out."

"All right."

"I'm sorry that happened. You didn't deserve those things Sarah said, and I certainly didn't mean to . . . I didn't know who was shining that lantern on us, and the first thing that occurred to me was to kiss you, to make it look like a romantic rendezvous." Elliot laughed bitterly. "Anyone who knows me well—as Sarah does—won't have any trouble believing I slipped out to the garden to meet a lady friend."

"I understand, Elliot," Roxanne said softly. "You did the right thing, I suppose. That was quick thinking." She laid a hand on his arm. "But you've probably ruined your engagement to Sarah. She was so furious, she'll no doubt call off the wedding."

"We had never set a date, not with everything so uncertain in the colonies right now. I don't know if we would have ever gotten married, even if this hadn't happened."

Roxanne could hear the deep disappointment in his voice as he spoke. Despite the brave front Elliot was putting up, he had been shaken by the night's events. Unless Sarah was more forgiving than Roxanne believed she was, Elliot had sacrified his relationship with her in order to preserve the secrecy of the work they were doing. If there had been any doubt in Roxanne's mind about Elliot's devotion to the cause of liberty, there was none now.

"You had better tell me the name of the ship and the

schedule she's following," Roxanne said quietly. "I'll contact the committee tonight and let them know about this."

"The ship is the *Carolingian* and she's due here in Boston early next week. I don't know the exact date, but I'll find out. I believe she makes one stop in New Hampshire first, then sails down the coast to Boston Harbor. I'll confirm that at the office tomorrow." He gave a snort of laughter. "My father is going to be a bit surprised at what an interest I'm taking in his business affairs again."

"Just be careful," cautioned Roxanne. "Don't make him suspicious."

"Don't worry. I know how to handle the old man."

She squeezed Elliot's arm and slipped out of the gazebo. "Good night," she called softly to him.

He waved but said nothing. When she glanced back before slipping through the rear gate, she saw him still standing there, his hands in his pockets, his shoulders slumped.

Roxanne hurried down the alley to her horse, thinking about what had just happened. Sarah's finding them in each other's arms was not the only surprise of the evening: When Elliot kissed Roxanne, she had felt her heart flutter, and a warmth had sprung up inside her that she had felt only once before—in the arms of Daniel Reed.

Avery Wallingford had been standing in a corner of the Markham ballroom, a glass of cognac in his hand. He was a slender young man of medium height, with a lean, aristocratically handsome face. His father was one of the leading bankers in Boston, as well as one of the most influential members of Tory society. Avery was invited to every party, and he had cut a wide swath through the attractive young women who traveled in the same circles. At one time, when they were both youngsters, he had been Elliot Markham's best friend.

Things had changed.

A few people remained in the ballroom, but the musicians had finished playing, packed up, and gone. Across the room, Avery saw Benjamin Markham, Theophilus Cummings, and his own father, deep in a discussion that probably concerned money and how they were going to use the coming war with the insurrectionists to make more profit than usual. Avery sipped his drink. *Trust that group to find a lining of silver—and gold—in all circumstances.*

The French doors banged open, and Sarah Cummings stalked in, leaving the doors ajar behind her.

Avery had rarely seen her look more beautiful, and he had never seen her as upset as she was at this moment. She was paler than usual and trembled as she made her way blindly across the room.

He moved away from the richly paneled wall and smoothly intersected Sarah's erratic course. Theophilus Cummings had not noticed how upset his daughter was, but that was all right, Avery thought; *he* would comfort her. He reached out to stop her.

Sarah flinched away from his touch and gasped in surprise. "Avery!" she exclaimed when her eyes focused on him. "It's only you."

"What a greeting," he murmured. "What's wrong, Sarah? You look quite shaken."

"I'm fine," she said, but her quavering voice betrayed the lie she spoke. "I—I need some air."

"But you just came in from the garden."

"Yes. The garden," repeated Sarah, her tone hardening.

Avery took her arm. "Come with me," he said firmly. "I think you need a friend."

She allowed him to lead her into the elegant high-ceilinged parlor. The painted faces in the family portraits on the wall opposite the fireplace stared down at them. The reflection in the gold-framed mirror over the mantel enabled Sarah to see Avery closing the door.

"You may be right," she said. "I think I do need someone to talk to."

"I'll certainly be glad to listen," Avery said as he walked toward her. "After all, we've been close for many years."

That was true. Sarah had been a part of the same group of well-to-do children that included Avery and Elliot. For a time Avery had been Elliot's rival for her affections, before she had decided that a match with Elliot would be more advantageous, since their fathers were business partners.

That pragmatic decision had not stopped her from accepting a carriage ride with Avery one day, nor had it prevented her from giving in to the sudden passion he had aroused in her. They had made wild love in the grass, underneath a tree—and not once in Sarah's moaning and thrashing had she called Elliot's name.

That thought made Avery smile with remembered pleasure. Elliot might have won the fair Sarah's hand, he thought, but he had sampled her gifts first.

"Now tell me," he said, holding her hands gently in his, "as one old friend to another, what happened?"

Sarah's self-control crumpled. Her lovely features twisted, and tears welled in her eyes. "I saw Elliot in the garden!" she sobbed.

"Did the two of you argue?"

"Worse! I saw them . . . I saw Elliot kissing that redheaded Darragh wench!"

Avery's eyes narrowed in surprise. "Roxanne Darragh?" he asked.

Tears rolled down Sarah's smooth cheeks.

"But I thought she and Daniel Reed—" Avery broke off his sentence and took a deep breath, remembering the scandal that had erupted a month earlier when Daniel Reed was exposed as an insurrectionist spy. Elliot had been furious that his cousin Daniel had used him to gain access to the Tories, Avery recalled, and the two of them had come to blows when the British major had arrived to arrest Daniel. Roxanne must have been humiliated by the discovery and in her shamed, upset condition turned to Elliot for comfort. It all made sense.

"I'm so sorry, Sarah," he went on, making his words sound genuinely sympathetic. He drew her into his arms and patted her lightly on the back. There was nothing sensuous about the embrace—not this time—but Avery was well aware of the sleek warmth of her body pressed up against his. "Do you know how serious they are about each other?"

"No," Sarah replied in a choked voice. "And I don't care, either! I don't want to have anything to do with either one of them anymore!"

"Poor, poor Sarah," Avery murmured. His brain was spinning, his thoughts clicking like the wheels of a racing wagon. How best to turn this situation to his advantage? He had to proceed carefully, he was sure of that.

"Perhaps you shouldn't be so quick to condemn Elliot. Things might not have been as they appeared."

"But I saw them!" Sarah straightened and looked up at him. "I saw him holding her and kissing her."

"She could have thrown herself into his arms and taken him by surprise. Or she could still be upset about Daniel, and perhaps Elliot was just comforting her as a friend—as I'm doing now with you."

"No, it wasn't that way. I'm sure of it. Roxanne's nothing but a shameless little trollop!"

Avery sighed. "Well, I think we should look into this further, Sarah. I'll tell you what I'll do: I'll keep an eye on Elliot for you and find out just how serious this is, all right?

Once I've discovered how deeply involved Elliot is with Roxanne, I'll tell you. I think you have a right to know."

"You'd do that for me, Avery?"

"Of course. I adore you, Sarah, you know that."

"Yes," she whispered, then rested her head against his chest.

This was not the moment to bring up the lovemaking they had already shared, Avery sensed. Let things remain as they were, he decided, with Sarah feeling sorrowful about Elliot and affectionate toward him. By defending Elliot, even halfheartedly, he had insured that Sarah would believe anything he told her concerning Elliot and Roxanne.

That would be the proper moment to strike and once more taste the sweetness Sarah possessed. And in time, she would be his and only his.

But between now and then, Avery was intensely curious about Roxanne Darragh. What had been going on between Elliot and her? He had always thought Roxanne was a lovely bit of baggage and certainly would not have minded a dalliance with the redhead. If she was upset about Daniel and looking for someone to comfort her . . .

It was no secret, Avery thought as he continued to hold Sarah tenderly: When it came to comforting beautiful young women, he was leagues ahead of Elliot Markham.

After leaving the Markham estate, Roxanne had hurried to the Salutation Tavern, only to find that none of the members of the Committee of Safety was there. The committee was shorthanded at the moment. Samuel Adams and John Hancock were away from Boston, and Dr. Joseph Warren had made himself scarce lately, as well. Dr. Benjamin Church was still in town, or he had been when he brought Roxanne back to Boston from the Parsons's farm. She knew where Paul Revere lived, but the British were watching him closely, and if she went to his house, she might compromise her effectiveness as an agent for the patriots.

She hesitated to trust the information in her possession to men she barely knew, such as Billy Dawes, James Otis, or Francis Rotch; she was well aware of the likelihood that there was a British spy on the committee.

Then she remembered Benjamin Tallmadge and Robert Townsend, friends and former classmates of Daniel's from Yale. Tallmadge and Townsend had helped persuade Daniel to join the patriots, and Roxanne decided her best course of action might be to contact them, although she hated to delay passing along the information about the shipment of British munitions. Better to wait than to tell the wrong person, she finally decided.

Physically and emotionally exhausted, Roxanne went home. But sleep did not come easily. She couldn't tell if her wakefulness was due to the shipload of munitions—or the passionate kiss Elliot and she had shared. She wasn't in love with him; it was her body and not her spirit that had responded to his touch. But could the two be so separated? Roxanne had never believed so before.

In the gray light of dawn she finally dozed off.

Chapter Four

The night had been a long one for Daniel Reed, although no one had approached the campsite during the night. Quincy had awakened him from a deep sleep to take the second watch, and Murdoch had relieved him three hours later. Daniel had fallen asleep again with no difficulty, and when Murdoch woke him the next morning, he was the last to rise. Quincy was already saddling the horses; Cordelia was nowhere in sight.

Daniel sat up abruptly in his blanket. "Where's the girl?" he asked Murdoch.

"She, um, had t' go tend t' herself. Anyway tha's what she told me." The big frontiersman looked a bit embarrassed. "She's on the other side of these pines."

Throwing his blanket aside, Daniel leapt to his feet. "I hope she hasn't run off," he said worriedly. "She's liable to run into those men who were looking for her."

"I think you're too suspicious of Cordelia," Quincy said as he turned away from the horses.

"And why shouldn't I be? Has she done anything so far but make trouble for us?"

"What trouble?" Quincy challenged.

Daniel picked up his blanket and folded it.

"Well, first of all she was the cause of us lying to those ruffians."

"She was unconscious at the time," Quincy pointed out. "You're the one who made that decision, Daniel."

"And it's one I pray doesn't come back to haunt us. She's done nothing but complain and make life miserable for us."

"You're wrong," Quincy said angrily. "You ought not to be so critical of her, Daniel."

"Why?" Daniel snapped. He was growing irritated. "Because she's soft and warm and has hair the color of corn silk?"

At that moment Cordelia appeared around the edge of the stand of pines and said tartly, "Anyone with eyes can see the color of my hair, Mr. Reed, but I'll thank you not to comment on things you have no knowledge of, such as how soft and warm I am!"

Daniel felt himself flush. He'd had no idea she would overhear what he was saying. The thought of being embarrassed by her only made him angry.

Cordelia walked over to Quincy and laid a hand on his arm. "Thank you for defending me, Quincy. At least someone in this group doesn't distrust me." She smiled sweetly at the young man, then glanced over her shoulder at Daniel.

He swallowed his anger and moved to the campfire Murdoch was kindling. Turning his back to Cordelia and Quincy, he asked, "How much longer do you think it'll be before we reach Bennington?"

"Hard t' say," grunted Murdoch. He was feeding large sticks to the snapping fire. "The country 'tween here and there isn't too bad, but 'tis hilly. We won't be able t' travel very fast. If we dinna get there late tomorrow, we should arrive the next day at the latest."

"That's fine. I want to get there as soon as we can, but there's no point in killing our mounts just to shave off a few hours."

"Aye," Murdoch agreed. He looked up from where he squatted next to the small blaze. "Especially since one o' the animals is carrying double."

Daniel would have been happier if Murdoch had not pointed out that fact. For the moment, he wanted to forget Cordelia Howard, her bad mood, and the trouble she had already caused them. He was going to get her off their hands as soon as possible after they reached Bennington, and good riddance.

Breakfast was salt pork and corn cakes, the same as the night before, but in the early morning hours of his watch, Murdoch had located a beehive, and they had wild honey on their cakes. After they had eaten and put out the fire, Murdoch and Quincy packed the remainder of their gear onto the horses.

"I hope I'll be riding with you again today, Quincy." Cordelia's voice was more than loud enough for Daniel to hear, but she managed to make the words sound soft and caressing. "You were so careful not to jostle me yesterday."

"I'm sure you can ride with me, M-Miss Howard," Quincy said. His eyes were downcast as he spoke.

"You don't have to call me Miss Howard," Cordelia said with a laugh. "My goodness, that makes me sound like some sort of old lady. Why, I'd wager I'm not more than a few years older than you, Quincy. My name is Cordelia, and that's what I want you to call me."

The boy beamed as he tightened the cinch on his horse's saddle. "Sure. I'd be glad to, Cordelia."

She looked at Daniel, but he kept his face expressionless and busily got his mount ready to ride.

Murdoch led the way as they left the camp, trailed by Quincy and Cordelia, then Daniel. Cordelia was speaking quietly to Quincy, talking almost directly into his ear, and she kept her voice so low that Daniel could not make out what she was saying. He could see that Quincy was blushing again, though.

Daniel put his horse into a trot and rode past them. *Let them bring up the rear for a while,* he thought.

He caught up to Murdoch and asked, "Do you recognize any landmarks around here?"

"Aye. Tha's Mount Greylock over yonder." He waved to the west, toward the stocky gray eminence of a mountain taller than any that surrounded it. As he swept his big hand around to the north and pointed a knobby finger, he went on, "And up there be th' Dome. Tha' one's over th' border in Ethan Allen's territory. We'll skirt it t' the east, probably in the morning."

"It doesn't look that far away," mused Daniel.

"Distances can fool a man out here. Ye'd do well t' remember that, Dan'l."

Ever since they had been forced to seek refuge on the Parsons's farm, Daniel had enjoyed being away from civilization with the woodsman. He had spent much of his childhood in Virginia outdoors, hunting and fishing, but Murdoch had gone over the Cumberland Gap with Daniel Boone and helped to found Boonesborough, in the Kentucky Territory; from there he had moved west, into the valley of the Ohio River. Daniel loved to sit by a fire and listen to Murdoch tell yarns about exploring, trapping, and fighting Indians. He knew there was much he could learn from Murdoch Buchanan about surviving in the wilderness.

As the morning passed, Daniel worried less about Perry

Faulkner and his henchmen. It was possible that they had doubled back and passed the camp unknowingly in the night and were now somewhere ahead of them. It was just as likely that the scoundrel had struck off in a different direction in his hunt for Cordelia.

Daniel caught her glaring at him after they had stopped to rest the horses. She seemed to despise him, and that was just fine with him. In less than two days they would arrive in Bennington, and then Miss Cordelia Howard would be someone else's worry.

When the sun was high overhead, Daniel called a halt for lunch. The day had warmed up, and Cordelia had removed her cloak. As she slid down from the back of Quincy's horse, her gray breeches tightened across her rounded hips, and Daniel looked away quickly. She might be wearing a man's trousers and shirt and a tricorn hat, but only a blind man would mistake her for a male. Not the way her breasts thrust so engagingly against her shirt—

What am I doing? Daniel thought. *This woman is nothing more than a good-looking annoyance. Roxanne is just as beautiful, and she's twice the woman this mindless, self-centered twit is.*

Cordelia sat down next to Quincy. Lunch consisted of cold leftovers from breakfast, and she made a face as she tore off a piece of corn cake and chewed it. The salt pork was even tougher. She swallowed, took a drink from the water jug Quincy handed her, then said, "This is not the way I'm accustomed to living."

" 'Tis not fancy, I'll give ye that," Murdoch agreed from his perch on a thick, fallen log. "But I've eaten a lot worse in my time."

"We'll be in Bennington tomorrow, with any luck," Daniel said as he sat down next to Murdoch. "Then you'll have all the comforts of civilization again, Miss Howard."

"It can't be soon enough to please me. I'm tired of living like some sort of barbarian."

"I'm sure Perry Faulkner would have been pleased to provide better accommodations for you," Daniel said.

She glanced at him, her blue eyes glittering with anger. "I doubt that," she replied acidly.

"Then stop your complaining, for heaven's sake! I've never met such an ungrateful, spoiled—"

"You've no call to talk like that, Daniel!" Quincy exclaimed. "Cordelia hasn't caused us any trouble, and she hasn't slowed us down."

Daniel took a bite of food and stared into the distance as he ate. After a long pause, he said, "I suppose not."

"What a gallant admission." Contempt dripped from Cordelia's words.

Daniel swallowed the last of his food and stood up. "I believe I'll take a walk, have a look around." He stalked into the woods beside the trail, eager to answer the call of nature and get away from Cordelia for a few moments.

He did not stray far, and when he felt calm enough to face her again, he started back. Out of habit, he was careful to make as little noise as possible as he approached the others.

It quickly became clear to him that Cordelia did not know he was close by. Daniel stopped to listen as she was saying to Quincy, "Tell me about your brother."

"What is there to tell? Daniel's a fine brother. He's taken good care of me the last couple of years. Sometimes a little too good. He acts like a mother hen, you see. Once, back in Boston, I got mixed up in some trouble—"

No! Daniel thought. *Don't tell her what we're involved in! We don't know her well enough to trust her!*

Something kept him from leaping into the camp and shouting those words out loud. He stayed where he was, frozen in position in the stand of pines, listening intently to hear what Quincy was going to say next.

"I wasn't attending my classes at the Latin School, you see," Quincy went on after a second's hesitation. "Things like that. But Daniel never got really angry. He just tried to make me understand the right thing to do."

"He seems very bossy to me," Cordelia said with a sniff.

Quincy chuckled. "As I said, he can be a mother hen. But he means well."

"It's a shame he's so obnoxious. He's rather handsome, you know."

"Daniel?" Quincy sounded just as surprised as Daniel felt. "I suppose a girl might think so. I've never thought about it."

"Well, you shouldn't be surprised. Good looks run in the same family, and you're quite an attractive young man, also, Quincy."

"Me?"

"Of course. I think you're adorable." Cordelia changed the subject by asking, "Where has Mr. Buchanan gone off to?"

"I imagine he's just taking a look around," Quincy told her. "Murdoch likes to do that. He says a man's got to keep his eyes open on the frontier if he wants to live very long."

After a moment, Cordelia said, "I hate this wilderness. I'll be glad when we get to a town."

"Don't worry, Miss Howard—I mean, Cordelia. We'll take care of you. We won't let anything happen to you."

"You're sweet, Quincy, but I'm not sure you understand exactly what's going on."

"You could tell me," Quincy prodded.

Daniel heard her hesitate before saying, "I really don't want to talk about it. It's just too unpleasant."

"Well, all right. If that's what you think is best. It's really none of our business, anyway."

Tired of eavesdropping, Daniel shuffled his feet back and forth to make some noise, then stepped around the pines and into the camp. "Where's Murdoch?" he asked.

"Off scouting in the woods somewhere, I guess," Quincy replied. "He's probably checking our back trail."

"Get ready to ride. I'm sure he'll return soon."

Murdoch tramped out of the forest a few minutes later and waved a big hand toward a hill not far off. "Been up yonder taking a look around," he said. "I did'na see anyone following us."

"We've given Perry the slip," Cordelia said happily. "He's probably miles away from here."

"We can hope so," Daniel said. "Let's mount up and get moving."

Toward midafternoon the trail widened, and Daniel was not surprised when they rounded a bend and spotted a crossroads with a small inn beside it. It was a sturdily built, two-story log and stone structure, with a hitching rail out front and a stable to one side. From the looks of it, the place was not busy; only two horses were tied at the railing.

"Civilization!" Cordelia exclaimed with a sigh. "Can we stop?"

Daniel turned around in his saddle to look at her. "It's only the middle of the afternoon," he said. "We could ride another couple of hours."

"I need some hot food and perhaps a cup of tea." Cordelia took a deep breath and made the visible effort required for her to say, "Please?"

Quincy added, "A bowl of stew would be mighty nice after all those corn cakes and salt pork, Daniel."

"I would'na mind a mug o' ale," the big redhead said.

"All right," Daniel agreed. "I don't think we're going to

make it to Bennington until the day after tomorrow, anyway. I don't suppose stopping here for a while will hurt."

Cordelia contented herself with an expression of smug self-satisfaction.

They rode up to the hitching rail and dismounted. The sign hanging over the door of the inn proclaimed it to be the Wild Boar, and there was a picture of just such an animal, snorting fiercely, underneath the words. The artist was talented, Daniel thought, and had captured the essence of the boar's charge. He could almost hear the animal's frenzied grunting and feel its hot breath.

Murdoch led the way inside, opening the door and stepping into the large public room. The floor was made of puncheons, and rough-hewn tables and benches were the only furniture. On the right-hand wall was a massive stone fireplace, while opposite it was a simple bar made of crudely hacked planks laid across several barrels. At the back of the room a flight of stairs led to the second floor, where lodgings could be rented. Daniel had seen dozens of inns such as this one; its only unique feature was the row of boars' heads above the fireplace.

There were just two patrons in the room, as well as an elderly man behind the bar. Judging from the dirty apron the old-timer wore, Daniel figured that he was the proprietor.

The man gave the newcomers a feeble smile and said loudly, "Come in, gentlemen and lady. Come in!"

"I can tell why th' old one's glad to see us," Murdoch muttered to Daniel. "Did ye ever see a place more in need o' some business? There's probably dust on the ale spigots!"

"We can hope not," Daniel said dryly. He motioned for Quincy and Cordelia to sit down at one of the tables, and then he and Murdoch strolled over to the bar. "My friends and I were hoping we could get something to drink and perhaps hot food."

The old man did not meet Daniel's eyes. Instead, he looked past Daniel's shoulder and said, "Got a pot of stew simmering over the coals in the fireplace. Will that do?"

"That'll be just fine," Daniel told him, "along with cider for my brother and the young lady, and ale for my friend and me."

"Right away, sir." Still the old man did not look at Daniel. He reached for wooden bowls and spoons on a shelf behind the bar.

Every instinct told Daniel that something was wrong, and a glance at Murdoch showed that he was also tense. Daniel trusted the Scotsman's hunches, but this time the warning came too late.

They heard footsteps on the stairs at the back of the room, and Cordelia let out a frightened scream.

"Perry!" she cried.

Daniel spun around. Perry Faulkner, cocked pistol in hand, stood on the stairway with two of his men behind him. Two more appeared in the doorway at the front of the building, while three more crowded into the room from a rear entrance under the stairs. All eight men had their guns drawn, as did the strangers who had been sitting at one of the tables. Those two were clearly part of Faulkner's group, even though they had not been with him the day before. All ten men trained their weapons on Daniel, Murdoch, Quincy, and Cordelia.

"I know you thought you could get away from me, my dear," Faulkner said to Cordelia, his narrowed eyes fixed on her. "But I've proven you wrong, just as I said I would."

Daniel tensed, ready to make a move, but Murdoch stopped him with a low-voiced growl. "Take it easy, lad. There be too many for us t' fight."

Cordelia lifted her hands to her mouth as Faulkner sauntered down the stairs and across the room toward her.

"You've led me on a merry chase, Cordelia," he said. His voice was deceptively calm. "But it's over now. You'll be going with me."

"No!" she said, her voice trembling with anger and terror. "I'm never going anywhere with you again, Perry!"

Quincy sat beside Cordelia, his face pale and his body rigid. Daniel kept a close eye on him, hoping he would not do anything foolish—such as try to jump Faulkner. From the look on that man's face, Daniel knew that he was seething with rage under his smooth exterior, and probably wouldn't hesitate to shoot anyone who crossed him, even a boy.

Faulkner paused a few feet from the table where Cordelia and Quincy sat. He pointed his pistol directly at them and said, "On the contrary, Cordelia, you're in no position to tell me what you will or will not do."

"Hold on a minute, mister," Daniel said.

Faulkner turned toward him quickly and lifted the pistol until it was trained on Daniel's chest. "I should have known that the three of you would be with my wife when I caught up to her. As soon as I laid eyes on you yesterday, I knew you were a bunch of lying bastards."

Daniel barely heard the insult. Instead he was focused on Faulkner's first comment to him. "Wife?" he repeated softly.

"That's right." Faulkner's lips curved in an arrogant smile. "Cordelia and I are married."

In shock, Quincy stared openmouthed at the blonde while Daniel peered at her curiously. She met his gaze for an instant, then dropped her eyes to the table in front of her.

"Wife," Daniel said again, his voice flat and angry.

"Indeed," Faulkner said crisply. "And not only have you aided and sheltered a runaway wife, denying me my husbandly right to do with her as I please, but you've helped a thief as well."

"What did she steal?" Daniel asked.

"That's none of your business."

Daniel waited for Cordelia to refute the accusation, but she continued to stare down at the table. She was pale, and she trembled slightly, like a deer caught in the sight of a rifle, wanting to leap away to safety but held where she was by an invisible bond.

"You're lying!" The words burst out of Quincy.

"No, son, I'm not," Faulkner said. "I'm not surprised she's taken you in, though. Cordelia can usually get a man to believe anything she wants him to." A hint of bitterness crept into his voice as he spoke.

"We had no idea she was married to you," Daniel assured Faulkner. Despite his instinctive dislike of the man, Daniel knew that he, Quincy, and Murdoch had no right to interfere in what went on between a husband and wife.

"As I said, I'm not surprised," Faulkner said. "But that doesn't really matter now, does it?"

"You've got her back, and that's the end of it, I suppose," Daniel agreed reluctantly.

"Not quite." An arrogant smile played across Faulkner's face again. "The three of you lied to me, deliberately deceived me."

Cordelia looked up sharply. "No, Perry! It's not their fault! Leave them alone, please!" She started to stand up.

Suddenly Faulkner reached out and brutally grasped Cordelia's shoulder, his fingers digging into her flesh and causing her to gasp in pain. He held her there, half-standing beside the table. "Stay out of this, Cordelia," he snapped. "This is between me and these three gentlemen who so gallantly tried to help you."

"Take your hand off her, mister!" Quincy said angrily.

"All right," Faulkner said, and without further warning, he released Cordelia's shoulder and swung his arm in a vicious backhand that cracked across Quincy's cheek and knocked him off the bench.

Furious, Daniel sprang forward, but nine pistols were instantly leveled at Murdoch and him. "You cowardly son of a bitch!" Daniel cried. "He's only a boy."

"He's grown-up enough to be taken in by my lying slut of a wife," Faulkner sneered. "Listen! No one lies to me or crosses me—even unintentionally—without paying for it. Do you understand?"

"I understand that ye be a yellow dog, mister," Murdoch said. "Why don't ye come over here and try t' knock me around like ye did th' lad?"

"I wouldn't dirty my hands on the likes of you." Faulkner tucked his pistol under his belt, grabbed Cordelia's arm, and jerked her toward the doorway with him. Over his shoulder he said to his men, "Teach the three of them a lesson that will stay with them the rest of their days!"

"No!" Cordelia wailed. She tried to pull away, but Faulkner shoved her out the door and followed closely behind.

Quincy scrambled up from the floor, but Daniel warned him to stay down. Then he realized it was not going to make any difference. Faulkner's men were putting their pistols away, grinning in anticipation of what he had given them permission to do. There were nine of them, so the odds were three to one in their favor—and nothing was going to stop them from having their fun.

"Still think there's too many of them to fight, Murdoch?" Daniel asked quietly.

"Aye," replied the big frontiersman. "But we're not going t' have a choice, are we? Times like this, ye got t' do the best ye can."

With a bellow of rage, Murdoch balled his fists and lunged forward. Daniel was right behind him, and Quincy, putting his head down, charged into one of the men near him. Their attack took Faulkner's men by surprise, and Daniel hoped it might be enough to offset the odds against them. His fist lashed out and connected solidly with a beard-stubbled jaw, sending one of the toughs staggering backward.

Murdoch had swept two of the men into a bear hug and crashed them together. The big Scotsman was still yelling. Daniel knew he enjoyed nothing more than a great brawl.

Quincy possessed a good deal of strength for such a wiry young man, and he was quick on his feet. He dodged one ponderous blow and struck a lightning-fast jab to his opponent's nose. The man howled in pain as blood spurted down his face and onto the front of his shirt. Quincy whirled away to find another target, but someone grabbed him from behind, arms binding him like iron. He was jerked upward, and his feet hung above the floor.

Daniel blocked a punch and slammed a fist into the stomach of the man facing him. He felt a blow to the side of his head, and it staggered him for a moment, but then he regained his balance and drove an elbow to the side. He experienced a satisfying sensation as the blow caught one of the men in the chest.

Murdoch's next move was an attempt to turn the odds completely around. As several of the attackers charged toward him, he grabbed a heavy, rough-hewn bench and, with a surge of strength that made the muscles in his back and shoulders ripple against his buckskin shirt, flung it as if it were nothing but a lightweight chair. The elderly proprietor of the inn cried out from behind the bar as the bench crashed into the oncoming men. They went down hard, and the bench tumbled to the floor.

Quincy, still held from behind, managed to kick out with his feet and knock a man down. His resistance came to an end, though, as the one who was holding him butted him head-to-head from behind, stunning him. Then fists thudded into Quincy's belly, and he could fight back no longer.

"Quincy! Hang on, I'm coming!" Daniel said when he saw what was happening to his brother. But before he could reach Quincy's side, a man tackled Daniel around the waist. He went down, and Faulkner's man landed heavily on top of him, driving the breath from his lungs. As he gasped for air, the man jerked Daniel's head up by the hair and smashed his head against the floor.

The world was wavering in front of his eyes. He summoned all his strength and tried to shake the man off him, but it was no use. Daniel felt himself sliding down a long, steep slope toward darkness. As he looked up, he saw Murdoch Buchanan flailing and fighting and shouting in the sheer joy of battle, even though he was surrounded by Faulkner's men and sinking beneath their furious assault.

Then Daniel reached the bottom of the slope and fell off into nothingness. His last thought was of how his luck had taken a definite turn for the worse on the day he first met the young woman who called herself Cordelia.

Chapter Five

It was warm, dark, and peaceful where Daniel was, and he did not want to leave. He moaned as shards of light penetrated the blackness surrounding him. Like brilliant daggers, the light stabbed at him, and when he tried to turn away from its annoying brightness, more pain exploded through his placid universe.

"He's coming around, he is. At least, I think so."

The voice boomed down at him, assaulting tender eardrums and making him wince.

"Give me that bottle. A wee dram will make the poor lad perk up."

Strong hands helped him hold his head up, and he felt the neck of a bottle being forced between his swollen lips. Liquid fire filled his mouth. He swallowed to keep from choking, and the blaze burned out of control all the way down his gullet and into his stomach.

Daniel opened his eyes, blinked, and stared up into the battered face of Murdoch Buchanan.

The Scotsman's wide mouth stretched in a grin. "Ah, ye be alive after all, Dan'l. Quincy and me, we were starting t' think ye had passed beyond the vale." Murdoch lifted the bottle toward Daniel's mouth again.

"N-no more," he rasped. "That stuff is awful!"

"Aye, 'tis homemade busthead, brewed right here at th' Wild Boar by Master Plemons himself. It has a good kick, and tha's what ye needed t' wake ye up."

With Murdoch's help, Daniel pulled himself into a sitting position and looked around. Moving his head sent waves of pain through him.

The evidence of battle was everywhere. Tables were overturned, crockery was shattered, and benches had been smashed into kindling. A few feet away, Quincy sat huddled on one of the few benches that had been left in one piece. He was holding a wet cloth to the right side of his face.

"Quincy!" Daniel exclaimed. "Are you all right?"

"I think so."

"The lad's bunged up a bit, but he'll be fine," Murdoch assured Daniel. The frontiersman bore his own cuts and bruises. He grasped Daniel's outstretched hand, lifted the younger man onto his feet, then helped him onto a bench.

Daniel drew a deep but painful breath and took the wet cloth offered to him by the elderly proprietor of the inn.

The old man looked nervous as he hovered around the three of them, eager to do anything he could to help. "Right sorry I am about what happened, lads," he said shakily. "If you need anything . . . "

Daniel pressed the cool cloth against his forehead. It helped to ease the ache a bit. "Just be quiet for a moment," he said to Plemons.

" 'Course, young sir, be glad to. Nobody can say that old Ike Plemons doesn't know when to shut his mouth—"

The man stopped short after Murdoch gave him a stern look.

For a few minutes Daniel sat, recovering a little of his strength. His stomach was queasy from the bad whiskey, but he had to admit the fire in his belly had helped bring him back from unconsciousness. He pushed himself to his feet, walked gingerly to the bench where Quincy was sitting, and sat down slowly beside his brother. "Let's have a look at you," Daniel said.

Quincy lowered the cloth from his face, and Daniel winced when he saw the huge bruise covering the right side of his brother's face. In addition, there were several smears of dried blood from cuts and scratches; his right eye was swollen shut.

Daniel supposed he looked just about as bad. He ran his fingers over his cheek and felt the sting of splinters embedded in his skin from a hard landing on the floor. "Neither of us is going to be very pretty for a while," he said dryly.

"Cordelia won't think we're so handsome now." Quincy returned Daniel's weary smile.

"I never figured they'd do this," Plemons said. "I knew they was bad, the way they came in here and took over, told me what I had to do when the three of you showed up. But I didn't know they'd come so close to killing you, I swear to that."

Daniel looked up at the old man. "They bullied you into going along with what they wanted, is that it?"

"That's it!"

Plemons was a little too quick to seize on that explanation, Daniel thought. It was more likely Faulkner simply bribed the old man for the use of the inn to set his trap. Not that it mattered. What was done was done; Cordelia was gone, and Faulkner had had his revenge. There was no point in taking out his anger on the elderly innkeeper.

Murdoch was sitting on one of the tables. He still had the whiskey bottle in his hand, and he tilted it to his lips for a long, healthy swallow. Daniel shuddered at the thought of putting that much whiskey into his body.

Murdoch merely wiped his mouth with the back of his hand. "Well?" he asked. "What do we do now?"

"What do you think we should do?" Daniel asked in return.

"I know exactly what we should do," Quincy said without hesitation. "We have to help Cordelia."

"She's his wife, Quincy. You heard Faulkner. She ran away from him, and she stole from him, too. You can't still feel sorry for her."

"Cordelia never said she did those things," Quincy protested.

"She didn't deny them, either."

"The lad's got a point, Dan'l. Could be the lass was too scared o' Faulkner t' refute what he was saying. Or maybe not. What really matters is that he had the bastards jump us. We cannot allow them t' get away with that."

"So we go after them and risk another beating because they already gave us one? I'm afraid I don't follow the logic of that argument, Murdoch."

"Logic, hell!" Murdoch pointed to the cuts and bruises on his face. "A Buchanan does not let a man get away with the likes o' this!"

"He's right, Daniel," Quincy said. "We've got a score to settle with those men—and with Faulkner. And it has nothing to do with Cordelia."

It has everything to do with Cordelia, Daniel thought. If they had not encountered her, they would not have had all this trouble. And they still had to get to Bennington in time to rendezvous with Colonel Ethan Allen before the campaign to take Fort Ticonderoga began. The smart thing to do would be to forget they had ever seen Cordelia Howard—or Cordelia Faulkner.

The only thing keeping him from saying so was the memory of how terrified she had looked as Faulkner shoved her toward the door. Wife or no wife, she had been afraid Faulkner would kill her. Daniel could not stand by and let such a thing happen, not when he could try to stop it.

"Which way did they go?" he wearily asked the old innkeeper.

"South. They took the south road," Plemons said.

"Where will that lead them?"

"There's another crossroads about five miles from here. The road to Pittsfield and the Manor of Rensselaer in New York Colony runs through there." Plemons shrugged. "Could be where they're going. I've got no way of knowing for sure."

"The important thing is that if Faulkner hasn't gone north toward Bennington, we'll have to go completely out of our way to chase him."

"What about it, Daniel?" Quincy asked impatiently.

"We'll take a look at the trail and see if there's any sign of them," Daniel said. "I'm not promising more than that." Daniel looked up at Plemons. "Get us something to eat before we leave," he said. "We never did get the hot meal we came here after."

The stew was greasy and filled with chunks of meat gristly enough to have come from one of the wild boar whose dusty heads hung over the fireplace. But the food was hot and, along with generous pieces of freshly baked bread, helped the men regain their strength. Daniel was sore and stiff, his head still hurt, and his cheek still stung from the splinters, but he felt human again when he finished the meal.

While they were eating, Plemons had gone outside to water their horses and give the animals some grain. Daniel was surprised—but grateful—that Faulkner had not stolen their mounts.

Plemons came back inside as Murdoch was sopping up the last bit of grease in his bowl with his bread. "Your horses are ready to go, lads. I wish you all the luck in the world."

"Unless Faulkner returns, eh?" Daniel took a coin from his pocket and flipped it to the old man, who plucked it out of the air with surprising deftness. "That's for the stew—and for keeping quiet about us in case anyone comes by asking questions."

Plemons frowned. "Who do you expect to be after you boys?"

"I don't expect anyone," Daniel replied. "That's just in case you see Faulkner before we do."

"Oh, he won't come back," Plemons said. "He got what he wanted here."

"Keep the money, just in case."

"Oh, yes, I'll keep the money, all right." Plemons glanced around at the debris littering the floor. "There's an unholy mess to clean up here. Going to take even more cash to put this place right."

"Ye'll have t' get it somewhere else," growled Murdoch. "We're not paying ye another penny for helping Faulkner that way."

"No, no, that's fine," Plemons said quickly. "I don't want any more trouble."

"Neither do we," Daniel said earnestly.

Plemons bit the coin and stowed it away in his apron pocket as the travelers left.

Quincy went straight to his horse, but Daniel and Murdoch stopped him from mounting up.

"Hold on," Daniel said. "We'll take a look at the tracks in the road first."

Walking carefully in order not to smudge any tracks in the dirt, Daniel and Murdoch could see where Faulkner's men had led their horses from the barn next to the inn. The riders had headed south, just as Plemons had suggested.

He and Murdoch went back to the hitching rail and swung up into their saddles. "All right," Daniel said, "let's go."

As they headed down the road he glanced up at the trees, trying to tell how much longer light would be filtering through the new growth on their branches. There could not be much more than an hour's worth of daylight left, he reasoned, but that would not matter. The light of the moon and stars would be more than enough to let them follow the trail.

With each step the horses took, Daniel was farther from his ultimate goal. He was brooding over that thought when Quincy said, "I want you to know I appreciate this, Daniel."

"I suppose you see yourself as a gallant knight trying to rescue his princess from her evil captor," Daniel said, eyeing his brother.

"We're going after Faulkner to help Cordelia. It's the right thing to do, and you know it," Quincy said, blushing furiously.

"What we're after, laddies, is vengeance, plain and simple," Murdoch said fiercely.

"Yes, but the main thing is to see that Cordelia is safe," argued Quincy. He turned back to Daniel. "I know you didn't get along with her very well—"

"That was her idea, not mine. She was the one who seemed to be naturally unfriendly."

"Not to me, she wasn't. And I think she liked you, too, Daniel. You just got off on the wrong foot."

Daniel thought back to the conversation between Quincy and Cordelia he had overheard and had to admit that her attitude toward him seemed to be softening a bit. But then, moments later, she had been as acerbic to him as ever. *No, Quincy has to be wrong,* he thought. *Cordelia harbors only bad feelings toward me.*

Soon the forested hills grew dusky as the sun fell lower in the sky and finally set. While the stars twinkled to life in the darkening sky, Daniel, Quincy, and Murdoch reached the crossroad Plemons had told them about. They reined in, and Daniel said, "What do you think, Murdoch? Did they turn west, like the old man said they might?"

"It would be better if there were a bit more light," Murdoch said as he leaned far over in the saddle to study the surface of the road. "There's not been much traffic along here." He straightened. "My best guess is they went west, just like the old skalleyhooter said."

"Then we'll head west, too." Daniel looked over at his brother. "You have to understand something, Quincy. If we find Faulkner and his men and can help Cordelia, that's fine. I hope we do. But we can't spend a week or more looking for them. We have a job waiting for us."

"I understand," Quincy replied quietly. "Don't worry, Daniel. I've got a bigger score to settle with the British than I do with Faulkner." He slapped his thigh where the musket ball had torn through it during the raid on the munitions warehouse in Boston.

"Let's go, then." Daniel heeled his horse into a trot and headed down the road to the west.

* * *

Only two hours after Roxanne Darragh had fallen asleep shortly before dawn, she awoke with a start, her heart pounding. Memories from the night before flooded into her consciousness and merged with what she had been dreaming, and for a moment she couldn't distinguish between the two. Had she actually kissed Elliot Markham? Had she really felt such intense desire for him? And how would that kiss change the course of Elliot's relationship with Sarah Cummings, and his future?

But those concerns faded when she recalled with a jolt what she had learned from Elliot: A ship loaded with munitions intended for the British was on its way to Boston. She had to find Benjamin Tallmadge and Robert Townsend and let them know. And the sooner the better.

She had no guarantee they were even in Boston; when Daniel had last spoken to them, their organization was operating primarily in Cambridge, Lexington, Roxbury, and other areas outside the city. She knew that Daniel had gotten in touch with them several times through a stationer's store near Faneuil Hall, and after she had dressed and eaten a biscuit and tea, she went there first.

Roxanne entered the store, bought several sheets of foolscap, and mentioned to the clerk that a friend of hers, one Benjamin Tallmadge, had recommended the establishment to her. She asked casually if Tallmadge had been in lately.

"Ben Tallmadge?" asked the clerk, scratching his head. "Don't know if I recall the fellow."

"He's a friend of Daniel Reed's," Roxanne told him and added meaningfully, "and so am I. My name is Roxanne Darragh."

She saw a flicker of recognition in the man's eyes.

"If I see this man Tallmadge, do you want me to tell him you're looking for him?"

"Could you?"

"I suppose there wouldn't be any harm in that—if you're really a friend of Daniel Reed's."

"I am," Roxanne said sincerely, hoping this gamble would pay off.

Less than an hour later a messenger arrived at her home, bringing an unsigned note containing an address and a time. Scrawled at the bottom of the paper were the words *second floor.*

Now, at dusk, with a light mist rolling in from the bay, Roxanne waited nervously in the doorway of a brick building on one of Boston's quiet side streets. She wore a respectable square-necked dress of dark green linen, with a matching green bonnet over her red hair, and a light wrap to protect her from the damp spring air.

She was waiting for Elliot Markham. As soon as she had received the note from Tallmadge and Townsend, she had sent a young boy to the offices of Markham & Cummings with a message to be delivered personally to Elliot. She had written the note on a piece of paper from her father's print shop, and she had folded it, sealed it with wax, and written Elliot's name on the outside in a square and masculine hand—all in the hope that anyone glancing at the note would assume it had something to do with business.

She spotted a figure hurrying down the cobblestone street, passing in and out of the squares of light cast by lanterns behind the windows of the buildings. It was a man, and as he got closer, Roxanne recognized Elliot, even though he wore an inexpensive black suit that was not much like his usual elegant garb. His tricorn hat, however, was cocked at its usual jaunty angle.

Elliot reached for her hands as he came up to her in the doorway. "I got your message. I must admit, I was surprised to hear from you again so soon. Were you able to get the information to the committee?"

"That's why I summoned you here. I wasn't able to find any of the committee members last night, so I've arranged a meeting with Benjamin Tallmadge and Robert Townsend."

In the shadowy doorway Roxanne could not see Elliot's face clearly, but he paused in surprise at her words. "Tallmadge and Townsend," he repeated. "Daniel told me about them. They met with Nathan Hale and him at the Hare and Hound a while ago, didn't they? He said their talk with him that night was one of the reasons he became involved with the patriot cause."

"I'm going to tell them about the *Carolingian.*"

"That's a good idea," Elliot agreed. "And you want me to talk to them as well?"

"Yes. You and I have already discussed the possibility that the British have an agent inside the committee. I think it's time we begin to work on our own. I feel wretched about going behind the backs of the committee members; after all, it was their influence that formed my ideas of liberty. But if there *is* a traitor in their midst, it's time for us to begin acting independently. Otherwise the revolution might be over before it's properly begun."

"We'll need to be very cautious," Elliot mused, "but I think you're right, Roxanne. Men like Tallmadge and Townsend might be able to put this information to better use than the committee." He looked past her at the entry to the building. "Is this where we're supposed to meet them? The place looks deserted."

"I was told to come to this address at six o'clock, to the second floor," Roxanne explained.

Elliot took her arm. "Well, then, let's go up."

She eased her arm out of his grip. "I'm going first. I

want you to wait outside in case there's any trouble. That way perhaps both of us won't get caught and exposed if this is a British trap."

"I'm not sure that's a good idea. You should wait outside, and I'll go in."

"They're expecting a woman," Roxanne pointed out quietly. "What I suggested is the only safe way to proceed, Elliot."

"I suppose you're right. But I'll only agree if you let me go inside the building with you. I'll stay back so they can't see me. I'm armed with a pistol, and if there's the slightest sign of trouble, call out to me. I'll be in there in an instant."

"All right," she agreed, anxious to get on with the rendezvous. "Let's go."

Elliot opened the heavy door, and they entered the building together. A faint light shone at the head of a staircase in front of them, giving off just enough illumination for them to find their way. Roxanne glanced around and saw that the foyer through which they passed was empty. There was a musty smell, suggesting that the building had stood abandoned for a while. She wondered if Tallmadge and Townsend had used it for other secret meetings.

Side by side she and Elliot went up the staircase, which seemed solid enough despite the deserted state of the building. When they reached the second floor landing, they saw that the light came from an open doorway to the right.

Roxanne put her lips close to Elliot's ear and whispered, "Wait here." She stepped toward the door and called, "Mr. Tallmadge? Mr. Townsend?"

"Is that you, Miss Darragh?" a man's voice asked from inside the room.

"Yes, it is."

"Come ahead, then. But I warn you, if this is a trick, I'm

armed. There'll be a pistol pointing at you as soon as you enter."

"It's no trick," Roxanne assured the man.

She walked into the room and saw two men seated on straight-backed chairs. They held flintlock pistols, and both weapons were trained on her. Through her nervousness she managed to smile, and she held her hands out slightly to the side. "As you can see, I'm unarmed."

They lowered their pistols, but she noticed that neither of them put the guns away. The men were young, in their twenties, and simply dressed. They reminded her of Daniel.

"I'm Benjamin Tallmadge," the one on the left told her, "and this is my friend Robert Townsend."

"Hello," he said, giving her a nod.

"And you'd be Roxanne Darragh—a good friend of Daniel Reed's. I'm inclined to trust you, Miss Darragh, because, in truth, the last time we saw Daniel he mentioned your name."

"I see," Roxanne said. She took the seat that Benjamin Tallmadge indicated.

"So why have you gotten in touch with us?" asked Townsend.

"I have some important information, and I'm no longer sure that the committee members can be trusted."

Both men were silent for a moment. Then Tallmadge commented, "That's a very strange thing for someone like you to say, Miss Darragh. You're not casting aspersions on the patriotism of those men, are you?"

"Not all of them," she replied bluntly. "Just one."

"Who?" Townsend asked sharply.

"I don't know. But I'm convinced the British have a man inside the committee."

Tallmadge grinned. "You're not the only one who's

come to such a realization, Miss Darragh. There's been talk for months now that the British have been finding out too many things that are supposed to be secrets. Did you know, for example, that when General Gage sent his men to Lexington and Concord to seize the supplies stored there, he had a map showing where everything was hidden?"

That was the first Roxanne had heard of such a thing. She'd had no idea Gage had been so well informed about the activities of the patriots.

"That's why the redcoats headed straight for Colonel Barrett's farm once they'd left Concord," Townsend added. "And such puzzling things are why we are no longer directly involved with the committee."

"But what is this important information you have?" Tallmadge asked. "I don't mind telling you, it wasn't easy for the two of us to slip into Boston tonight. We did it only because we knew you had been working with Daniel before he had to leave the area."

"As I said, I've found out something vital to our effort. I will tell you what I know as an act of faith, but you must allow me and my friend Elliot Markham to help you in the future."

"Markham!" Townsend exclaimed. "Surely you're not talking about the son of Benjamin Markham? He's the son of one of the best-known Tories in Boston! Why, they say the boy's a rounder, with a terrible reputation with both women and business."

"That doesn't mean I *am*."

The quiet voice from the doorway made Tallmadge and Townsend jump up from their chairs. They reached for their pistols and snapped up the muzzles. Roxanne moved quickly, bolting from her chair to put herself between the weapons and the doorway, where Elliot had just stepped into the room. Over her shoulder she cast an annoyed glance at him.

His hands were empty. He held them out at his sides in plain view and went on, "You can put up your pistols, gentlemen. I'm on the side of liberty and have been for months now. Roxanne can vouch for my patriotism."

"Yes, but who besides Daniel Reed will vouch for Miss Darragh's?" Tallmadge snapped.

Roxanne lifted her head and said angrily, "Samuel Adams, for one. Mr. Revere, the silversmith, for another, as well as Dr. Warren, Dr. Church, Mr. Hancock—"

Slowly Tallmadge lowered his pistol and motioned for Townsend to do the same. "Point well taken, Miss Darragh," Tallmadge said. He cast a skeptical glance at Elliot. "But what about you?"

"The members of the committee know that I've been working with Daniel and Roxanne ever since the night we sprang Daniel and Quincy Reed from the Brattle Street jail," Elliot said. "And would I be here telling you how to get your hands on a ship's cargo of British guns and ammunition if I weren't trustworthy?"

Tallmadge and Townsend exchanged a glance. "What about British guns and ammunition?" Tallmadge asked.

"They can become rebel guns if you like," Elliot said. A mocking grin appeared on his face. "All you have to do is take them off a Markham and Cummings ship that will be arriving on Monday, four days from now—if it hasn't been delayed at sea."

"A Markham and Cummings ship?" repeated Townsend, clearly confused. "One of the vessels belonging to your father's company?"

"You'd better explain yourself, Mr. Markham," Tallmadge said.

"That's why we're here, gentlemen. It's precisely what we're trying to do." Roxanne's tone indicated how annoyed she was.

"Just listen for a moment," Elliot said. Quickly, he filled Tallmadge and Townsend in on everything he had learned from Major Dorn at the party the evening before. The two men listened intently as he spoke.

"If we could only take over that ship before it reaches Boston—" Townsend said when Elliot was finished.

Tallmadge took up the thought. "—we could capture the guns and considerably weaken the British!"

"Exactly," Elliot said. "I did some investigating today at my father's office and discovered that just as I thought, the *Carolingian* is scheduled to dock at Portsmouth, New Hampshire, on Sunday evening before sailing to Boston on Monday. Somewhere between those two ports is the place to take it."

Tallmadge put away his pistol, slipping it under his coat, and resumed his seat. He gestured for Roxanne and the others to sit. "You're right, Mr. Markham. Not in Portsmouth itself," he said, frowning and thinking it through as he spoke. "But somewhere between Portsmouth and Boston."

"Yes," agreed Townsend. "We'll take the ship while it's at sea."

"Wait a moment," Roxanne said. "What if this is a trap? What if this Major Dorn told Elliot about the munitions deliberately, so the British could lure us into attacking the ship?"

"Major Dorn is too much of a dunce to be trusted with a complicated scheme like that, Roxanne. He was telling the truth." Elliot was confident he had accurate information.

"As far as *he* knows it," Roxanne pointed out.

"You're right, Miss Darragh," Townsend said. "The British could be orchestrating a complex scheme."

"Then the best thing to do," Elliot suggested, "is to get an agent aboard the ship at Portsmouth to make sure the guns—and not a shipload of British troops, say—are really on board. Then, if everything is as it should be, our man can signal at the appropriate time, and you can have boats ready to sail out from the coast to take the ship."

"An excellent plan," Tallmadge agreed. He cocked an eyebrow and went on, "But whom do you think should be trusted with the assignment? It's going to be a delicate job."

"It certainly is. That's why I should do it."

Roxanne stared in surprise at Elliot as he made the firm declaration.

"That's what occurred to me right away, and I'm sure it did to Benjamin, too," Townsend said. "You'd be perfect for the task, Mr. Markham. It should be quite a simple matter for you to board the *Carolingian* in Portsmouth. After all, your father's company owns the vessel."

Elliot looked at Roxanne. "What do you think?"

She took a deep breath. "I think you've forgotten one thing," she said. "I'm going with you."

"What did you say?" Elliot asked, caught off guard by her bold statement. Tallmadge and Townsend looked equally surprised.

"I said I'm going with you."

Elliot stared at her. "Impossible. There's no reason for you to go along, no reason at all."

"Oh? Then how are you going to explain how you came to be in Portsmouth, begging a ride on one of your father's ships?"

"I won't have to explain anything," Elliot snapped. "No one is going to deny my right to be on the vessel."

"Perhaps not," Roxanne admitted. "But they might wonder *why* you're on it."

"She's right about that," mused Tallmadge. "We've got to come up with a good story, so that the captain and the crew won't be suspicious. We don't want to tip our hand until we're sure the weapons are on board—and this isn't an elaborate trap."

"You mean you still don't trust me," Elliot stated.

"We didn't say that," Townsend responded. "But even if you are telling us the truth, the whole thing could be a British snare, just as we've discussed. However, Mr. Markham, you have to admit that all we have to go by is what you claim to have learned from this Major Dorn."

"He was at a party in my own home, and I've told you exactly what he told me," Elliot insisted. His face was mottled with anger.

Tallmadge held his hands up, palms out. "Please, Mr. Markham. We mean no offense. Caution has been ingrained in us in a fairly short span of time. However, it does strike me as a good idea that she accompany you."

"And how am I supposed to explain her to the crew of the *Carolingian*?" Elliot asked.

"I'm right here," Roxanne said coolly. "You don't have to speak of me as if I'm not in the room."

"Sorry," Elliot muttered. "It's just that I don't know what to make of this."

"You've just had an argument with Sarah," she said to Elliot and saw the flash of pain that flickered across his face. "It seems perfectly logical under the circumstances that you might take a different young woman on a short journey."

"You—you mean like a lovers' jaunt?"

"Exactly."

"You know such a thing wouldn't be good for your reputation," Elliot pointed out.

Tallmadge agreed. "He's right about that, Miss Darragh. You should carefully consider what you're suggesting."

"What does a reputation matter if none of us is free? I *have* considered it, gentlemen, and I think my idea is perfectly reasonable. The men on the ship are not going to suspect us if they believe our main reason for being there is—is a mere dalliance." She hoped Daniel Reed didn't hear about this before she had a chance to tell him herself and explain the logic behind the plan.

"All right, it's settled, then," Tallmadge said. "The two of you will go to Portsmouth and board the ship. You'll have Sunday night to determine that the munitions are on board, and if there are no British troops, you can signal our boats the next morning. We'll have them waiting at the cove near Marblehead Neck. From the top of the promontory a lookout will easily see a signal from the ship. Are you familiar with the place?"

Reluctance still visible on his face, Elliot said, "Yes, I know it well. What sort of signal did you have in mind?"

"How about a bright red pennant unfurled from the mast?" suggested Townsend. "That ought to be easy enough for our men to spot."

"Won't the captain think it strange to fly a flag other than the English Red Ensign?" Elliot asked.

"I'd certainly think so," Roxanne said quickly. "I have a better idea. If the lookout uses a spyglass, he will easily see the ship's quarterdeck. Tell him I will stand on the starboard side, and I'll wear a bright red, hooded cape if the munitions are on board. Should the cargo be trade goods, I'll wear a black cape." Now that they had settled on the plan, she did not want to give them the chance to back out.

"Done," Tallmadge said emphatically. He extended his hand to Elliot. "We're glad to have you with us, Markham. I just hope you've told us the truth."

"You'll see," Elliot said coldly, but he took Tallmadge's hand.

"Is there anything else?" Roxanne asked.

"Not that I know of," Tallmadge answered. "We'll be in touch with you if we need to pass along any more information. And you can get in touch with us by leaving a message at the stationer's shop, as you did today. If you don't hear from us, proceed with the plan just as we've laid it out here tonight."

Townsend ushered them to the door. "In the name of liberty, good night," he said solemnly.

"Good night," Roxanne replied.

Without adding his farewell, Elliot took her arm and propelled her down the stairs and out the door. When they reached the street, he could no longer contain his temper. "Those pompous, arrogant little tin gods!" he exploded.

"You're wrong about them," Roxanne said bluntly. "They have to be careful. The British would have them shot for treason if they knew what was going on right under their noses. How do you expect them to act toward us?"

Elliot shrugged. "Perhaps you're right. And I suppose I can't blame them for not fully trusting me. My father is one of the most influential Tories in the city, just as they said. Still, I'm not sure I care for their attitude."

"That will change," Roxanne said, her voice little more than a whisper, "once we have proved ourselves to them and those guns and ammunition are in our hands."

"True enough." He looked around through the fog at the shadowy street. "I think I should escort you home."

"No," Roxanne said quickly. "That won't be necessary."

Elliot glanced at her in surprise. "What do you mean? You shouldn't be out by yourself at this time of night, Roxanne."

"I got here by myself," she said. "I can get home the same way. I don't think we should be seen together too much."

"But why not? If we're going to pretend to be—well, lovers, I'd think it would look even more strange if we weren't together."

"Don't forget we're only pretending," she reminded him tartly. "When we make that journey to Portsmouth, that will be soon enough to resume the masquerade."

"All right, but I don't like the idea of your being out here by yourself at this time of night."

"Thank you, Elliot," she said, placing a hand on his arm as they stood there together in the doorway. "You're very kind. But I promise you I'll be just fine."

He bent over slightly to brush her cheek with his lips. "Good night," he murmured. "I'll pick you up Sunday morning, and we'll go to Portsmouth in one of my father's carriages."

"I'll be looking forward to it," she said, and she meant it. It would feel good to be doing something again, rather than just skulking around Boston.

Elliot squeezed her shoulder gently, then turned and walked away, vanishing swiftly in the night as Roxanne stayed behind to let him get ahead of her.

Chapter Six

As Roxanne Darragh stood in the doorway, waiting for Elliot Markham to walk away from the building where they had met with Townsend and Tallmadge, she watched the dim lights of the few carriages that traversed the streets through the thickening fog. She was breathing rapidly, and her mouth was dry. The audacity of their plan to sabotage the *Carolingian* shipment left her reeling; the consequences of their actions would alter the future of the colonies—whether it succeeded or not.

Her association with Elliot in the affair somewhat distressed her. Pretending to be romantically involved with him when they went to Portsmouth was for the good of their common goal, she told herself; as a partisan for the patriot cause, she was prepared to make whatever sacrifices were required. But what she had felt when he kissed her the previous night hardly fell into that category. What she had felt was desire, nothing but raw, naked desire—mixed with a large amount of guilt.

Roxanne sighed loudly. She was filled with remorse, and she had not betrayed anyone yet. Elliot was a gentleman, and she was sure he would not repeat what had happened between them in the garden—unless she encouraged him.

And that was the real problem, she realized. She did not know what she wanted Elliot to do.

She took a step into the street and turned to the right. Elliot had been gone long enough now. Anyone seeing her walking along the road would not connect her with him.

There was a busy avenue only a few blocks away, and she was not worried about anyone accosting her after she reached the thoroughfare. If anyone did bother her, she could cry for help and someone would come to her assistance. The narrow side street she was on now was a different story. She walked quickly; the heels of her shoes clicked on the cobblestones. As she hurried to reach the safety of the busy road, the fog drifted in thicker from the harbor, and the eeriness did not help her nerves.

Still, she was not really concerned until she heard the faint sound of footsteps behind her. They were not very close, but as Roxanne slowed her stride she could tell whoever was back in the shadows was drawing nearer.

She picked up her pace. She was tempted to break into a run, but if she did and the person behind her turned out to be harmless, she would feel and look foolish. For an instant she wished she had accepted Elliot's offer to walk her home.

Mentally Roxanne scolded herself. This fear of a stranger walking behind her, just because it was a foggy night, was ridiculous.

But the sharp rapping of the footsteps came steadily closer. . . .

She looked over her shoulder and gasped as a person loomed out of the fog. Fear jolted through her as she saw a man striding quickly toward her, one arm outstretched, his hand reaching for her. She did not cry out, but her muscles pulled her forward.

"Roxanne!"

The voice made her stop short. She recognized it but for a moment could not recall the owner.

"It's me, Roxanne, Avery Wallingford."

"Avery!" Roxanne exclaimed. A great feeling of relief flooded through her. She had not known whether the follower was intent on robbing or molesting her, or if he was a British soldier who had somehow found out about her espionage activities.

But now she could relax. She knew Avery Wallingford, though she did not particularly like him. He had always been at the parties she had attended with Daniel; Avery was as much a part of Tory society as Elliot was.

That thought made her smile faintly. Avery, like all the young wastrels in his circle of friends, would be shocked if he knew what kind of person Elliot had become.

"What in the world are you doing here, my dear?" he asked. "This is hardly the sort of neighborhood where a respectable young woman should be walking about after dark."

"I know," Roxanne said. "I ran an errand for my father and thought I was taking a shortcut back home. I seem to have lost my way, though."

"Do you know where you are now?"

"Oh, yes," Roxanne assured him. "I can make it home without any trouble."

"Perhaps I should escort you."

"That won't be necessary."

"I insist." Without waiting for her permission, Avery linked his arm with hers. "Come along, and I won't hear another word of argument."

Roxanne sighed. It would be easier to put up with Avery than it would be to run him off, she sensed. "All right," she said.

He chattered for a moment about mutual acquaintances from her party-going days, then asked smoothly, "Seen much of our friend Elliot lately?"

"No, not recently," Roxanne replied warily.

"Oh, really? That's not the way I heard it. In fact, I know you met him tonight. A romantic rendezvous is the best reason to be out on a dank night like this, eh?"

Roxanne felt a surge of panic. Coldly she said, "I don't know what you're talking about."

Avery stopped, and since his arm was still linked with hers, she was pulled to a halt. He turned to face her and said, "I know what you were doing tonight."

Fear washed through her. How could Avery know about the meeting with Benjamin Tallmadge and Robert Townsend?

"I know what happened between the two of you in the garden of the Markham estate last night. There are no secrets from Avery Wallingford, my dear."

Sarah, she thought. Sarah must have told Avery what she had seen in the garden. Roxanne stifled a sigh of relief. Avery might be an annoyance, but he was not a serious threat to the mission she and Elliot were undertaking. *But he might prove to be a threat to me personally,* she thought.

He was backing her toward a building, steering her into the dark recessed entrance to a closed store. She remembered all too well Avery's reputation as a ladies' man, a reputation in which he took great pride.

She backed away from him but came up against the door of the shop and could not retreat. He stood disturbingly close to her.

"I want some answers, darling Roxanne," Avery said, and despite the smoothness of his voice, there was menace in the words. "Tell me what's going on between you and Elliot Markham."

"You seem to know already. There are no secrets from you, remember?"

"True, true. I know you were in Elliot's arms last night, kissing him. What I want to know now is how serious it is?"

"I don't see that it's any of your business."

He tightened his grip on her arm, stopping just short of making her cry out. "Listen, you little doxy," he grated, all pretense of politeness gone. "I don't care if you and Elliot have jumped over the bundling board a dozen times. That doesn't mean anything. I know Elliot, and he's perfectly capable of bedding you and then sweet-talking his way back into Sarah's good graces. What I want to know is whether or not he intends to do that."

"You mean, are he and I in love, or just—lovers?"

"Exactly," Avery hissed.

"Elliot and I are in love," Roxanne said quietly.

Avery clenched his free hand into a fist. "I knew it!"

Roxanne drew a deep breath. Not only had she told Avery what he wanted to hear, but this unpleasant encounter could even turn out to be useful. The news that she and Elliot were romantically involved would spread quickly now and could only lend credence to their reason for traveling to Portsmouth together.

"I've told you what you wanted to know," she said to Avery. "Now either let me go, or escort me home as you said you would."

"Oh, I'll take you home, all right, my dear, but not until I'm finished with you. I have a little tradition, if you will, that I'm establishing. You see, my good friend Elliot doesn't get you—until I've had you."

"You wouldn't dare," she said in a cold, angry voice.

"Oh, wouldn't I? Come on now, darling, what harm can it do? Other than to make you spend the rest of your life pining for the touch of a real man."

She felt his hot breath on her face, smelled the brandy he must have drunk earlier in the evening. Even as she tried to twist away from him, he tightened his grip and thrust his body against hers. His face dipped toward hers, and his mouth opened to kiss her.

She tensed her leg, intending to bring her knee up into his groin with as much force as she could muster. He could kiss her if he wanted, but, by God, he was going to pay for it!

"Here now, what's all this? Come out of that doorway, you two!"

Avery stepped quickly away from Roxanne, spinning around to face the newcomer. "Who the devil?" he snapped. "How dare you—"

A large man with a cloak draped about his broad shoulders moved closer to them. "Is that you, young Wallingford?" the man demanded. "I should have known as much when I saw someone hiding in a doorway and mauling a young lady."

"How dare you, sir!" Avery exclaimed, his voice trembling with rage. "If I were not a gentleman—"

"If you were a gentleman, you wouldn't have been doing what you were doing," the man cut in coldly.

Roxanne found her voice. "Good evening, Dr. Church."

"Church?" Avery repeated in surprise. He knew who the physician was, even though they did not travel in the same social circles.

"Good evening, Miss Darragh," Dr. Benjamin Church

said as he moved into the doorway and swept his tricorn off his powdered wig. "How good to see you again, even under these less than auspicious circumstances."

"See here, Doctor," Avery began, trying to work up a semblance of righteous indignation, "you've no right to interfere in this. Miss Darragh is a grown woman, and her business is with me, not you."

"Is that so? Well, let's just see what the young lady has to say about that, shall we?" Church turned to Roxanne. "Would you like me to leave you in the company of Wallingford here, Miss Darragh, or would you rather I escort you home?"

"I'd be honored if you'd walk with me, Doctor," she said.

Church held out his arm, and Roxanne gratefully linked hers with it. Although she could tell that Avery was seething, he made no move to stop her.

"You haven't heard the last of this, or of me, Roxanne," Avery said as they walked away.

Church paused and turned to stare at Avery. "If I ever hear of you bothering this young woman again, Wallingford, I'll personally see to it that you regret your actions for the rest of your days. Do you understand?"

Avery just glowered at Church and Roxanne, then turned on his heel and stalked off into the fog.

"Thank God he's gone," Roxanne said with a heartfelt sigh.

The physician chuckled. "I don't believe he'll bother you again, Miss Darragh. His kind is brave only when the odds are all on his side."

"I know. Thank you, Doctor."

"I'm just glad I happened along when I did. I must admit, however, that I was surprised to see you. What are you doing out and about this late, especially in a neighborhood like this? Something for the patriot cause, I've no doubt."

"I had to meet someone," Roxanne said, keeping her voice low.

"Young Mr. Markham, I'd wager," Church commented.

"Yes, I saw Elliot. We talked to Benjamin Tallmadge and Robert Townsend."

As soon as the words were out of her mouth, Roxanne realized she should not have spoken about the two men who operated independently of the Committee of Safety.

"Tallmadge and Townsend, eh?" the doctor said. "Fine young men, from what I've heard, and certainly devoted to the cause of liberty."

"They're old friends of Daniel's," she said quickly. "It was more of a, ah, social meeting than anything else."

"Well, I hope they're careful. The British would like to catch up to those two, judging from the rumors I've heard. I won't ask you about this meeting, my dear. I don't want you to betray any confidences. We all have to be very careful these days."

"I know. But someday things will be different."

"Of course they will," Church murmured.

Less than a quarter of an hour later Roxanne said goodbye to Dr. Church on the sidewalk in front of her father's house. The tall, attractive doctor tipped his hat to her and bid her farewell. "I'd try to avoid that Wallingford boy if I were you, Miss Darragh. I fear he's up to no good."

"I think you're right, Doctor. Good night, and thank you."

"Good night, my dear."

Roxanne started up the walk to her house, then paused and looked back at Church as he strode away into the foggy night. She was very grateful that the doctor had come along when he did—but she was puzzled as to how he had come to be there at just the right time. Avery Wallingford had been spying on her; was it possible, she wondered, that Dr. Church was doing the same thing?

There was a frown on Dr. Benjamin Church's handsome face as he walked along the streets of Boston after leaving Roxanne at her house. It was a quiet night, but he knew the peace would not last much longer. Boston—the whole expanse of the colonies, for that matter—was like a powder keg with a narrow, flame-sputtering trail of black powder leading to it. Sooner or later, an explosion would rip apart the flimsy façade of peace.

And he was doing his part to contribute to the sparks that would ultimately set off that blast.

Tallmadge and Townsend, for instance. There had been hints that the two young men, along with their friend Nathan Hale, were trying to establish their own intelligence network to further the patriot cause. If they were making contact with Roxanne Darragh and Elliot Markham—agents who, up until now, had worked solely for the Committee of Safety—that might mean Tallmadge and Townsend were ready to put their espionage ring into operation. That development would bear looking into.

But for the time being, he would keep the information to himself, Church decided, rather than pass it along to Major Cane, his contact in the British army.

It would be more impressive—and more profitable—to uncover the identities of all the young intelligence agents . . . before he betrayed them.

The last of the twilight had faded, and the moon had not yet risen. But the starlight allowed Murdoch Buchanan and the Reed brothers to move at a good pace in pursuit of Perry Faulkner and his men—and Cordelia. Daniel wondered if Faulkner had called a halt for the night or pushed on. It was more likely, he decided, that Faulkner had stopped; the man did not strike him as the type to worry too much about what was behind him. To Faulkner's way of thinking, any threat represented by Daniel, Quincy, and Murdoch had already been dealt with.

When the brightly glowing moon finally rose, they were able to make better time. Less than two hours after the sun set, Murdoch's keen eyes spotted the yellow gleam of lantern light a hundred yards ahead at the side of the road. At his signal, Daniel and Quincy slowed their horses.

"There's a building up yonder," Murdoch said quietly. "Could be a tavern or another inn. Ye two stay here, while I take a look around."

"All right," Daniel agreed. "But be careful. If we hear any sounds of trouble, we'll come as quickly as we can."

Murdoch urged his horse forward at a walk, keeping the animal on a bed of pine needles at the side of the road where its hoofbeats would not be so loud. Within moments, his big form was a dark, indistinct shape in the shadows.

"Do you think we've caught up to them, Daniel?" Quincy asked anxiously.

"No way of knowing yet. Let's just wait until Murdoch gets back."

The scouting mission did not take long. In fifteen minutes Murdoch returned on foot. "Left my horse tied up in the trees out back o' the place," he told Daniel and Quincy. " 'Tis an inn, all right, and the stable's full o' horses. I think I recognize the two that were tied up in front o' the Wild Boar. I'd bet money Faulkner's there, or I've lost my senses."

Daniel did not think that was likely. "Did you take a look inside the place?" he asked.

Murdoch shook his head. "I did'na want t' get too close until I told the two o' ye what I'd found, just in case anything happened."

"Smart thinking," Daniel told him. He glanced over at Quincy. "Are you ready to do a little scouting?"

"Let's hurry up and get started. We're wasting valuable time."

At Murdoch's suggestion they swung down from their saddles and led the horses, veering away from the road and entering the woods as they approached the inn. Murdoch led them unerringly to the spot where he had left his own mount, and Daniel and Quincy tied their horses to nearby saplings. The soft lights of the inn shone through the screen of trees.

A dog barked, and several others joined in, creating a clamor. Daniel put a hand on Murdoch's arm and whispered, "Are they barking at us?"

"Who can tell? Mongrels like t' bark, and they're going t' do it whether they have a good reason or not."

"We'll let them settle down before we get any closer."

The door of the inn opened, and a man stuck his head out and shouted, "What the hell are you mutts barkin' at?" The dogs barked louder, and after a moment the man waved a hand at the night, cursed, and went back inside. Watching from the woods, Daniel released the breath he had been holding.

Finally, the barking and howling quieted, then stopped. Daniel motioned Murdoch and Quincy forward. They eased toward the building, a sturdy two-story wood structure with three dormer windows extending from the gambrel roof. The shutters were open on several of them, letting in the night air and allowing lamplight to escape.

Crouching, Daniel, Murdoch, and Quincy ran to the side wall of the building and leaned against it, hugging the clapboards to make themselves less visible. Daniel motioned for Quincy and Murdoch to stay where they were, then edged toward the nearest window. He took off his tricorn and dropped it on the ground as he reached the opening and stooped beneath it.

Daniel straightened until he could peer inside. He saw a big public room with a fireplace and a bar. Unlike the barroom at the Wild Boar, quite a few drinkers crowded the benches and tables here. Daniel spotted Faulkner sitting by himself, staring broodingly into a mug. His men were scattered around the room, roistering and drinking and pawing some of the inn's serving girls. Judging by the looks on the faces of the women, they were too frightened of these rough-looking customers to do anything but submit meekly.

Daniel felt anger flare up inside him. Two apron-clad men, one middle-aged, the other considerably younger, stood behind the bar and watched the raucous goings-on with undisguised dismay, but they made no move to interfere. There was a strong resemblance between the two men, and Daniel pegged them for father and son.

But he could see nearly the entire room from his vantage point, and there was no sign of Cordelia. *She's probably locked in one of the upstairs rooms while Faulkner gets drunk in the barroom,* Daniel thought.

He grabbed his hat, moved away from the window, and glanced up at the huge sycamore tree growing near the building. From its branches, a person could look right into several of the upper windows.

He hurried back to Quincy and Murdoch and put his mouth next to his brother's ear. "Can you see through your swollen eye well enough to climb that tree and look in the windows on the upper floor?" he asked, gesturing at the sycamore that towered only a few feet from the wall of the inn.

Daniel mouthed the words *Be careful,* and Quincy hurried over to the tree, studied the branches for a moment, then stretched up on his toes and selected his first handhold. He pulled himself up, swung his leg over a branch, and disappeared into the new spring foliage.

Below, Daniel and Murdoch waited impatiently, peering upward to catch a glimpse of Quincy. Daniel hoped his brother would select his handholds and footholds with care, since one misstep could send him plummeting. The fall itself could be dangerous, but, in addition, the commotion it created would draw the attention of the men inside the inn.

Long minutes dragged past. *At least the dogs are still quiet,* Daniel thought. Then he heard a rustling in the branches over his head, and Quincy dropped lightly to the ground beside him. Daniel put out a hand and grabbed Quincy's arm to steady him.

"Did you find her?" he asked in an urgent whisper.

Quincy nodded and pointed toward the middle dormer window. "She's in that room right there," he whispered.

"Is she alone?"

"She's lying on the bed crying. I swear, Daniel, I've never seen such a pitiful sight. She must be scared out of her wits."

Daniel jerked his thumb toward the woods. "Come on. Let's get away from here so we can work out a plan."

They crept away from the building, and Daniel began to breathe a little easier when they were safely concealed in the shadows of the trees. When they reached the small clearing where they had left the horses, Daniel said quietly, "Get your guns, and make sure your pistols are primed and loaded."

"I like the sound o' that. Just what did ye have in mind, Dan'l, me boy?"

"We'll have to get Cordelia out of that room," Daniel said, "without alerting the men downstairs. That sycamore is our best route for doing that. I just hope she can climb down a tree."

"I'd wager she's more afraid of Faulkner than climbing," Quincy put in.

"That's what I figure, too. Once we've got her out of there, we'll scatter the horses so Faulkner and his men can't come after us. The noise will draw their attention, so we'll want to keep them pinned down for a while inside the building, to give us time to get away. A few well-placed shots ought to make them lie low."

"So I'm to go back up the tree to fetch Cordelia while you and Murdoch get ready to run off the horses?" Quincy asked.

"No, you'll help Murdoch. I've climbed a few trees in my time, little brother. I'll take that job."

"Why not me?" Quincy protested. "I can do it."

"I'm sure you can. But Faulkner could decide to go up to Cordelia's room at any time. For all we know, he'll be up there by the time we get back. There could be trouble."

"I can handle it," insisted Quincy.

"Sorry," Daniel said flatly. "That's my decision. Now, are you going to help Murdoch or not?"

"Sure," Quincy said after a second's hesitation. "Whatever you say, Daniel. But that doesn't mean I have to like it."

"No, you don't. You just have to do your job, and maybe we'll all come out of this alive."

"I'm just glad ye did'na ask me t' shinny up the tree," Murdoch said. "I'm not built for climbing."

Daniel clapped the big man on the shoulder. "Here," he

said, taking his rifle from where it was slung on his saddle and handing it to Murdoch. "You'll have two rifles, one musket, and three pistols between you. Six shots without reloading will make those men inside think there's a sizable force out here. We'll take our horses close to the building, so we can make a quick getaway. Cordelia will ride with you again, Quincy, just like before."

"And I'll reload a couple o' these guns and cover your retreat," Murdoch said. He gathered the reins of the three horses in his big right hand. "I'm ready whenever the two o' ye are."

The companions crept through the trees toward the inn. Daniel checked his pistol to make sure it was loaded. He did not expect to encounter any trouble, but if he did, he would not hesitate to use the firearm—not after what Faulkner and his men had done to them.

With the exception of the huge old sycamore and several maples, a strip twenty feet wide had been cleared away between the trees and the building. They hurried through the open area. Then Daniel motioned for Murdoch and Quincy to head for the barn. He went to the base of the sycamore, reached up, grasped a limb, and started climbing. Every muscle he used ached with soreness.

He had left his hat and vest hung on the saddle of his horse so they would not get caught on the branches. Tree climbing, Daniel found, was harder work than he remembered, especially in his bruised and beaten condition. He was breathing hard and his pulse was pounding in his head by the time he reached the level of the second-floor dormer windows. Lying face down, grasping a limb with his arms and legs, he eased his way farther out on it. He pushed aside a newly budded branch and peered into the chamber where Cordelia was being kept.

She was there, all right, but so was Perry Faulkner.

Cordelia was sitting on the bed, her eyes red and puffy from crying, yet filled with anger as she looked up at Faulkner. He stood at the foot of the bed, his hands clasped together behind his back.

"No point in being foolish about this, Cordelia. You're my wife, and you'll do as I say."

"I may be your wife," she said, "but that doesn't make me your slave."

"That's where you're wrong, my dear." Faulkner smiled smugly. "For all intents and purposes, that's exactly what you are, and you shouldn't forget it. You have no rights other than those I'm willing to grant you, and after what you've done, I'm in no mood to give you any more chances to hurt me or my business."

Judging from the expression on Cordelia's face, given half a chance, she would have clawed Faulkner's eyes out. "If my father had only known what you're really like, he never would have insisted I marry you."

"Your father is a bumbling old fool," Faulkner snapped, "but it serves my purposes to deal with him, just as it serves my purposes to have you for my wife."

"But why? You don't love me! You don't even . . . you don't even take me to bed anymore."

Faulkner's features hardened into a stony mask. "I'm a busy man with a great deal on my mind. I don't always have time for everything."

"You have time for murder! You spend all your time planning and plotting, Perry. Ever since you found out about that British wagon train filled with muskets, you've been a different man. But I never thought you'd kill that poor major. That was the last straw. I knew then I had to get away!"

"So you stole gold and money from me and ran off like

a frightened little girl." Faulkner's voice dripped with contempt. "I know you, Cordelia. You're not that much different than I. You intended to get to a safe place and then blackmail me with what you know, didn't you?"

"No! That thought never occurred to me. I just . . . wanted to get away from you."

"Hah!" Faulkner snorted in disbelief. He strode around the end of the bed and stepped close to her. "You'll never get away from me, Cordelia." With his left hand, he reached out and cupped her chin, while his right dropped to her bosom. She closed her eyes and shuddered as he squeezed her breast. "I think it's time to exercise those husbandly rights you so mockingly referred to."

The information Daniel had just overheard put a new complexion on the matter. This was not just a marital dispute, nor was Faulkner merely a ham-handed husband with a recalcitrant wife. He was a killer, and since Cordelia had knowledge of some scheme of his concerning a wagon train and some British guns, he might decide to dispose of her. Daniel could not in good conscience leave her in Faulkner's hands.

He hoped Murdoch and Quincy were ready to move.

Inching backward on his belly, Daniel edged along the branch to the security of a thicker limb closer to the trunk of the old sycamore. He stood up and climbed higher in the tree until he reached a branch that hung over the peak of the roof. Crouching on all fours, he wormed his way farther out on the branch. For one horrible moment, he felt it sag and thought it was going to break, but he managed to steady himself and dropped silently next to Cordelia's window. Holding on to the eaves of the dormer, he crept forward until he was in position, ready to leap through the open window and rescue her. He slid his pistol from under his belt and, taking a deep breath, flung himself into the room. At the same time he shouted as loudly as he could, "Now, Murdoch!"

Daniel's feet hit the sill of the window, and he tumbled through the opening.

Faulkner was still struggling with Cordelia. He heard Daniel's cry and whirled around; his hand went underneath his coat to grab for his pistol. A gunshot blasted, deafeningly loud in the small bedchamber. The pistol ball missed Daniel, and he rolled over and came to his feet. In the same motion his arm lashed out, and the barrel of his pistol thudded against the side of Faulkner's head. Daniel considered putting a ball through the man's heart, but, unwilling to be a cold-blooded murderer, he discarded the idea. Instead he reached out, caught hold of Cordelia's arm, and jerked the young woman to her feet.

She stopped screaming long enough for Daniel to hear shouts from below and the thunder of hoofbeats: Quincy and Murdoch were taking care of their end of the job. Hard on the heels of the hoofbeats came more shots. Someone downstairs let out a howl of pain, and Daniel knew one of the shots must have hit home.

"Come on!" he said, urging Cordelia toward the window. "We've got to get out of here."

She tore her startled gaze away from Faulkner's crumpled form and looked at the window. "Out there?" she asked in a high, thin voice.

"There's no other way," Daniel told her. He tugged her to the window without giving her a chance to resist. "Just step up on the sill and climb out. Hold on to the eaves of the dormer and reach out for the nearest limb. The branches are within easy reach. Grab hold of one of them, and I'll be right there to help you."

"But—but I can't!"

"You've got to." Daniel tucked away his unfired pistol. He would shove Cordelia out the window if he had to. Staying where they were meant certain death.

Summoning up all her courage, she followed Daniel's directions and climbed out onto the same branch he had used. She wrapped her arms and legs around it and hung on for dear life as her weight made the limb bob up and down wildly. She cried out in terror.

Daniel had to jump to a smaller, less accessible branch. He pushed back his own fear and leapt. His fingers raked against the rough bark, and the branches bent beneath him as he tried to find a hold. His hands slipped for a moment, but then he found a suitable purchase and scrambled toward the trunk of the tree, where the limbs were sturdier.

Cordelia was just above him and to the left. He reached out to steady her and said, "Come on. Crawl toward the trunk."

She inched along with her eyes closed. When they were both in secure positions, Daniel swung up to the same branch that supported Cordelia.

"It's not far to the ground," he assured her, sliding a hand under her elbow. "Let's go."

More shots cracked through the darkness. *Murdoch and Quincy do sound like a small army,* Daniel thought.

Awkwardly, he and Cordelia descended the tree, and when they reached the lowest limbs, he told her, "We'll have to jump from here. I'll go first so I can catch you when you come down."

With that he lowered himself to the limb, scooted over it, and, still holding on, let his body hang for a moment. He dropped to the ground with a quiet thud.

"Your turn," he called softly.

"I—I can't!"

"Yes, you can," Daniel said firmly. "You can if you want to live. Otherwise I'll have to leave you here for Faulkner."

That jarred Cordelia into action, and she dropped six feet to the ground. Daniel caught her and stumbled. Holding her tightly to protect her, he was aware of the warm fullness of her body as it sagged against his. Then he caught his balance and pulled her toward the woods. "The horses are over here!"

They found Quincy waiting just inside the edge of the trees. He was holding the reins of four horses. "We took one of Faulkner's mounts for Cordelia to ride!" he said as Daniel and Cordelia approached. "Get on!"

"Good idea. What about Murdoch?" Daniel asked. A flurry of shots from the trees near the corner of the inn was his answer.

Quincy said, "He wants us to go on! He said he'd cover us so we can get a good head start!"

Daniel boosted Cordelia into the saddle of the newly acquired horse. Quincy had already mounted. Grasping the horn of his saddle, Daniel swung up quickly, banged his heels against the animal's flanks, and cried, "Come on!"

With Cordelia and Quincy trailing him, he galloped around the front of the inn to the road. A musket boomed from inside the building, and he heard the whining passage of a ball close to his head. Leaning over the neck of his horse, he urged it on to greater speed.

He caught sight of Murdoch boiling around the corner of the inn. The big Scotsman turned in his saddle, controlling his mount with his knees, and fired his pistols toward the building.

That will make Faulkner's men lie low for a few minutes, Daniel thought.

They had rescued Cordelia from Faulkner—again. But

when Faulkner regained consciousness and found her gone, he would come after them, even though scattering the horses would delay the pursuit considerably. If he caught up to them, Daniel knew, Faulkner would not be content until they were all dead.

But that confrontation would have to wait. For now, they were free, making their way through the dark woods as fast as they could, putting the inn far behind them.

Chapter Seven

Cordelia was exhausted by the time Daniel called a halt several hours later. He could tell by the way she swayed in the saddle that her reserves of strength were gone, and without rest she would collapse. He told Murdoch to find a place to camp, near a stream, if possible, and the Scotsman located a clearing in the woods, well away from the road, with a small waterfall nearby.

They had retraced their route and, in the middle of the night, passed the Wild Boar once again. Daniel had considered stopping but decided against it. The Wild Boar was dark when they rode past, and Ike Plemons was probably asleep inside. If questioned by Faulkner, the old man could honestly say he had not seen the fugitives since they had ridden out late the previous afternoon.

Once Murdoch had led them to the spot where they would stop for a few hours, Quincy hurried over to help Cordelia dismount. She gave him a tired smile and said, "Thank you."

"You're welcome," he replied eagerly.

"We'll rest here for a while," Daniel said, "but then we'll have to get moving again. We all know Faulkner is going to come after us."

"Perry won't rest until we're all dead," Cordelia murmured.

"Are you really married to him?" Quincy asked.

The moon was almost down, and not much of its light penetrated the clearing, but Daniel could see the faint, rueful smile on Cordelia's face as she said, "I'm afraid so. We all make mistakes, Quincy. They don't all turn out as badly as mine, though."

"Well, you shouldn't have to stay married to him," the youngster declared. "He's an evil man."

"I can't argue with that."

"I think we can risk a small fire," Daniel said. "A little food and drink before we turn in is probably a good idea."

Murdoch used his tinderbox to kindle a small blaze in the center of the clearing while Daniel and Quincy watered the horses, unsaddled them, and rubbed them down. Leaving the animals hobbled so they could graze, the brothers joined Murdoch and Cordelia by the fire. Murdoch made an extravagant but much-needed pot of tea and put it aside to steep.

"Don't you think it's about time you told us the truth about everything?" Daniel asked her. "I overheard enough before I came bursting through that window to know that this isn't just some squabble between a husband and wife."

Cordelia sighed. "I suppose you're right. I wasn't concealing things because I didn't trust you. I just thought you'd be safer if you didn't know what kind of man Perry really is. I didn't want to give him any reason to kill the three of you as well as me."

"He wants to kill you?" Quincy asked, disbelief evident in his voice.

"Well, perhaps not at first, but he can't afford to have me wandering around loose now, knowing what I know. He's afraid I'll tell someone about his plan and ruin everything for him."

"That's why he killed the major?" Daniel asked.

She looked at him sharply. "You did hear quite a lot, didn't you?"

"Ye mean this fella's already been killing folks?" Murdoch asked.

"He murdered a British major named Simonson. You see, Simonson told Perry about a British wagon train that's taking guns, powder, and ammunition to Fort Johnson in New York Colony. Perry plans to attack the supply train and steal the goods it's carrying," Cordelia went on. "He has wagons waiting to carry the guns away, wagons he got from my father."

"Then your father is part of this scheme with Faulkner?" asked Daniel.

"Not really. My father owns the biggest wagonyard in Saratoga. Perry proposed they go into the freighting business together, and he promised to provide the first shipment. He just didn't tell Father that his wagons would be carrying stolen guns." She grimaced. "Father was so taken with the idea that when Perry suggested he and I get married, Father was all for it. He thought if he and Perry were going to be business partners, that Perry should be part of the family as well."

"Sounds like Faulkner is a smooth-talking gentleman," Daniel commented.

"There's nothing gentle about him," Cordelia snapped.

"He's a brutal, horrible man. He'll kill anyone who interferes with him. He's murdered dozens of men already."

Daniel blinked in surprise. "Dozens of men? Are you sure?"

Cordelia looked up at him. "I found out after we were married that Perry used to be a wrecker. Do you know what that is?"

Daniel had heard plenty of stories about scoundrels who placed false warning lights along the coastline to lure merchant ships into crashing on the shore or on nearby reefs. Once the ships had been wrecked and the crews killed in the catastrophe, the wreckers would move in and salvage the cargo for themselves. It was a vicious arrangement and well deserving of the hanging it warranted when wreckers were caught.

"I know about wreckers," Daniel said grimly.

"He gave that up when he became too well-known along the coast. The constables and the British authorities were after him, so he went inland and set up this scheme to steal the guns."

"What is he planning on doing with them?" Murdoch asked.

"He's going to sell them to the rebels," Cordelia said bitterly. "Perry says insurrectionist money is as good as any."

Daniel, Quincy, and Murdoch exchanged glances over the dancing flames of the campfire. From the tone of her voice, they all realized that Cordelia had little or no sympathy for the patriots.

"You're a loyalist?" Quincy asked.

"Of course. England has never done anything to hurt me. The colonies belong to the Crown, and they're wrong to want to break away."

Cordelia's reply had a practiced quality to it that made

Daniel suspect she was repeating what she had heard someone else say.

She went on, "I imagine Perry will sell the supplies, especially the guns, to the highest bidder. If the British decide they're willing to buy back what Perry steals from them, he'll deal with them. I'm sure of that."

Daniel stared into the fire. The information Cordelia had just revealed further tangled an already complicated situation. The idea of patriot forces in New York getting their hands on British supplies was appealing, but allowing Perry Faulkner to profit by it was not. But if they tried to put a stop to Faulkner's plans—as Daniel's instinct was crying out to do—they might be dealing a blow to the hopes of their fellow patriots in New York.

The tea was ready, and Murdoch filled their tin cups. As she sipped the hot brew, Cordelia stated, "Next time Perry won't be content to capture me and take me back with him. He'll just kill me and be done with it."

Daniel agreed with her. "What more can we do to help you?" he asked.

"As I said, my father lives in Saratoga. Perry and I were on a business trip when I found out what he's up to. When I fled, I didn't pay any attention to which way I was going, but I had hoped to get back to Saratoga. If I tell my father what Perry is really doing, he'll help me. I'm sure of it. There's a British garrison in Saratoga, too. I could tell the officer in charge about Perry's scheme. I know the British would take steps to stop him."

"I imagine so," Daniel said. "You want to go to Saratoga, then."

Cordelia leaned forward anxiously. "You'll help me get there?"

Daniel did not reply. Quincy looked as though he

wanted to say something, but he struggled to keep his mouth shut. Murdoch just sat there, his craggy face unreadable in the flickering light of the fire.

"You'll have to come with us to Bennington," Daniel finally said. "As I said before, I'm sure once we get there, you can make arrangements to travel on to Saratoga. Will that be all right?"

"If that's the best you can do," she said, disappointed.

He expected Quincy to challenge his decision, but the youth remained quiet. "That's the best we can do," Daniel said. "I'm sure you'll be all right, though. You can hire a carriage and some guards to protect you from Faulkner, just in case he happens to catch up before you reach Saratoga. To be honest, I don't think that will happen. He doesn't know which direction we went when we escaped."

"He'll find me," Cordelia said fatalistically. "He seems to have a mystical ability to track me down. But if I can reach Saratoga ahead of him, I'll be safe. My father will see to that, once he knows what kind of man Perry really is."

For her sake, Daniel hoped she was right.

Murdoch got the last of the dried beef out of his saddlebag and handed around the tough strips of meat, which they ate as they drank the hot tea.

"Why don't you go ahead and get some sleep, Cordelia?" Daniel said when she had finished her tea. "The rest of us will take turns keeping watch."

"All right. Thank you."

She looked at him, and the hostility he had sensed before seemed to have vanished. "I really do appreciate everything the three of you have done for me."

"We were glad to do it," Quincy said as he handed a blanket to Cordelia. She took it and wrapped it around herself gratefully before lying down. Judging from her deep, regular breathing, she was asleep almost immediately.

Daniel waved Quincy and Murdoch away from the woman and said quietly to them, "We need to talk about this."

"Aye," rumbled Murdoch. "The lass has put us in a bad spot. We cannot let her talk t' the commanding officer o' the British garrison at Saratoga."

"Why not?" Quincy asked. "Don't we want to keep Faulkner from getting away with what he has planned?"

"Do we?" Daniel's question was blunt. "I don't want him killing the girl, or us, for that matter, but I'd like to see those British guns in the hands of the patriots."

"They would be a mighty help in the fighting t' come," Murdoch pointed out.

Quincy looked down. "I know," he admitted. "I just hate to see somebody like Faulkner profit from what he's doing."

"I can't argue with that sentiment," Daniel told his younger brother. "We have to weigh how we feel personally about Faulkner against the good his scheme could do for the revolution. All right, this is the way I see it," Daniel went on. "We have to avoid Faulkner ourselves. We can't let him get his hands on Cordelia again."

"That's right," Quincy said emphatically.

"But at the same time, as long as there's a chance the rebels could wind up with those guns, I don't think we can let her go running to the British, either." They all were silent. In the distance an owl hooted, its call cutting through the sound of the waterfall.

Finally Daniel said, "When we reach Bennington, instead of sending her on to Saratoga, we'll keep her with us."

"Against her will, you mean?"

"If need be."

Quincy picked up a twig and threw it to one side. "I guess you're right."

"I'm not happy about this either," Daniel said. "I wish we could help her do exactly what she wants to do. But we have to think about larger concerns than our own personal problems."

"Don't worry, Daniel." Quincy summoned up a smile. "I know you're right, but I'm not sure Cordelia is going to feel the same way."

Murdoch looked across the embers of the fire to where Cordelia lay. "Aye," he said with a smirk. "The lass will be none too happy."

"Watch out! Watch out, damn it!"

The man who had shouted grabbed at the trailing reins of the horse that galloped past him. He caught the lines and was jerked off his feet as the big beast plunged through the woods. The weight at the end of the reins gradually slowed the horse, and as it came to a halt, the man leaned against the animal and breathed heavily.

Another man sprinted up, panting. "I think that's the last of 'em," he said.

"Come on," said the man holding the reins. "Let's get back and find Faulkner."

Together they led the horse through the forest. An early morning mist hung over the trees and curled around the trunks. The two men, along with the rest of Faulkner's hired henchmen, had spent the night searching for and rounding up the horses that had been scattered by the three troublemakers who stole their leader's wife.

When the two men led the last of the stampeded horses into a clearing in the woods, they saw their companions huddled silently around a meager campfire. The recaptured horses were tied to trees nearby, and Faulkner was stalking back and forth, his handsome face set in cold, angry lines.

He stopped his pacing as the two stragglers entered the clearing. He glared at them and snapped, "It's damned well about time."

"Sorry, Mr. Faulkner," said the man leading the horse. "We had some trouble running down this nag."

"Well, you're back. I suppose that's the important thing." Faulkner clasped his hands behind his back and looked around at the group of toughs. "We still have a problem, however. There are eleven of us—and only ten horses."

One of the men spoke up. "We been talkin' about that, sir, and we figger that gal rode off on one of 'em. There were tracks of four horses leavin' that inn, and them bastards who grabbed her only had three mounts earlier."

"Yes, yes," Faulkner said impatiently, "that's a foregone conclusion, you fool. The question is, what are we going to do about it?"

"Well . . . I reckon a couple of us could double up."

"No! That would slow us down, and I can't afford the time." A flinty expression settled on his face. "Which of you is without a horse?"

The men looked around the clearing, studying the mounts that had been recaptured. Finally one man cleared his throat and said, "I reckon it's me. I don't see my horse here."

"All right," Faulkner said calmly. He took his hands from behind his back and reached into his coat.

The man whose horse was missing grinned broadly, exposing the jagged yellow stumps of his teeth. "Mighty nice of you to offer to pay me for the animal, Mr. Faulkner."

"It's only what you deserve," Faulkner said.

He took a pistol from under his coat, pointed it at the

man, and pressed the trigger before any of the men knew what was happening.

The unexpected blast froze them where they stood, and they gaped in shock as the ball slammed into the chest of their horseless companion. He staggered back, his hands going to the dreadful wound. Blood welled between his fingers, and he fell loosely, flopping grotesquely for a moment before the stillness of death settled over him.

"There," Faulkner said, putting the pistol away. "That settles the problem. The rest of you, get mounted. We'll be riding long and hard today. By the way, that man's pay—it will be split among the rest of you."

For a moment the men hesitated, stunned by what they had seen, angered at the cold-blooded murder of their companion.

But the man's death meant extra coins all around, and there was something to be said for that. Besides, Faulkner was right: Two men doubling up on one horse would delay the group's progress.

One by one, they swung up into their saddles, ready to follow wherever Faulkner wanted to lead them.

Avery Wallingford was in a buoyant mood as he stood in the parlor of Theophilus Cummings's Beacon Hill mansion, a few blocks from Benjamin Markham's house. Avery had given his hat and cloak to the butler and been assured that Miss Sarah would join him momentarily in the parlor. For once, Avery did not mind waiting. Any impatience he felt was offset by the anticipation of Sarah's reaction when he broke his news to her.

He walked across the richly decorated room and struck a few notes on the spinet piano Sarah played so well. Then he settled in front of the fireplace in one of a pair of red brocade wing chairs, with ornately carved ball-and-claw feet. Two built-in corner cabinets held Mrs. Cummings's collection of blue and white porcelain dishes brought to the colonies by Markham & Cummings ships from far-off China. The wall-paper had been hand painted to match the pattern of the Canton ware.

Avery took his elegant surroundings for granted. He stood and poked at the fire, then heard a soft step, and the double doors leading into the parlor opened. Sarah stepped through, as lovely as ever in a soft beige dress with a scooped neckline outlined in intricate white floss embroidery. The cut of the bodice revealed the swell of her ivory bosom. Avery remembered nuzzling those breasts greedily as Sarah clutched his head and entwined her fingers in his hair.

Soon he would be doing that again . . . and more.

"Good evening, Avery," she said as she gently pushed the doors closed behind her. "Harrison said you wanted to speak to me."

"That's right." Avery smiled. "You look lovely this evening, Sarah."

"Thank you, but surely you came to do more than compliment me."

"Where are your mother and father?" he asked in a low voice.

"Mother has already retired for the evening, and Father is working on his ledgers in the library. We don't have to worry about being disturbed."

"What about Harrison?"

"He knows better than to come in here while I'm entertaining a guest."

I'll wager that's true, Avery thought, suppressing a smirk. He hurried on, "I've been keeping an eye on Elliot Markham for you, just as I promised."

Sarah's carefully maintained façade slipped for an instant, and Avery saw the flash of pain and anger in her eyes. Then she recovered and asked coolly, "And just what have you found out? Not that it's of any great importance to me, of course."

"Of course," Avery murmured. "I just thought you'd like to know that two nights ago, I followed Elliot to a rendezvous with Roxanne Darragh."

At the mention of Roxanne's name, Sarah clenched her hands into fists, and Avery knew her fingernails were digging into her palms. She kept her features composed and said quietly, "That doesn't surprise me. Another romantic assignation, I presume?"

"I know of no other reason for them to be meeting in such an out-of-the-way part of town." Avery hesitated, then said, "I talked to Roxanne."

Sarah caught her breath and lifted her chin. "And what did she say?"

Putting an expression of deep sympathy on his face, Avery said, "She told me that she and Elliot are in love."

"I . . . I see." She could not prevent a shudder from running through her slender frame at hearing the words stated so baldly. "To tell you the truth, Avery, I expected no less. I knew when I saw them in the Markham garden that evening that what Elliot and I once had was destroyed."

Despite her statement, Avery could tell she had not been completely convinced that Elliot had abandoned his love for her. She had been hoping desperately that Avery would tell her something else, something that would allow her to cling to a shred of hope. Instead, his news had swept away the last bit of support under her feet. Emotionally, she was adrift, and Avery intended to catch her.

"There's more, Sarah," he said, stepping closer to her.

Sarah did not look as if she could take much more, but she managed to say, "What?"

"I saw Roxanne with Dr. Benjamin Church."

"Dr. Church?" Sarah sounded puzzled now. "The insurrectionist, the one who makes all the speeches and writes those pamphlets with that awful doggerel?"

"Exactly."

"But why would Roxanne—" Sarah broke off her question and lifted a hand to her lips in shock as the realization came to her. "You mean she's involved with those traitors? And Elliot . . . ?"

"I'm afraid she may have seduced him into getting mixed up with some bad company, Sarah," Avery said solemnly. "I hate to say it—Elliot's been my friend for many, many years—but a man sometimes does foolish things for the love of a woman."

That was the last straw for Sarah. She was devoted to the Crown, and to hear that not only had she lost the man she loved to another woman, but that he was betraying his country as well—it was too much for her to bear. She covered her face with her hands and sobbed.

Avery drew her into his arms. "There, there," he murmured as he patted her back and cradled her head against his chest. "Don't cry, darling. Don't waste your tears on that rotter."

Sarah hiccuped a time or two, then said, "I thought you said he was your friend."

"Well, any man who would treat a wonderful girl like you the way he has doesn't deserve my friendship. And he certainly doesn't deserve you."

"I—I'm not wonderful."

"Yes, you are," Avery said, cupping her chin and tilting her head back so he could peer down into her blue eyes. "I probably shouldn't say this right now, but I've been madly in love with you for a very long time, Sarah."

"Oh, Avery! I know what we did—"

"I'm not talking about that," he said urgently. "Our passion for each other carried us away, but I'm talking about something deeper, something real." He hurried on before she had a chance to protest. "I never said anything about how I really feel because Elliot was my friend. At least I thought he was. And I didn't want to come between the two of you when you seemed so happy together. But now . . ."

"Now it's all over between Elliot and me," Sarah said dully.

"It can be the beginning of something even better." There was no point in holding back, Avery thought. "Sarah, will you marry me?"

She gasped in surprise. "Marry you?" she repeated. "Now?"

"We'll wait long enough to satisfy the bounds of propriety. But since your engagement to Elliot is over, and since you know now how I feel about you . . . please say yes."

"I don't know what to say. This has all come as such a shock."

"Then at least promise me you'll consider it," Avery urged.

"Yes, I can do that. I will think about it, Avery."

His lips brushed hers in a gentle kiss, then captured her mouth in a harder, more demanding fashion. She responded as she always did, tightening her arms around him and pressing the softness of her breasts and belly against him. A moan came from deep in her throat.

Avery broke the kiss and lifted his hand to stroke her cheek, just brushing against her breast in the process. "I hope you'll let me know your decision soon," he whispered. "I'm not sure I can stand the waiting."

"I—I will," Sarah promised.

As she gazed up at him, Avery wanted to laugh. She was so trusting, so easily manipulated. If only she realized that she had never stood a chance against him! But he was sure such a thing would never occur to her.

And that move was only the beginning. Sooner or later, he would take everything that had ever mattered to Elliot Markham. The rivalry that had existed between them since they were children, the competition that had started out in such a good-natured manner, would reach the only conclusion that was possible: Avery Wallingford would win.

Chapter Eight

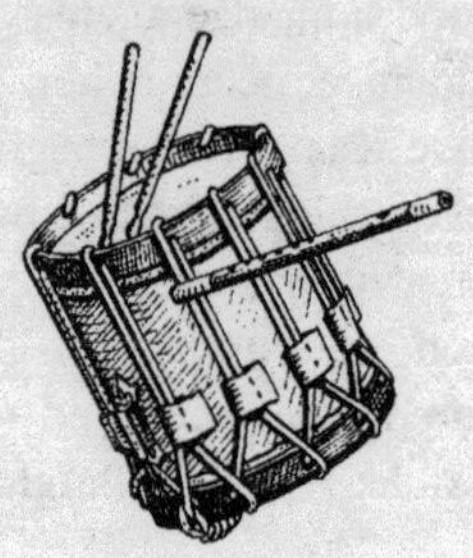

After they had decided what to do about Cordelia, Daniel, Quincy, and Murdoch took turns standing watch, but no one slept for very long. It was well before dawn when Daniel awoke to the clamor of birds, loudly announcing the beginning of a new day. He roused Cordelia and told her to get ready to travel. She got up without complaint, but Daniel knew from the slow, stiff way she moved that she needed more rest.

At least she had not had to endure the beating they had suffered at the hands of Faulkner's men the day before, Daniel thought. He was still sore, and there was a dull ache behind his eyes that the short stretch of sleep had done little to help.

They did not light a fire. While it was unlikely that Faulkner could be anywhere nearby—he and his men were probably still trying to catch all their horses, Daniel realized with a slight smile—there was no point in taking chances. In the chill of the damp predawn darkness they prepared to ride and moved out only a short while later as the night gradually faded into the grayness of early morning.

They rode in silence, Murdoch leading the way to the trail. He turned north, toward Bennington, and the others followed, Daniel bringing up the rear. His flintlock rifle was balanced across the pommel of the saddle in front of him, primed, loaded, and at half cock. He kept a watchful eye on the winding trail behind them.

The spring air was refreshing and cool, and the sunlight soon cut through the branches to sparkle on the dew-laden young leaves.

"Can we stop and eat something now?" Cordelia asked.

"I don't see why not," Daniel replied as he reined in.

They dismounted and led their horses to the side of the road. Then everyone scattered in different directions to stretch their legs.

Nearly ten minutes later, when they had regrouped and were ready to unload the food, Murdoch said quietly, "Somebody's coming, Dan'l."

Daniel peered down the road behind them, fearing he would see Perry Faulkner and his hired toughs galloping toward them. Instead, he saw two ox-drawn wagons coming around a bend; several men walked beside each team of oxen, prodding the massive animals to keep them moving.

"Just some pilgrims," Murdoch said. "I dinna think we need t' worry about them."

"Perhaps they have some decent food they'll share with us," Cordelia said.

Daniel gave her a hard look. "I'm sure these people need what supplies they have, and I don't think we should ask them for anything."

"Well, it wouldn't hurt," Cordelia snapped. "I'm getting

awfully tired of corn cakes, and Murdoch said last night that was the last of our dried beef."

Our dried beef? Daniel thought.

Several minutes later, as the wagons pulled even with them, Daniel and Murdoch raised their hands in greeting. The men herding the oxen reached out, grasped the animals' harnesses, and hauled the teams to a stop.

"Hello, friends," one of them said. "It's good to see fellow travelers out here. We've not run across anyone for several days now." He held out a hand. "I'm Matthew Alford, and this is my family."

As Daniel and Murdoch shook hands with him, the man went on to introduce his brothers, Edward, Noble, and Thaddeus. Their wives and children were riding in the wagons, he explained, crowded in with the goods the families had brought from their former homes in eastern Massachusetts. The entire family had decided to move to Vermont.

"We just didn't like the way things have been going in Massachusetts lately," Matthew said, looking solemn now. "With all that fighting going on around Boston, it's plain to see there's going to be a war with England sooner or later."

The war has already begun, Daniel thought. *And Murdoch and I were in Concord to see its bloody birth.*

"I'm Daniel . . . Ramsey, and this is my brother, Quincy." Caution was becoming a habit with Daniel. Gesturing toward Murdoch, he went on, "And a friend of ours—"

"Call me Buck," Murdoch broke in, quickly picking up on Daniel's deception. He grinned broadly at the travelers, and several of the small children in the wagons giggled.

"And this is my wife, Cordelia," Daniel announced, slipping his arm around her.

He was afraid she would explode with anger and ruin

the little masquerade, but she managed to smile and say sweetly, "I'm so pleased to meet you."

Daniel had no doubt she would have cheerfully plunged a knife into him and twisted it, but no one would have known that from her pleasant expression.

"Where are you folks headed?" one of the Alford brothers asked.

"We're on our way north to Bennington." Daniel could see no harm in telling the truth about their destination.

"We're headed there, too," Matthew Alford said. "Not planning to stay, mind you. We want to push on farther north and put as much distance as we can between us and the fighting. You don't think the troubles will reach all the way up into Vermont, do you? We know Ethan Allen and the Green Mountain Boys have an occasional scuffle with the Yorkers, but before long we expect Allen and his boys will make the territory of Vermont free from the taxes and laws of both New York and New Hampshire."

Reinforcing his discouraging opinion that violence would spread throughout the colonies would serve no purpose, Daniel decided. He said honestly, "I hope there won't be widespread violence."

"Well, since we're headed in the same direction, no reason we can't travel together, is there?" the man asked.

Daniel hesitated and looked at Murdoch and Quincy. By attaching themselves to a larger party, there was a chance that Faulkner would not risk attacking them again. On the other hand, as desperate as the former wrecker was to stop Cordelia from jeopardizing his plans, he might attack the Alfords as well.

A decision had to be made. "That sounds like a fine idea," he said to Matthew Alford, "but we have to be in Bennington tomorrow, and I'm afraid at the pace your oxen move, we wouldn't arrive in time."

"Too bad," Matthew said. "We would have enjoyed your company. But best of luck to you anyway!"

"Let's mount up," Daniel said to his companions.

Cordelia glanced up at him, and he saw an angry flash in her eyes. "We stopped for—"

"For a short rest, and now we've had it," Daniel finished for her, urging her toward her horse. "Here, let me help you, dear."

With their backs to the travelers, Cordelia gave him a murderous look as he assisted her into the saddle. Quincy and Murdoch swung up onto their own horses.

"Good luck to you!" Daniel called to the Alfords after mounting his horse. The men waved, as did the women and children inside the wagon, and Matthew called out a farewell. Daniel, Quincy, and Murdoch returned the waves, but Cordelia kept her eyes straight ahead.

"Those folks are going t' think ye're a mite unfriendly, lass," Murdoch told her.

"I don't care what they think." She glared at Daniel. "I'm hungry, and I'm tired. And what if Perry finds those people and asks them if they've seen us? They'll send him right on to Bennington."

"You're right. It would have been better if we hadn't encountered them. But we did, and there's nothing we can do about it now." Wearily, Daniel rubbed a hand over his face and laughed hollowly. "You know, I remember a time when life was simple. Seems like ages ago now."

"Life's never simple, lad," Murdoch told him. "Sometimes 'tis just resting up before it pulls its next wee surprise."

* * *

The road became busier the next morning as they started on the last leg of the journey to Bennington. Several men on horseback overtook them, heading toward the settlement some miles ahead. Each time the riders approached, Daniel, Murdoch, and Quincy put their hands on their weapons, in case the newcomers turned out to be Faulkner's men. The travelers were strangers in every instance, however, bent on their own business, and other than a few waves and called-out greetings, no one paid attention to Daniel and his companions.

They passed several wagons driven by farmers returning home after having been to market in Bennington. Some were empty, and others laden with livestock or supplies. Again, they exchanged greetings and went on their way.

"Ought t' be there by early this afternoon," Murdoch said. "We can stock up on food and anything else we need when we get there."

Daniel glanced toward Cordelia. It would not be long until she discovered they would not be parting company in Bennington after all, he knew. Perhaps he should tell her. . . .

But before he could say anything, Quincy spoke up. "Look! There's a travelers' hostel up ahead."

"Thank God," Cordelia said fervently. "If I never see another corn cake, it will be perfectly fine with me."

"We can only stop long enough to eat," Daniel said. *And after we have eaten a good, hot meal, I'll tell her about our plan*, he decided, hoping that she would be in a more cooperative mood once her hunger was satisfied.

Several horses and wagons were tied up in front of the wayside inn, which appeared to be a much busier place than either of the establishments they had visited in the past few days. They reined in and dismounted.

"The three of you go on inside," Cordelia said, looking

at a small building to one side of the inn, at the edge of the woods. "I'll join you shortly."

Daniel was about to protest when he spotted the half moon carved in the door and recognized the building as a privy.

He and the other two men went inside the inn. The place was doing a brisk business, but they found a spot at the bar and ordered cider and meat pies for themselves and Cordelia. After mugs of hot cider had been served, they took them to the vacant end of one of the long tables to wait while the food was being prepared.

The men talked idly, and a quarter of an hour had passed when the proprietor stepped out from behind the bar, carrying a platter of four steaming meat pies. He set the platter on the table and looked at the untouched mug of cider. "Where's the other one?" he asked.

"She'll be here shortly," Daniel said, his voice curt.

"No offense, mister. I was just wonderin'."

"The lady went t' use the outhouse," Murdoch explained.

The proprietor frowned. "Not that old two-holer out there, I hope."

"Why not?" asked Quincy.

"Well," he said slowly, "it ain't the most fragrant place in the world to start with, mind you, but a skunk crawled up in there this mornin'. One of the serving girls surprised him—but not as much as he surprised her. I reckon it'll be a week or more 'fore the air in there is bearable again."

Daniel exchanged a confused glance with Murdoch and Quincy.

"But I don't reckon her whereabouts are any of my affair, mister, as long as you and your friends got the money to pay for the food an' drink."

Impatiently, Daniel dug a coin out of his pocket and clattered it on the table. The proprietor skillfully scooped it up.

"Come on," Daniel said as he stood up. "I want to see about this."

"What about your food?" asked the proprietor.

"Leave it here. We'll be back in a minute . . . I hope."

Trailed by Murdoch and Quincy, Daniel stalked out the front door and turned left, toward the privy.

"No need t' check over there," Murdoch said, stopping Daniel by putting a heavy hand on his shoulder. "Look at th' horses."

Daniel's heart fell as he saw that Cordelia's horse was gone. "Damn it! I should've expected something like this," he said bitterly.

"I don't understand," Quincy said. "Where could she have gone off to?"

"Who knows? Perhaps she's heading west toward Saratoga on her own."

"But why? I thought she was too afraid of her husband to leave on her own."

"I guess the lass was no' asleep like we thought the other night," Murdoch said. "She overheard that we were planning t' keep her with us, so she's been biding her time, waiting for a chance t' slip away."

"I'm afraid you're right, Murdoch," Daniel agreed grimly. "And now we've got even more trouble than before."

He turned to Quincy. "Go back in there and get those meat pies. If we've got to go chasing after Cordelia again, at least we're going to have some hot food along the way."

Quincy hurried into the building.

"Which way are we going, Dan'l, toward Bennington or Saratoga?" Murdoch asked.

"Both," Daniel answered shortly.

Murdoch's bushy red eyebrows lifted in surprise. "Splitting up, are we?"

"I don't see that we have a choice." Daniel gestured toward the crossroads. "She either headed north, toward Bennington, or west toward Saratoga. We can't all go in both directions at once."

"Aye, tha's true. I'll go t' Saratoga, and ye and the lad can head on up t' join the Green Mountain Boys."

Daniel was deep in thought. After Quincy had returned, his hands full of meat pies, Daniel said, *"I'll* start toward Saratoga, Murdoch. You and Quincy will go on to Bennington."

"What?" Quincy exclaimed. "What are you talking about, Daniel? I thought we were going to stick together."

"Your friend Cordelia has made that impossible," Daniel said bitterly, his voice pitched low. "We have to stop her from warning the British about Faulkner's raid on the supply wagons. We must see to it that those guns wind up in patriot hands."

With a dubious expression, Quincy said, "You may be right about that, but I don't like us splitting up. I especially don't like you going one way and me another."

"Murdoch will watch out for you."

"Damn it, Daniel, that's not what I'm worried about, and you know it! If Faulkner finds you again, he'll kill you, and I might never find out what has happened to you."

Daniel sighed. "I understand, Quincy. But we can't lose sight of our original mission. One of us has to reach Bennington and find Colonel Allen. You can handle that while I search for Cordelia. It's more likely she went west and is trying to reach Saratoga on her own."

Quincy glared at him for a second, then accused, "You

don't think I can stop her, do you? You think I'd let her do whatever she wants to do. You think I've forgotten everything that's important just because a pretty girl smiled at me," Quincy went on hotly.

"She's a mighty pretty lass," Murdoch pointed out.

"Just do as I say, Quincy."

For a long moment Quincy said nothing. Then he shoved two meat pies into Daniel's hands. "Here," he snapped. "Take Cordelia's, too, in case you catch up to her."

"Thanks, Quincy. Remember, I'm trusting you to find Colonel Allen and report to him. I'll catch up as soon as I can."

"Sure." Quincy turned away, then hesitated and swung back to face his brother. "Be careful, Daniel," he said softly.

Daniel embraced him and held on as long as he could. "I will," he promised. "You, too."

Daniel had been riding for well over an hour when the sudden bark of a gunshot made him jerk his mount to a halt. He waited tensely, but there were no more shots. He could faintly hear angry voices, however.

Turning his horse toward the side of the road, he followed the sound until he could tell what direction the shouting was coming from. A hundred yards ahead of him the road twisted to the right, and if he cut through the trees, he figured he could reach the road near the spot where the trouble was. The thick woods would offer plenty of concealment as he approached, so he would be able to see what was going on before he blundered into the middle of it.

The undergrowth was sodden and spongy, causing his horse some difficulty and making Daniel suspect that he might be close to a bog. Not wanting to take a chance on an accident, he dismounted, tied the animal to a sapling, and unslung his flintlock rifle. He made sure it was loaded, then out of habit patted his powder horn and shot pouch, assuring himself he had plenty of ammunition. Tugging the tricorn down on his head, he slipped carefully through the soggy undergrowth, putting his boots down as silently as possible with each step.

The angry voices had gotten louder, and he recognized one of them as Cordelia's. When he neared the road, which had bent around just as he expected it would, he found several large boulders, deposited long ago by glaciers, to hide behind and carefully peered around one at the people in the byway.

Cordelia stood in the center of a group of men, her face pallid except for a red spot of rage that shone on each cheek as she glared at Faulkner. Two of the toughs held her arms while her husband stalked back and forth in front of her. "—never interfere with my plans again!" he shouted.

"I've no interest in interfering with your plans," she told him coldly. "All I want is to be left alone. If you let me go, Perry, I promise I'll never say anything to anyone about what you're doing."

"You're damned right you won't! I'm tired of this endless game, Cordelia. You're a lovely woman, but there are things more important to me than beauty."

"Money," she said bitterly. "Money and power."

"One and the same," Faulkner returned arrogantly.

Daniel leaned out slightly, trying to see how many men Faulkner had with him. Two were holding Cordelia, and he could see at least two more. Others might be outside his range of vision. The odds against him would be at least five to one if he attacked, but he did not know what else he could do. He could not turn away and leave Cordelia's fate in Faulkner's hands.

"I've been racking my brain trying to decide what to do with you, my dear. Killing you out of hand seems to be such a waste," Faulkner said.

"Go ahead and do it," spat Cordelia. "I'm sick and tired of running from you."

"It won't be that easy, I'm afraid. You've inconvenienced me a great deal, and you're going to have to pay for your troublemaking." He smiled icily at her. "I've decided to let the men have you. They can do whatever they please—as long as you're dead by nightfall so we can get on about our business."

To Daniel it was beyond belief that Faulkner could plot such a fate for his wife, a woman he had loved at one time. But not only had she outlived her usefulness, she had also become a hindrance to his plans.

Daniel's instinct screamed out for him to put a rifle ball through Faulkner's brain. He could do it easily at this range, before the others could stop him. But then they would swarm over him and kill him, and Cordelia would be no better off than she was now.

No sound alerted him, nothing but a silent warning bell in the back of his mind. Daniel turned around to see what had set it off.

The prick of a knife point in the small of his back stopped him short. An arm looped around his throat and tightened with a jerk. In a whisper he could barely hear, a strange voice said in his ear, "Don't make a move, mister, or I'll shove this pigsticker clean through you."

Chapter Nine

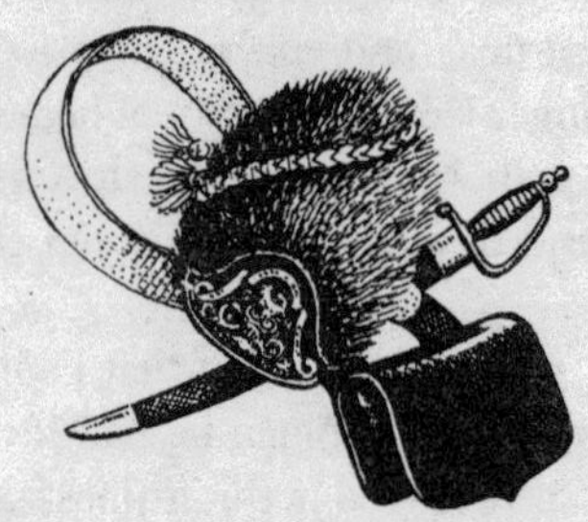

Roxanne Darragh looked at the small grip she had packed. The bag, sitting on the floor at the foot of her bed, contained a change of clothes, some cosmetics, and the red hooded cape that would serve as the signal should the munitions be on board the ship. She had decided to wear her black cape on the journey.

Tomorrow she would take the valise with her when she and Elliot left for Portsmouth, New Hampshire, to rendezvous with the *Carolingian.*

She sighed and turned to face the mirror on her dressing table. Picking up a whalebone-handle brush, she ran it through her long red hair. The task occupied her body but not her mind, and her eyes strayed once again to the bag, this time studying its reflection.

Things had been moving so quickly she'd had little time to think about the course on which she had embarked. A combination of bizarre circumstances had cast her in the role of Elliot Markham's lover, and the trip to Portsmouth would be the final reinforcement of that. When her parents found out what she had planned, they would question her morals as well as her intelligence.

For long, long months now, they had put up with her comings and goings at odd hours, her disappearances with little or no warning, and they had tolerated her behavior because they trusted her, the youngest of their six children, to maintain the family's respectability. They knew no details of what she had been doing, but they had assumed that she was involved in the movement to obtain liberty for the colonies, and only a few weeks ago their suspicions were confirmed.

But what she was about to do was different. This escapade would ruin her reputation publicly and forever. One day the truth would come out about the real purpose of the trip, Roxanne told herself, so it should not matter what anyone thought about her now. This was a time of war, and she was only doing what she thought was right.

But it *did* matter. It mattered a great deal what her family thought of her. And what if Daniel ever found out?

"He'll just have to understand," she said out loud. "I'm sure he'll understand. . . ."

She laid the brush on the dressing table, then looked up in surprise as she heard a sound from downstairs. Her parents had gone out for the evening, to attend a party honoring the twenty-fifth wedding anniversary of close friends, and Roxanne was not expecting them back until much later. Alone in the house, she had planned on going to bed early and was already wearing her nightgown.

She heard the sound again, and she stood up. It was not her imagination; a knocking noise was coming from somewhere on the ground floor of the house. She felt a shiver of apprehension.

With the tension gripping Boston those days, there was a

feeling that anything could happen. Though General Gage tried hard to maintain military discipline, many of the British troops who walked the streets of the city were looking for an excuse to cause trouble, and Roxanne knew that some of the soldiers were little better than common hoodlums.

Nervously, she reached for her robe and quickly shrugged into it. Next to the fireplace downstairs there were several stout iron pokers, and anyone trying to break into the house would find a rude welcome.

To Roxanne's surprise, she found herself hoping for some trouble. After struggling with her confusion about the trip, it would feel good to do something as simple as swinging a poker at an intruder's head.

Quietly, she opened the door of her room and stepped out into the upstairs hallway. Again she heard the noise. Now that she could hear it better, she recognized the sound for what it was.

Someone was knocking on the front door.

Feeling rather foolish—and vaguely disappointed—she called out, "Coming!" and ran down the stairs. Tightening the belt of her heavy, white cotton robe, she went into the parlor and picked up a poker from the stand beside the massive fireplace.

She clasped the poker tightly as she went to the door and called through the thick panel, "Who is it?"

The reply was muttered, and she could not make it out other than to recognize the voice as that of a man. Leaning closer to the door, she said again, "Who's out there? I'm not opening this door until I know who you are."

This time the voice croaked harshly, "It's Elliot!"

What is Elliot doing here? Roxanne thought, and for a second she considered the possibility that someone else might be using his name to get her to open the door. But he went on: "For God's sake, Roxanne, let me in! I don't feel well."

She leaned the poker beside the doorway and fumbled with the latch. When she swung the door open, she found Elliot leaning against the side of the recessed entranceway. From the sound of his voice she thought he might be injured, but as her eyes scanned his disheveled form she saw no sign of a wound.

She realized as soon as she saw the bottle dangling from his right hand, that he was probably not in any pain whatsoever.

"You're intoxicated."

"Very little escapes the eye of an experienced spy such as yourself, does it, my dear?" He leered at her.

"Keep your voice down. The neighbors might overhear you. I thought you said you were sick."

"I am," Elliot insisted. "Heartsick." He peered blearily past her, down the hallway leading from the foyer. "Are you here alone?"

"My parents are out for the evening," she admitted, not sure whether to be angry or sympathetic.

"Good. Then I'll come in and tell you all about it. After all, we're comrades-in-arms, aren't we?"

She could not deny it, or him, and stepped back quickly as he stumbled into the house.

"You can come in for a moment," she said as she closed the door behind him. "But you can't stay, Elliot. It wouldn't look respectable."

"And traveling with me to Portsmouth tomorrow will look respectable?"

Roxanne blushed at his question and followed him into the parlor. Elliot took off his coat, threw it over a chair, sank down on the overstuffed divan, and rested his head on its cushions. A shudder ran through him, and he sighed.

"Finally, a safe haven."

"I wouldn't count on that," Roxanne told him. "You had no right to come here like this, Elliot. You've been drinking too much. What if my parents had been here and seen you like this?"

"I have a confession to make." He grinned crookedly. "I knew they were gone. I saw them leave earlier."

"You were here earlier?" Roxanne asked in surprise. "Why didn't you come in then?"

"I was . . . working up my courage, I suppose you could say."

"Finding it in a bottle, more likely."

"I admit I visited a few taverns tonight, in between my trips past your house." He sat forward. "But the important thing is that I'm here."

Crossing her arms across her chest, Roxanne said tartly, "Indeed you are."

Elliot became serious. "I'm sorry if I'm causing a problem for you, Roxanne. That wasn't my intention. It's just that I've had some bad news this evening. It's nothing I wasn't expecting, mind you, but still that doesn't lessen the blow. I wanted to talk to someone, and since Daniel's not here anymore, I thought I could come to you."

A pang of sympathy went through Roxanne. Elliot was blinking rapidly, and beads of sweat had popped out on his forehead. He leaned over and put his head in his hands.

She sat down next to him. "I'm sorry, Elliot. Of course you can talk to me. What's wrong?"

"As I said, nothing I didn't know about. Theophilus Cummings stopped by my father's house late this afternoon on business. He happened to mention that Sarah is now engaged to Avery Wallingford."

Roxanne's eyes widened in surprise. "My, that was fast! She hardly waited a suitable interval since ending her engagement to you, did she? Why, she must have changed her mind—almost overnight!"

"I can't blame her, not for any of it. Most of it was pure bad luck, and what wasn't ill fortune was my own fault. I should have convinced Sarah that things weren't what they seemed to be."

"Between you and me, you mean," Roxanne said softly.

He sighed. "Exactly."

"You only did what you had to do to preserve our secret."

Elliot met her gaze. "Do you really think that's true, Roxanne? Was there nothing else I could do to salvage the situation in the garden but kiss you?"

"I don't know, Elliot."

He scrubbed his face with his palms, then stood up and paced back and forth across the parlor. "After I overheard what Cummings was telling my father, I left the house and went to see Sarah. I knew it was a mistake even as I left, but I couldn't stop myself. I had to find out if it was true, had to hear for myself—from her own lips—that she was going to marry Avery."

"You saw Sarah?"

Elliot stopped his pacing, leaned against the fireplace, and looked bleakly at her. "She wouldn't talk to me—wouldn't even see me. I told her mother that all I wanted to do was ask Sarah if it was true. It didn't do any good. Sarah refused to budge from her room. I finally gave up and left. That's when I came here the first time. And from here I went to a little tavern I know."

"I think I can guess how the rest of the evening went," Roxanne said dryly. She crossed the room to where Elliot stood, reached out, and took his right hand in both of hers. "I'm very sorry. I wish you had never lost Sarah. But one day this war—this revolution—will be over. Surely once you explain everything to her, she'll have to understand."

"A devoted loyalist such as Sarah? Not bloody likely. No matter how the struggle turns out. No, I'm afraid it's over forever. That it's for a good cause doesn't make me feel better right now."

He was voicing the same arguments Roxanne had used against herself earlier. Someday the war would be over. Surely their loved ones would understand.

Acting on impulse, Roxanne put her arms around Elliot. "I'm sorry," she whispered as she drew him against her. "I'm so very sorry."

There was no thought in her mind but to comfort him. He was in pain, and she had reached out. He returned the hug, patting her awkwardly on the back.

"Everything will be fine," she said. But she did not believe the gentle lie told to help the grieving young man.

They stood there, embracing, pressed together. Then Elliot leaned back slightly in order to look down into Roxanne's eyes. His eyes were moist from the tears he blinked away. "Thank you," he said huskily. "I know I had no right to come here tonight, but I felt that I had to see you."

"I'm glad you came," Roxanne whispered. "We're friends now—comrades-in-arms."

"Is that all?"

"What—what do you mean?"

"I've been thinking about you ever since that night in the garden," Elliot said, his voice quivering. "When I kissed you. I think it wasn't just because Sarah discovered us and I had to protect our mission."

"What are you saying?" asked Roxanne, barely able to get the words out.

"I'm saying that I'd been wanting to kiss you for a long time."

And with that, his mouth came down on hers.

Roxanne struggled slightly in his arms, as surprised as she had been when he kissed her in the garden of the Markham estate. Then she had been shocked as well by the sudden glare of the light shining on them. But now, the remarkable flood of feelings that surged through her was in response only to Elliot's lips moving hungrily against hers and his arms tightening around her. Her breasts pressed against his chest as he drew her to him. She could feel the almost painful sensation of her nipples hardening against the heavy cotton fabric of her nightdress and robe. Surely he could feel them, too, she thought wildly, and the heat of embarrassment welled up within her.

No, not embarrassment, she realized. This was an entirely different kind of heat. . . .

Gasping for breath when Elliot finally broke the hard, demanding kiss, Roxanne lowered her head to rest on his chest. One of his hands was still splayed on her back, holding her to him, but the other had strayed down to caress the swell of her hips under the gown. As he touched the small of her back and then moved lower, a quiver went through her. An unfamiliar noise surprised her by coming from low in her throat.

A part of her brain screamed at her that this was wrong, that she should pull away from him now, while she still had the chance, but she ignored the warning and slid a hand between their bodies, and slipped it into his shirt so she could feel the warmth of his skin.

"I think I had better leave," Elliot whispered huskily.

"No! You don't have to go."

"Despite what you may have heard about me—despite the way I've acted at times in the past—I'm not a cad, Roxanne. If I stay, I don't think I can trust myself with you. You're so beautiful, so intelligent . . . so dedicated." He smiled sadly. "But Daniel—"

"Daniel is far away," Roxanne interrupted, "and this is wartime. We don't know if he'll ever return to us, Elliot. For that matter, we don't know if you and I will be coming back from the mission to Portsmouth."

"Those sound like arguments I should be using on you."

"That's because you realize I'm right."

"It is only natural, I suppose, that at a time like this we should turn to each other. We have to take what comfort we can in each other."

Roxanne nodded wordlessly.

He kissed her again, and her lips parted to let his tongue dart into her mouth with a hot, wet urgency. Her hand was still inside his shirt, her fingers trailing through the mat of fine hair on his chest. Her fingertips traced the outline of his muscles. An insistent heat grew in her belly until it was blazing like flames fanned up from glowing embers. There was no turning back now. She had to have Elliot, and she was going to try very hard not to think about Daniel Reed for the next few hours.

The man who was holding the knife against Daniel's back edged deeper into the woods, away from the boulders, and Daniel had no choice but to go with him. The arm that was locked tightly around his neck prevented any struggle.

His captor made as little noise as possible as they moved away from the spot where Faulkner and his men were detaining Cordelia, causing Daniel to discard the thought that he had been captured by one of Faulkner's hired toughs. The man was just as interested in avoiding discovery as he was, he realized.

They had backed away fifty yards over a hill when the man whirled around and shoved Daniel in front of him. Someone else caught Daniel's arm and, while he was off-balance, flung him to the ground. The move knocked the breath from Daniel's lungs. As he lay there gasping for air on the wet bed of leaves, the second man came down hard with his knees on Daniel's chest and put a knife to his throat.

"Who are you?" the man asked.

Still trying to get air into his lungs, Daniel stared up at him. In appearance, he resembled Faulkner's henchmen: rough looking, with several days' growth of beard stubble, ragged clothes, and a stained, battered tricorn tilted to the back of his head. He held the long-bladed hunting knife at Daniel's throat with an easy familiarity.

Looking past the man's shoulder, Daniel could see his original captor peering down at him. The two men's eyes were suspicious and hostile, but their gazes lacked the dull coldness of hired killers.

Breathing shallowly because of the knife at his throat, Daniel managed to choke out, "If you'll move that blade, I'll tell you what you want to know."

"You'll tell us anyway. Are you with that bunch of devils who're holding that woman?"

"Would I have been hiding in the bushes if I were with them?"

"He's got a point, Asa," whispered the first man. "When

I jumped him, he didn't act like he wanted them to know he was there."

The other man glared at Daniel. "I still don't trust you. Why were you skulkin' around, damn you?"

"I wanted to—to help the girl."

Asa seemed unconvinced, but he moved the point of the knife away from Daniel's skin. "Seen any redcoats around?" he asked sharply.

It was still hard to breathe with the man's knees in his chest, but Daniel felt better without the knife point prodding the soft flesh of his throat. "I haven't seen any British soldiers since I left Massachusetts."

"Thought you sounded like a Massachusetts man."

"Then I suppose I've been up in this part of the country too long. I was born and raised in Virginia."

"Let him up, Asa. He's no British spy."

"Sure of that, are you, Jasper?" Asa snapped. "He wouldn't be much of a spy if he was paradin' around in lobsterback red and talkin' like a damned Cockney, now would he?"

"Believe me, I'm no British spy," Daniel said emphatically.

At last Asa stood up and stepped back, although he held his knife at the ready in case Daniel tried to double-cross them.

Wearily, Daniel climbed to his feet and brushed the wet leaves and dirt off his clothes.

"Who's that girl to you?" Jasper asked.

"She's a friend," Daniel said. That was a lie; Cordelia was no friend of his, but he did feel responsible for her. And knowing about her life with Faulkner had made him sympathetic to her, despite her obstinate attitude.

"Who're them gents shoving her around?" demanded Asa.

"The well-dressed one is her husband. The others work for him."

Both of Daniel's captors looked surprised.

"Husband, you say?" Asa exclaimed. "I've heard some men claim that their wives need a thrashing now and then, but I never heard tell of nobody who hired men to do it for him."

"Perry Faulkner's not like other men," Daniel said bitterly, "and he's only after Cordelia because she knows his plans."

Asa squinted at him. "What plans?"

Daniel was going to have to take a chance. "Plans to steal a British supply train full of guns."

Asa and Jasper were clearly startled by Daniel's words. They stared at each other for a good minute before Jasper said, "You'd better come with us and tell the colonel all about it. You and him can hash it out." He grasped Daniel's free arm to lead him away.

"But what about the girl?" Daniel asked anxiously, shaking his arm free and halting.

"She'll have to wait until you've talked to the colonel," Asa said from behind him, giving him a gentle shove.

Daniel made an effort to curb his impatience. The men who had apprehended him were armed with pistols and long knives, and they had him at a disadvantage. He had to go along with their wishes.

"I need to get my horse before I talk to anyone," he said. "And just who is this colonel you keep talking about?"

"He's a militia officer from Connecticut," Jasper said, "and he's leading a bunch of us boys up to Lake Champlain to fight the bloody British. His name's Benedict Arnold."

Chapter Ten

Once they had decided what to do with Daniel, Asa and Jasper became friendlier. Jasper was downright talkative as they escorted Daniel through the woods toward the column of men led by Colonel Benedict Arnold.

"Asa and me, our farms are next to each other back in Connecticut," he explained after they had retrieved Daniel's horse and their own mounts. "When the trouble came to Massachusetts, Colonel Arnold went from Connecticut to Cambridge, where the Committee of Safety told him he could raise a force of four hundred men and head west to meet up with Ethan Allen. So Arnold sent out the call for volunteers, and we both joined the militia." He paused as he led them around a large fallen tree. "Figured it was the right thing to do. Somebody's got to show the British they can't push us around."

Daniel did not say he had been present when "the trouble" came to Massachusetts, as Jasper expressed it. That was putting it mildly, Daniel thought, remembering the bloody, brutal battle that had begun at Concord bridge on a day that seemed long, long ago.

"When we got to Cambridge, General Artemas Ward and some of the other officers suggested we head up toward Lake Champlain. I got a feeling that's where the next fighting's going to break out," Jasper went on. "The colonel says we're going to take a British fort at a place called Ticonderoga."

Asa and he had been sent out as scouts, Jasper told him, in order to make sure the militiamen would not encounter anyone who might warn the British of their troop movements. Since leaving Massachusetts, Arnold's force had stuck to back roads and narrow trails, avoiding settlements, so their arrival at Fort Ticonderoga would take the British completely by surprise.

Benedict Arnold sounded like a shrewd and effective leader, from what Daniel could tell.

He grinned, feeling almost gleeful at his luck. He had fallen in with colonial forces heading for the very spot that was his destination. At least it had been before this business with Cordelia and Faulkner.

Daniel winced as he thought about the predicament Cordelia was in. He had heard Faulkner announce his intention of turning his wife over to his men to be molested, raped, and eventually murdered.

An idea began to form in the back of his mind. If he could persuade Colonel Arnold to lend him a hand, he could help Cordelia and insure that the patriots got hold of the weapons. In order for his plan to work, Cordelia would have to cooperate with him, of course, but considering her grim alternative, Daniel thought he could convince her to give up her churlish attitude and work with him.

After half an hour of traipsing through a forest floor

thick with rotting leaves and brittle twigs a sudden hail from a clump of birches made all three men stop abruptly. "It's just us, Jim," Asa called out to the sentry who had challenged them. "We're coming in, and we've got a prisoner with us."

Another militiaman clutching a flintlock musket emerged from the cluster of trees. He eyed Daniel and asked, "Is he a redcoat spy?"

"Says he's not," Jasper replied. "I believe him, but the colonel will have the final say." The scout frowned in puzzlement. "Has the company stopped? Why aren't you marching?"

"We're taking a rest, all right, but not the colonel. He's not even here."

"Not even here?" Asa exclaimed. "Where the devil is he?"

"Rode on to Bennington by himself." Jim was walking toward them, stepping high over dead branches and clumps of ferns. "Said he could make better time that way and couldn't afford to wait any longer. If you ask me, he's afraid the Green Mountain Boys are going to get to the lake first and the fighting'll be all over by the time he gets there. No glory in that, is there?"

"Who's in charge now that your colonel's gone?" Daniel asked.

Jim stopped in his tracks and squinted at him. "And what business is it of yours, mister?"

"I have some very important information for whoever is in charge."

"He was going on earlier about a wagon train of British guns," Asa added, casting a dubious glance at Daniel. "I reckon we'd better let him talk to the commander."

"That'd be Captain Page," Jim said. He jerked a thumb

over his shoulder. "He's back yonder about two hundred yards."

"Thanks," said Asa. "You can go back to your lookout now. We'll escort the prisoner."

They were challenged by another sentry as they approached the halted column of militiamen, most of whom were clad in brown and green, though none could be said to be wearing a uniform akin to those worn by the British. The guard passed Daniel and his captors on after a moment of explanation, and within a few minutes he was brought before the officer in command.

"Found this fellow in the woods, Captain," Asa said. "He was acting mighty suspicious, so we thought we'd better bring him back here for the colonel to talk to. Hear tell the colonel's gone."

"That's correct," the captain said as he got to his feet. He looked curiously at Daniel. "I'm Captain Norvell Page, temporarily in command of the First Connecticut Militia. And you, sir, are . . . ?"

"Daniel Reed, originally from Virginia, lately from Massachusetts. I'm pleased to meet you, Captain. I think we can be of great service to each other."

"Really? And how is that, Mr. Reed?"

"I know where you can put your hands on a wagon train full of British guns and ammunition," he said bluntly. "Or rather, I know someone who can tell you how to go about it."

"What the deuce are you talking about?" Page hissed.

Quickly Daniel explained about Cordelia and the dangerous plight in which she found herself. Page interrupted to ask the scouts if they could confirm what Daniel was saying.

"We saw the girl and those men pushing her around, sure enough," Jasper said. "Couldn't say for sure who she was, though, or if any of the rest of this fella's story is true."

"It is true, all of it," Daniel said solemnly. "If we can rescue Cordelia Faulkner, she can tell us where that British supply train can be found. Then we can get to the weapons before her husband does."

"You're going to have to back up even farther in your story to convince me, I'm afraid, Mr. Reed. Exactly who are you, and what's your connection with this man Faulkner and his wife?"

"I'm on assignment from the Committee of Safety in Boston." Daniel breathed in sharply and said, "My brother and I, along with a friend of ours, were supposed to go to Bennington and accompany Colonel Ethan Allen on his assault against the British at Fort Ticonderoga. We got involved in this mess with the Faulkners strictly by accident—but we're in a position now to turn things to our advantage."

"Your brother and your friend—where are they?"

"They've gone on to Bennington," Daniel told the captain. "Just like your Colonel Arnold."

Page turned his back on Daniel and, rubbing his chin, took ten steps, stopped abruptly, pivoted, and walked back to him again.

"This is quite a farfetched story you've told us, young man," the captain said, "but it has the ring of truth about it. Unfortunately, I don't see how I can help you. Colonel Arnold's orders are to proceed to Bennington and thence to Lake Champlain, and with his absence, that responsibility falls to me. I can't depart from that course."

His mind racing, refusing to accept a decision that would doom Cordelia, Daniel asked, "Tell me, Captain, is Colonel Arnold an ambitious man?"

"I'd say that describing the colonel as ambitious would be an accurate portrait," Page replied. His voice had taken on a caustic tone. "He's proven his mettle as a commander of men, and now he wants his just due."

"Then think about how much glory will accrue to him—and you—if you capture that shipment of guns," Daniel told him.

Page mulled that over. "Just a moment," he said curtly and motioned for his fellow officers to withdraw a few paces for a whispered conference. Finally Page nodded to the men and turned back to Daniel. "I suppose I could spare a small detail to go along with you. This whole thing still seems a bit harebrained to me, but the chance of capturing the British guns makes the risk worthwhile." His voice hardened. "However, I warn you, Mr. Reed. If this is some sort of trap that you intend to lead my boys into, I'll personally see to it that you are hunted down like a dog and hanged."

"It's no trap," Daniel assured him. "At least not for the patriots."

"Very well. I'll give you ten men."

A flood of relief surged through Daniel. "Thank you, Captain. Thank you. I'll be glad to take whatever help you and your men can give me."

Raising a finger, Page added, "You understand, Mr. Reed, that I can't ignore my own mission. The rest of the company will proceed to Bennington as planned. You can catch up to us either there or on the way to Lake Champlain."

"All right," Daniel agreed. "I'll be happy to have whichever ten men you pick to go with me."

"Me and Jasper are two of them," Asa said, taking Daniel by surprise. "You'll need gents who can move quiet when they have to."

Daniel smiled faintly at the scout. "Does this mean you're starting to trust me, Asa?"

"It means I don't trust you at all," Asa snapped. "By

going along on this wild goose chase of yours, I can keep an eye on you."

"I believe you, lad," Jasper said, clapping Daniel on the shoulder. "At least, I want to. I'm hoping you won't let me down and turn out to be a liar."

"You won't regret coming with me, Jasper. I promise," Daniel responded.

"If you capture any supplies from the British, you're to turn them over to Colonel Arnold or myself as soon as possible. Do you understand?" Captain Page asked.

"Of course, sir. That's what I intended to do all along."

Page held out his hand toward Asa and Jasper and said, "These two soldiers can select the other men to accompany you. Their judgment is sound. I wish you luck, Mr. Reed. I have a feeling you're going to need it."

Half an hour later, after Daniel looked over the group that had been picked to accompany him on his mission, he felt they just might have a chance against Faulkner. Six of them had, like Asa and Jasper, been farmers before joining the militia. The other two were city men and carried themselves with an air of competence.

"The first thing we have to do," Daniel said to the two men assigned to be scouts, "is find out where Faulkner took Cordelia. It's already getting dark, so they couldn't have gotten far."

"Ayuh," Jasper agreed. "We don't know this part of the country very well so there's no way of guessing which way they went. We'll try to pick up their trail, but it won't be easy."

"We had better get moving," Daniel said, spurred on by fear for Cordelia.

The men took their leave of the main column and headed for the place on the road near the boulders where

Daniel had last seen Faulkner and Cordelia. The small troop marched out quickly in the gathering dusk. They were all on foot, with Daniel, Asa, and Jasper leading their horses. Daniel carried his rifle canted across his shoulder, ready for quick use if it was needed.

As he walked he looked up at the sky. Clouds were gathering, making the hour seem later than it was. He had been hoping for a clear night with plenty of moonlight; it was the only way they would have enough illumination to track Faulkner's band.

By the time full darkness had fallen, the men had reached the road. Asa and Jasper studied the area by the dim light of the newly risen moon, as yet unobscured by clouds.

"They headed south," Asa announced dourly. "At least I think so, and Jasper agrees with me."

"Then we'll go south, too," Daniel said firmly. That meant heading away from Bennington and Lake Champlain, but the backtracking could not be helped.

Quincy and Murdoch are probably in Bennington by now, having supper with Ethan Allen and the Green Mountain Boys, Daniel thought, convinced that splitting up had been the right thing to do.

Gradually the clouds shrouded the moon and stars, leaving the night cloaked in thick shadows. Asa and Jasper kept the group on the road as they marched south, but there was no question of tracking now. It was just too dark.

Hours later, Daniel figured that they had to be getting close to the Wild Boar, run by Ike Plemons, where he, Quincy, and Murdoch had been waylaid by Faulkner before.

In a low voice Daniel explained to Asa and Jasper that Faulkner probably thought Daniel and his companions had ridden on and forgotten all about Cordelia. He hoped Faulkner would have had enough confidence in his assumption to be comfortably settled in at Ike Plemons's establishment for the night.

After mulling it over, Jasper said, "I think you could be right, Daniel."

"They could have made a camp in the woods," Asa pointed out skeptically.

"That's possible, of course," Daniel said, "but I don't think it's likely. Faulkner strikes me as the type who would want a roof over his head and a soft pillow under it, if he could get it."

"Well, we'll keep our eyes open. We should be getting to this Wild Boar soon," Jasper said.

The lights of the inn came into view less than half an hour later, and while the rest of the group stayed hidden in the shadows of the forest a hundred yards away, Asa slipped forward to reconnoiter.

It seemed to Daniel that Asa was gone for a long time, but when he finally returned, the scout said grimly, "There's a dozen horses in the barn, and I could hear a big ruckus going on inside the place. Looks like you may have been right, Reed."

Instinctively Daniel knew he *was* right. He had caught up to Faulkner, and this time, he vowed to himself, it would be the final confrontation with the wrecker.

"All right," he said quietly, taking command as the men gathered around him. "We'll approach as silently as possible. Range yourselves around the building, near the windows. I'll go inside, and you'll wait for my signal to fire."

"Inside?" echoed Jasper. "Into that lion's den, you mean?"

"We don't know that Faulkner and his men are in there," Daniel pointed out. "We have to make sure before any fighting starts, so no innocent people get hurt. Besides, I want a chance to get Cordelia out of harm's way."

One of the men chuckled. "Sounds like you're a little sweet on this girl, Reed."

"Hardly," Daniel replied tartly. "But I don't want to see her come to any harm. For one thing, I'm counting on her to be able to tell us where to find that British supply train."

"Makes sense. I guess you've proved yourself, Reed. You do have the best interests of the patriots at heart."

"I hope it works out, and we all don't die in there," Daniel said fervently. His hand was sweaty on the stock of his flintlock rifle. He tightened his grip on the weapon and said, "Get your weapons ready. Let's go."

Leaving the three horses, the men crept forward. Silently Daniel motioned for the men to spread out on each side of the building. On this warm spring night, the shutters were open on the windows, and they could hear the laughter coming from inside. From the raucous sound, the patrons were drinking heavily.

Gripping his flintlock rifle tightly, Daniel took three steps onto the inn's porch. He full cocked the gun, poised the weapon, then lifted his booted foot and drove it against the door. It slammed open, and Daniel strode into the barroom.

The unexpected entrance made everyone in the big public room freeze in surprise and stare blearily at him. Daniel was horrified at the sight of Faulkner and his drunken men gathered around a long table upon which stood Cordelia, totally nude.

She was trembling; lines of humiliation and misery were etched on her face. At the moment Faulkner's men seemed to be content merely to stare at the brazen display of her naked charms. Ike Plemons, the proprietor, stood behind the bar, his frightened eyes fixed on the lewd sight.

The momentary glimpse Daniel allowed himself was enough to make his heart charge wildly in his chest. The sight of Cordelia's smooth, creamy skin, the firm high globes of her breasts topped with large brown nipples, the swell of her hips and thighs . . . were imprinted indelibly on Daniel's brain.

"My God!" Perry Faulkner exclaimed from where he sat at one of the tables. "It's you again! Are we never to be done with you?"

While keeping most of his attention focused on the criminal's henchmen, Daniel watched Faulkner out of the corner of his eye. The man had a mug of ale in front of him, and it was apparent he had been sitting there enjoying his wife's torture.

"Don't anyone move," Daniel said firmly, his voice betraying none of the nervousness he felt. "I'll kill the first man who tries anything."

"And then the rest of us will kill you," Faulkner snapped. He stood up and stepped around his chair. "You've become quite boring, my young friend. I was prepared to let you live, even after everything you've done, simply because it was more convenient for me that way. Now, though, I think you're going to have to die, just so you won't keep annoying us."

Daniel ignored the arrogant threat and said, "One of you give your jacket to the lady. Now!"

He held the rifle rock steady in his hands, the muzzle trained on the men to give his threat weight. One of them stripped off his jacket and handed it up to Cordelia, who quickly shrugged into it and pulled it tightly around her.

"Step out of the way and let her down off the table," Daniel commanded. "I'll shoot anyone who lays a hand on her. And despite what your employer said, I've got a loaded pistol in my belt, so a second man will die, too, if you try anything."

The mercenaries moved carefully aside as Cordelia stepped down from the table. There was no pretense of dignity in her actions; she was shaking and on the verge of hysteria.

"Come over here, Cordelia," Daniel said.

Perry Faulkner raised his arm and offered loudly, "Fifty pounds to the man who kills them both."

The exorbitant bounty was too much for his men to resist. For a fraction of a second longer, they hesitated. Then one of them lunged toward Cordelia, jerking a knife from his belt as he leapt forward.

Smoothly Daniel tracked the barrel of his rifle slightly to the side and pressed the trigger. With a flash of powder and a puff of smoke, the flintlock blasted, sending its ball into the man's chest. Thrown backward by the impact, he dropped the knife only when the ball exploded out his back after boring straight through his heart, killing him instantly.

"Now!" shouted Daniel, and the men who had surrounded the building opened fire from the windows.

Daniel flung himself toward Cordelia, dropping his rifle as he sprang forward. With his left hand, he reached for her, while his right snatched the pistol from behind his belt. He caught hold of her arm and went down, dragging her to the floor with him as a storm of lead howled through the room. He rolled under one of the tables, pulling Cordelia with him.

From that vantage point, he saw Faulkner's men being riddled by the shots of the Connecticut militiamen. They tumbled to the floor in bloody, lifeless heaps. It was an out-and-out massacre, but Daniel could not bring himself to feel sorry for them.

A few of Faulkner's men were still on their feet. Asa,

Jasper, and the rest of the militiamen came pouring into the room to finish the fight hand-to-hand. Pistols boomed and knives flashed in the lamplight. Shielding Cordelia with his own body, Daniel looked around for Faulkner, then caught a glimpse of him ducking behind the bar, knocking aside the terrified Plemons.

With his pistol, Daniel snapped off a shot at Faulkner, who stumbled as though he had been hit. But then the man vanished through a doorway behind the bar, and Daniel could not be sure.

Peering around the smoke-hazed room, Daniel realized the fighting was over. Faulkner's men lay scattered about in various attitudes of death. A few of the militiamen had suffered minor wounds in the battle, including a bloody scratch over Jasper's right eye, but none of the injuries was serious.

Asa and Jasper grinned at Daniel when he and Cordelia emerged from under the table.

"Pretty good fight while it lasted," Asa said with grim good humor as he handed Daniel his rifle.

Gratefully Daniel put his pistol under his belt and took the long rifle. He wiped the sweat off his forehead. There was no such thing as a good fight in his opinion—only necessary ones.

"Are you all right?" he asked Cordelia, who clutched the jacket tightly around her.

She was still trembling. Daniel cupped her chin in his hand and lifted it, tilting her head back so he could look into her eyes. He saw fear as well as rage, along with her usual intelligence, and he knew the ordeal she had gone through had not unhinged her mind.

"Some of them already . . . had their way with me," she said, her voice stronger than he had expected it to be. "But

I'm not hurt. They would have gotten around to that later, after they were through parading me around the room."

"I'm sorry," Daniel said softly. "I got here as soon as I could." He made his tone more businesslike. "Where are your clothes?"

"In the first room at the top of the stairs."

Daniel looked at Jasper, who said immediately, "I'll fetch them for you, ma'am."

"Plemons!" Daniel said sharply. "Where the hell are you?"

The innkeeper nervously poked his head up from behind the bar. "Would—would you be needing something, sir?" he asked tremulously.

"Where did Faulkner go?"

"I—I'm sure I wouldn't know—"

"That door behind you," Daniel said impatiently. "Where does it lead?"

"Into a storeroom," Plemons replied.

"Is there any way out of there?"

"Oh my, yes. There's a door leading outside."

Daniel bit back the curse that sprang to his lips. Unless Faulkner was wounded more seriously than he thought, the man had had plenty of time to reach the barn, grab a horse, and escape.

"Would you take a look around outside, Asa, just to be sure Faulkner's not lurking anywhere nearby?"

"Sure." He jerked his head at two of his companions, and the three militiamen hurried out of the inn, their reloaded muskets held at the ready.

Daniel turned to Cordelia. "You're safe now," he told her. "Even if Faulkner gets away, he's lost all his men. He won't be a threat any longer."

"You don't know him the way I do, Daniel. He always finds a way to get what he wants."

"Not this time," Daniel declared.

"Where are Quincy and Murdoch?" Cordelia asked. "Who are these men?"

"Connecticut militiamen. They were part of a column on its way north to engage the British at Lake Champlain. Murdoch and Quincy have gone north to be part of the same effort." He told the truth bluntly, curious to see what her reaction would be.

"You mean—they're insurrectionists?"

"And so am I," Daniel said. "But you should remember—we're insurrectionists who just saved your life."

"Yes . . . yes, you're right." A faint smile appeared on her face. "You've risked your life for me several times if I remember correctly, Daniel Reed. Perhaps I've been wrong about you and your kind."

"Patriots, you mean."

"Yes," Cordelia said quietly. "Patriots."

Jasper brought Cordelia's clothes to her, and while she was dressing in the storeroom behind the bar, Asa and his two companions came back into the inn through the front door.

"No sign of Faulkner anywhere around," Asa told Daniel. "But there's blood on the ground behind the building and in the barn, and a horse is gone. I'd say you nicked him pretty good, Reed, but not good enough to keep him from getting on a horse and riding away from here."

"I was afraid of that. Well, as I told Cordelia, I doubt if he's much of a threat now. He's hurt and alone. He'll go find a hole where he can lick his wounds." But Daniel had a nagging sense that the job had been left partially undone.

Cordelia emerged from the storeroom wearing pants,

shirt, and cloak. She held the cloak around her to cover up the rents where Faulkner's men had torn the blouse when ripping it off her. "Are we going to Saratoga now?" she asked.

"We're not going to Saratoga at all," Daniel told her. "We're going after that British supply train. And you're going to tell us where to find it."

Chapter Eleven

Bennington was a good-sized village on the Walloomsac River, the largest settlement Quincy and Murdoch had seen in over a week. It was bustling with activity as they rode in, and judging from the number of men on the streets, the population had grown considerably in recent days. There were more people than there were buildings to house them, and many of the men were camped on the village green. Most wore either rough homespun shirts and breeches or tunics and trousers made of buckskin. A few coonskin caps like the one on Murdoch's thatch of red hair were also in evidence.

"I like th' looks o' this, lad," Murdoch said as he surveyed the men on the green. "These are my kind o' folks."

"Halloo," one of the men greeted them. "Where you bound, gents?"

"Looking for a man name o' Ethan Allen," Murdoch replied as he reined in. "Is he hereabouts?"

"Aye," the man said, pointing. "Over yonder on the

other side of the green, in the Catamount Tavern. He'll be wearing buckskin trousers and a blue jacket."

"Much obliged." Murdoch turned his horse, and Quincy followed closely. They rode across the green toward the large building the man had indicated. The tavern was made of logs and rough-hewn planks, and in front of it, perched on a twenty-foot tall platform, was the stuffed mountain lion that gave the place its name. The animal's teeth were bared, and it faced west, toward New York.

Quincy and Murdoch tied their horses at the railing next to the big cat. When they stepped inside the tavern, they saw several men gathered around a long table. One stood at its head and appeared to be in charge. Stocky and clean-shaven, he wore the same style buckskin trousers as Murdoch, with a military-looking blue jacket and a black tricorn. As Quincy and Murdoch approached, he lifted his freckled face and glanced at the newcomers.

"Good day to you, gentlemen," he said. "Can I help you?"

"We're looking for Colonel Ethan Allen," Quincy said.

"You've found him, lad. What can I do for you?"

"I'm Quincy Reed, and this is Murdoch Buchanan. We've come from Boston—Cambridge, really, since we're wanted by the authorities in Boston. We've been sent here by the Committee of Safety. They have word that you're planning to march on Lake Champlain and attack the British at Fort Ticonderoga."

"That's correct," Allen said to Quincy after a moment. "I wasn't aware that our plans were so widely known, but I suppose they're no great secret, either."

"The committee ordered us to report to you and join your expedition," Quincy said. "We're to go back to Boston after the mission and let them know what's going on up here."

"A wise move," Allen said. "If we're going to be successful against the British, we colonials have to work together, think and act as one rather than as scattered groups." He made a face and added, "Much as it pains us independence-minded soldiers to work with a bunch of New York squatters."

The men around the table laughed, and Quincy remembered that the Green Mountain Boys had been formed in response to a border dispute between the New Hampshire Grants and New York Colony. They had fought to claim the land that ran the length of the mountain range as well as the surrounding valleys. But they had put aside their hostility toward their former enemies in order to combat a much larger evil.

Colonel Allen continued, "Let's sit down and rest a bit, my friends. I'll have someone bring over some food and drink while we talk."

Murdoch straddled one of the benches. "Much obliged, Colonel. Me and the lad have been riding many days now t' reach ye."

"You're a frontiersman, anyone can see that. Ohio River valley?"

"Aye, amongst other places." Murdoch grinned at Allen. "Name it, and I probably been there."

"You remind me of my good Green Mountain lads, Mr. Buchanan. I'd be glad to have you with us." The colonel looked at Quincy. "I'm not so sure about you, young Master Reed."

Quincy stared at him in surprise. "What do you mean?" he asked.

Allen took off his tricorn and scratched his head.

"Well, we don't have any lads quite as young as you in our militia, son. And while I'm sure whoever gave you that black eye looks at least as bad as you do, and you can probably hold your own against the enemy, we don't know what we're going to run into up there at the lake. Could be some pretty bad fighting. I wouldn't want to take the responsibility—"

"Excuse me, sir," Quincy interrupted, making an effort to hold his temper. He laid a hand on his thigh. "I've got a good-sized scar on this leg, and as Murdoch can tell you, it came from a musket ball fired by a British Brown Bess. That was the same night I helped blow up a warehouse filled with British munitions and then escaped under fire from the Brattle Street prison in Boston. So as you can see, I have some experience with danger. And in perilous times like these, anyone old enough to carry a rifle has a job to do."

"Well said, lad!" the colonel exclaimed, grabbing Quincy's hand and shaking it heartily. "And you're absolutely right. We can't afford to proceed without a soldier like you."

For a second, Quincy thought Allen was making fun of him, but he detected nothing other than sincerity on the colonel's face and in his voice.

"Welcome to the Green Mountain Boys," Allen said. "I've a hunch both of you will make fine temporary Vermonters, even if you are from Massachusetts."

"The lad was born in Virginny, and myself in bonnie Scotland," Murdoch said. "But I reckon we're all one people now."

"God willing," said Colonel Ethan Allen. "But the British, damn their hearts, are going to have something to say about that."

* * *

"I'm going to what?" Cordelia demanded.

"You're going to tell us how to find that British supply train," Daniel told her calmly.

He took Cordelia's arm with one hand and turned her away from the bodies sprawled lifelessly around the inn's public room, and he motioned for the Connecticut militiamen to remove the corpses from the building. He steered Cordelia to a table and sat her down facing away from the grisly scene.

"Listen," Daniel said urgently as he sat down beside her, keeping his hand on her arm, "I know how you feel about this war and about what your husband was planning to do."

"And now that he's gone, you're going to take up where he left off, is that it?"

"Not exactly," Daniel said grimly. He signaled to Plemons to bring them something to drink. "Your husband wanted those guns so he could sell them to the highest bidder, whether colonial or British. I want them so they'll be out of the redcoats' hands and where they'll do the most good."

"In the hands of the insurrectionists, you mean."

"In the hands of men like the ones who just saved your life."

"You're right," Cordelia whispered. "You did save my life, and not for the first time. But you're asking me to go against the Crown."

"I'm asking you to help a cause that deserves your aid." Daniel leaned close to her. "You *do* know the route of that wagon train, don't you?"

Slowly and deliberately Cordelia whispered, "I saw the map Perry was using to plan his ambush. I . . . I have a good head for such things."

"You could draw us another map?" Daniel asked eagerly.

"I'm sure I could." She looked up from the table and met his eyes. "Better still, Daniel, I could take you there."

"I promise you, it's the right thing to do," he said. "It'll be dangerous, but I'll try to keep you out of the fighting."

"It couldn't be any worse than what I've already been through," she said hoarsely.

"Cordelia, the patriots and I—we will owe you a great debt of gratitude."

"We'll have to head south," Cordelia went on, "but I think we can intercept the wagons without any trouble. How many men do you have?"

"There are ten militiamen, as well as myself," Daniel told her.

"All right. We can move rapidly, then. We should be in position by day after tomorrow."

"Are you sure about this?" Daniel asked her.

"As sure as I've ever been about anything in my life. But considering how most of my decisions have worked out, I'd be pretty worried if I were you, Daniel Reed."

The spring rains had rutted the roads around Boston, but the uncomfortable journey was not the reason Roxanne Darragh had been silent for several hours on the ride to New Hampshire. She found it difficult to meet Elliot's gaze. When she did, she saw the same anxiety, confusion, unhappiness, and uncertainty she was feeling.

Their lovemaking the previous night had been gentle and furious, demanding and giving. Elliot had taken her virginity in the most tender manner, but their passion had become urgent, galloping along to a thunderous conclusion that had left them trembling, breathless, and sated.

And then he had left, hurriedly pulling on his clothes, saying almost nothing as he dressed and leaned over the bed to kiss her on the forehead. He had told her the hour he would pick her up in the carriage, and that had been the extent of the conversation.

She wished she had never allowed it to happen.

Passion had carried her away, but in the long, cold, sleepless hours after he had left her, she knew it had been a mistake. Despite the tenderness, despite the need for comfort, despite the genuine affection she felt for him, her heart belonged to Daniel Reed.

"We're almost there," Elliot said, breaking into Roxanne's reverie. "If . . . if there's anything that needs to be said between us, I think we should say it now. Once we arrive at the ship, all our thoughts should be on our mission."

"I agree completely," Roxanne said. "And I don't think there is anything we need to discuss." She hesitated, then added, "Do you?"

"I suppose not. The mission is the important thing, after all."

She swallowed hard. "Yes, you're right," she said. *Had what happened between them meant nothing to him?*

Portsmouth, New Hampshire, at the mouth of the Piscataqua River, well protected from the ravages of the Atlantic Ocean, was a bustling port. As their carriage rolled toward the city, Roxanne and Elliot passed old, weathered saltbox houses as well as sprawling colonials such as the Wentworth Mansion, home of the former royal governor. From this location they could see every ship in the harbor. They drove by Queen's Chapel at the corner of Court and Pleasant streets.

Once they arrived at the dock area, Elliot pointed out the Sheafe Warehouse to Roxanne. It was a large frame building used by Markham & Cummings to store trade goods. Several nearby warehouses were made of brick.

Roxanne enjoyed the familiar cries of seabirds and the

sound of men loading and unloading ships, along with the clip-clop of hoofbeats from the horses pulling the other carriages and wagons that thronged the avenues. Even on a Sunday afternoon, Portsmouth was busy.

The carriage rolled to a stop near one of the wharves, and through the window Roxanne could see the *Carolingian* riding at anchor. It was a fine-looking vessel with three tall masts made from trees cut in a forest nearby, Elliot told her.

He did not wait for the driver to hop down to open the carriage door. He swung it back himself and stepped lightly out of the vehicle, then turned to assist Roxanne. Elliot wore his best dark gray cut-away coat, a light gray silk waistcoat, and matching breeches, and his powdered wig was as white as his stockings. Roxanne's fashionable, long black cloak protected her elegant green silk dress when she stepped in a puddle a few feet from the carriage. She and Elliot gave the appearance of a sophisticated, handsome, well-to-do couple.

He took her arm, then snapped his fingers and gestured for the driver to unload their bags. After instructing the man to return immediately to Boston, Elliot led Roxanne up the gangplank onto the deck of the *Carolingian.*

The large doors into the hold had been thrown back, and the crewmen were scurrying about unloading crates from the ship's bowels. Dockworkers stood ready to take the burdens and carry them off the vessel. Several of the ship's officers, including the captain, kept an eye on the proceedings. He turned in response to a tap on the shoulder and a crewman's pointing finger that indicated the well-dressed new arrivals.

The captain, a burly man with graying black hair and the rolling walk of someone who had spent a lifetime at sea, hurried over to them. "Young Mr. Markham! What are you doing here?"

"Why shouldn't I be here, Captain Ralston? After all, this is one of my father's ships."

"Aye, of course it is," Ralston agreed. "I'm just surprised to see you away from Boston."

"I get out of the city occasionally."

"Well, naturally, sir." Ralston's eyes darted to Roxanne.

"Captain, this is a dear friend of mine, Miss Roxanne Darragh," Elliot said. "We've been visiting friends in the area and were wondering if you would be so good as to give us a ride back to Boston. That is your next port of call, isn't it?"

"Yes, it is, but you know as well as I, Mr. Markham, that the *Carolingian* is a cargo vessel, not a passenger ship."

Elliot waved his hand indifferently. "That doesn't really matter. I'm sure you can supply some suitable accommodations for us."

"Well . . . " Ralston looked dubious. "I suppose I could."

"Good. That's settled, then." To Roxanne he said, "You see, my dear, I told you that you could take your first sea voyage on one of *my* ships."

"Thank you, Elliot," Roxanne said. "I'm sure I'll enjoy it." She turned to the captain. "And thank you as well, Captain Ralston, for your hospitality."

"Glad to do it," Ralston mumbled unconvincingly.

"You know, Roxanne," Elliot said, "there's an old superstition that says a woman on a ship is bad luck." He grinned at Ralston. "You don't believe that, do you, Captain?"

"Of course not," the ship's commanding officer answered promptly. "Not in this day and age."

Roxanne laughed lightly. "I'm glad to hear that, Captain. I would hate to think I brought ill fortune to anyone, especially you and your sailors."

"Don't waste a second thinking about it, Miss Darragh," Ralston said, mustering up a few shreds of charm. "Welcome aboard the *Carolingian,* and I hope your voyage is a pleasant one, even though it will be short."

Elliot leaned closer to him. "By the way, Captain," he said in a low voice, "if you can only find one cabin for us, that will be sufficient."

"Of course, sir." Ralston reddened slightly. He was a tough old salt, but blatant immorality, especially aboard his ship—and by his employer's son—bothered him.

Roxanne was embarrassed, but she knew her pose as Elliot's lover had to continue until they had confirmed that the *Carolingian* was carrying the guns, powder, and ammunition the patriots were counting on.

Chapter Twelve

The *Carolingian* was at sea, plying the coastal waters between Portsmouth and Boston. Night had fallen several hours earlier, and after waiting for the proper opportunity, Elliot Markham had taken a lantern and slipped into the dark cargo hold to verify that the ship was actually carrying British arms.

The guns were there, packed neatly in long, narrow crates, as were the casks of powder and the boxes of shot. All he'd had to do was move a few crates of trade goods to uncover the vessel's real cargo. It was clear to Elliot that the British had depended on secrecy to protect the cargo and had not taken great pains to conceal the munitions. Neither had they taken into account the loose tongue of Major Philip Dorn.

Elliot and Roxanne had already determined that there were no soldiers on board to guard the special cargo, only the regular crew.

However, these were hardened sailors, accustomed to

fighting pirates, the elements, and each other. Elliot worried that when patriot forces arrived to take over the ship, they could meet with dogged resistance.

"Cross that bridge when you come to it," he muttered to himself as he set the lantern down on a nearby crate. Now he had to put things back as they had been, so no one would know he had come down to the hold.

As Elliot picked up a crate to replace it the hatch leading into the hold squealed slightly as it was lifted.

His heart pounding, he leaned over and blew out his lantern, hoping as the light died and thick shadows closed in around him that whoever was there had not noticed the flickering yellow illumination. He stood motionless as footsteps sounded on the rungs of the ladder leading down into the hold.

Flint struck sparks in the darkness, and Elliot closed his eyes so he would not be blinded if the person struck a light. Dropping into a crouch behind one of the crates, he waited.

The visitor lit a candle and held it up for a moment. The small circle of light cast by the tiny flame revealed a bearded, hatchet-faced sailor. Elliot could see the crewman, but he doubted that the man could see him. The glow from the candle would not reach all the way into the shadowy corner where Elliot crouched.

Satisfied that he was alone, the sailor placed the candle on a nearby stack of crates and sat down on a box. He pulled something from his pocket and lifted it to his lips.

Elliot wanted to laugh aloud when he saw the candlelight gleam on the small flask the man was holding. One of the rules on ships of the Markham & Cummings line was that the crewmen were not allowed to drink except in port, but this thirsty sailor had snuck into the hold to down a jot of rum.

While he waited for the man to finish his drink and leave, Elliot mulled over the wild thoughts that had raced through his brain during those first frantic seconds of near discovery. His biggest concern was Roxanne.

He loved her; there was no denying that. And yet, it was not the same sort of love he had felt for Sarah Cummings. Roxanne's heart belonged to Daniel, and he had been wrong to go to her house after he had been drinking. He had been wrong to take her into his arms and kiss her and let his senses swim with the taste and smell and feel of her. He admired Roxanne Darragh more than any woman he had ever known, but in the end that admiration had been expressed in all the wrong ways. And now she probably hated him for it.

The uneasy silences between them had been almost more than Elliot could bear, but he had no idea what to say to her, no notion of how to go about making things right between them again. So far, they had been able to put aside their personal feelings well enough to be able to carry out their mission, but sooner or later they would have to talk about it to each other. He resolved that he would beg her forgiveness, vow never to touch her again, and plead with her not to hurt Daniel by telling him what had happened. But, Elliot asked himself, was that the coward's way out? For years, he had been taking just that course whenever possible without ever feeling an iota of guilt over it, but now he could hardly stand the thought. *Could it be that you've grown up?* a voice in his head asked him.

"Ahhhh . . ." The sailor let out a long sigh of satisfaction, shoved the cork back into the neck of the flask, stowed it away, and blew out the candle. A moment later, the hatch opened, then closed, and Elliot knew he was alone, safe, and undiscovered.

* * *

Roxanne was waiting anxiously, sitting upright on the cabin's single bunk. The sacrifice of her reputation and her love for Daniel Reed would be worth it if Dorn's information had been correct and they were able to get the munitions to the rebels.

A step in the corridor outside the captain's cabin, in which she and Elliot were quartered, made her stand up. The doorknob turned, and the door swung open. Elliot stepped through quickly and silently closed the door behind him. The triumphant smile on his face told Roxanne what she needed to know.

"They're on board," he said softly. "Just as we thought. There must be two dozen crates of muskets, fifty casks of powder, and I don't know how many boxes of shot. There are enough weapons in the hold to supply a regiment!"

"That's wonderful. What do we do now?"

"Wait until tomorrow morning, I suppose, so that we can signal the men Townsend and Tallmadge promised to have waiting." He chuckled dryly. "I certainly hope they're where they're supposed to be."

"They'll be there," Roxanne declared. "I'm sure of it."

He moved a step closer to her. "I had a close call while I was in the cargo hold," he said. "One of the sailors nearly caught me down there. I had to blow out my lantern and hide in the dark."

"He didn't see you, did he?" Roxanne asked anxiously.

"I'm sure he didn't. He just went down there to sneak some rum. But I did some thinking while I was waiting for him to go away."

"Thinking?" Roxanne repeated tentatively. "Thinking about what?" Her hand went to the collar of the dressing gown she wore and drew it tight around her throat.

For a long moment, Elliot said nothing. Roxanne

thought she saw resolve shining in his eyes, but then it flickered and died. Finally, he said dully, "Thinking about our mission. I believe it's going to be successful, Roxanne."

"I do, too," she whispered, well aware that he had decided to keep his thoughts to himself.

He sank down in a chair across the room. "You'd better get some sleep," he advised her, his voice stronger now that he had reached a decision. "I'll stay here in this chair," he said firmly.

And as she stretched out on the bunk and pulled the blankets over her, she came to a decision of her own. A decision about what she intended to do the following day. It was a decision that would separate Elliot and her and forever remove them from temptation.

The morning was overcast, and the scent of rain hung in the air. Both Roxanne and Elliot worried as they went on deck with their baggage. He took her arm, walked toward the the starboard rail, and stared out across the water toward the Massachusetts coastline a half-mile away. Roxanne's bright red hooded cape was a colorful contrast to the thick gray clouds that scudded before the wind.

Taking her valise from her, Elliot set their bags on the deck. "A squall might ruin everything," he said in a voice only she could hear.

"Then we'll have to pray for clearing weather," she answered quietly.

A storm could blow them off course or make the captain head for shore to seek shelter. Fog or rain might make it impossible for the waiting patriots to see the signal from the *Carolingian,* even with telescopes.

"Good morning, Master Markham, Miss Darragh," said Captain Ralston from behind them. With an effort, Roxanne prevented herself from starting in surprise, and beside her Elliot did the same. They turned around calmly and greeted the captain with smiles.

"Good morning, Captain," Elliot said. "Looks like we may be in for a bit of a blow, eh?"

"This?" Ralston nodded at the clouds and the choppy water. "I don't believe it will amount to much as storms go, and we could just sail out of it as we go south. If you're worried, don't be. Should the water get too rough, we can always run in to a cove. They're plentiful along here. Have you and the lady had breakfast yet, Master Markham?"

Elliot smiled wanly. "No, and considering how turbulent the water is, it might be better not to tempt fate this morning. Neither Miss Darragh nor I have the strongest pair of sea legs."

"Aye, I understand," Ralston said with a smug, superior smile. "Well, let me know if I can do anything for you, sir." He strolled away, leaving Elliot and Roxanne at the railing.

Roxanne did feel rather queasy. How much of it was nerves and how much the ceaseless motion of the ship, she did not know. It was not important, either, she told herself; all that mattered now was that the bad weather lifted and the patriots could carry out the raid as planned.

As the morning passed, the clouds thinned and the wind became a steady breeze. Roxanne's spirits rose as the weather improved. She pulled the red cape tight around her, grateful for the warmth it provided, since she had to stay on deck long enough to be spotted by the rebels at Marblehead Neck.

Elliot and Roxanne studied the landmarks along the shoreline. They stood together at the railing when a distinctive-looking promontory came into view. Easily recognizable from a map Elliot had taken from his father's office, the cove had a rocky bluff just to the north of it and a long, sandy beach to the south.

The time had come.

Elliot turned to Roxanne, but she was already striding toward the ship's stern. A gust of strong wind caught her bright red cape, whipping it in the breeze. It made a popping sound as she climbed the stairs to the quarterdeck.

He followed her.

"I prefer not to have passengers on the quarterdeck, Mr. Markham. I like an unobstructed view of my ship and the sea she sails on," said Captain Ralston, holding steady to the wheel.

"Yes, Captain," Roxanne said, "but I wanted a better view. That is Marblehead Neck just ahead, is it not?" She danced back and forth along the deck close to the rail, praying she could be seen easily from the bluff.

"Aye. That is the inlet at Marblehead, Miss Darragh." He eyed her curiously, then said to Elliot, "Please take the young woman below, Mr. Markham."

"I don't see why we can't stay up here, sir. The day has cleared, and I promise we won't get in your way. I will accept full responsibility should anything untoward happen. Resume your duties, Captain."

Barely able to hide his anger, Captain Ralston turned his full attention to the wheel. He muttered, "It's bad enough I have to take orders from the owner's son. Now I'm supposed to be grateful she didn't climb the rigging to the crow's nest!"

Roxanne stopped flitting about, slipped her arm through Elliot's, and leaned against him. Through his jacket, she could feel his heart beating. His pulse was racing almost as fast as hers.

A moment later, Elliot gripped her hands, his fingers

tightening as he spotted sails emerging from the inlet. Roxanne saw them, too, and her breath caught in her throat as the boats angled out from the shore, their course set to intercept the *Carolingian.*

There was no outcry from the crew as the patriots' boats drew closer. This was a shipping lane, and although it was not as busy as it had been before the troubles in Boston prompted General Gage to close the harbor for a time, it was still not unusual to see other vessels in this stretch of water.

But after a few moments, one of the lookouts posted in the rigging shouted down, "Six ships comin' to starboard, Cap'n!"

Ralston strode to the rail, not far from Elliot and Roxanne. "That's odd," they heard him muse. "I wonder where they're bound."

The patriots' fishing vessels were smaller and more maneuverable than the large cargo ship. Elliot squinted and saw that cannon had been mounted on the decks of two of the boats. Where Tallmadge and Townsend had found cannon for this mission, Elliot didn't know, but he was impressed with their resourcefulness.

When Ralston noticed the cannon as well, the lines in his forehead deepened. "My God, what are they up to?" he muttered. "They wouldn't dare—"

One of the cannon boomed.

Roxanne flinched against Elliot, and he held her close as the sound of the blast carried across the water. The cannonball whistled in front of the *Carolingian* and sent up a geyser to port as it struck the ocean's surface.

"To your posts, men!" bellowed Ralston. He turned and snapped at Roxanne and Elliot, "Get below, both of you! I can't be responsible for your safety if you stay topside!"

"Come on, Roxanne," Elliot said, urging her toward the stairs down to the main deck.

With unexpected strength, she pulled away from Elliot. She reached into a deep pocket in her full skirt, removed a flintlock pistol, and trained the weapon on Ralston.

"Stand where you are, Captain!" she cried.

"Roxanne!" Elliot exclaimed.

Ralston's face was brick red with outrage, but he did not move as he asked, "What is the meaning of this, Miss Daragh?"

Roxanne advanced slowly, the pistol's muzzle never wavering as she approached. The lock was at full cock, and her finger was tense on the trigger. Several of the crewmen who had joined them on the quarterdeck were prepared to leap toward her to disarm her, but they did not dare take that risk. The slightest pressure of her finger would send a ball through Captain Ralston's head.

"The meaning," she said, ignoring Elliot for the moment, "is that your ship—filled with British munitions for good Tories such as Mr. Elliot Markham here and his father—is about to be taken over by my friends. If you want to live, I suggest you and your men surrender without any resistance."

Trembling with anger, Ralston switched his gaze to Elliot and demanded, "What do you know about this, Markham?"

"I don't know anything, Captain," he said, deciding to play along with Roxanne. "I'm as surprised as you are."

"Of course he's surprised," Roxanne added. "Elliot Markham is nothing but a Tory dupe."

He understood what she was doing, but he was upset and wished she had talked it over with him first. This changed things irrevocably. He said grimly, "I can't believe you're doing this, Roxanne. You tricked me!"

"Yes, I did," she said coldly.

Pleased with her performance but dismayed by the look on Elliot's face, Roxanne let the barrel of the pistol stray from its aim. It drooped only slightly, but it was enough to encourage one of the ship's junior officers to reach for the hilt of his sword. He had pulled several inches of the blade from its scabbard when Roxanne snapped back to attention and centered the pistol on Ralston's forehead.

"I warn you, I'll kill him!" she cried.

"Blast it, be careful, Dobbs," the captain muttered to the young officer. Beads of sweat popped up on his face. "Can't you see she means it?"

"Sorry, sir," the man said, letting his sword slide back into the scabbard.

With effort, Roxanne kept herself from heaving a sigh of relief. Letting her attention stray again could prove fatal, not only to her but to the mission that had brought her here.

Elliot glanced at the boats. They were within cannon range, and the railings of the vessels were lined with men training rifles and muskets on the *Carolingian.* Within moments, the boats would be close enough for the colonial forces to board the Markham & Cummings vessel.

"Captain," Elliot said emphatically, "I urge you not to fight these brigands."

"Not fight?" echoed Ralston. "You propose that I surrender my ship? By God, sir, I'll let this wench shoot me first!" He swung around. "Prepare to repel boarders! Cannoneers to the ready!"

Roxanne's finger tightened a fraction more on the trigger, stopping just short of the necessary pressure to fire.

"Captain Ralston!" Elliot shouted. "I command you to surrender!"

White-faced now, Ralston glanced at Elliot. "You dare—"

"I do," Elliot shot back. "You may be the captain, but my father and his partner own this ship, and I daresay they don't want it sitting on the bottom of the sea with cannonball holes blasted clear through it. No matter what sort of cargo you're carrying, Captain Ralston, it's not worth the loss of this ship." He added as an afterthought, "Or the lives of the crew."

Ralston stared at Elliot for a moment, then sighed. "You're sure this is what you want?" he asked.

Elliot nodded. "I'm sure."

"Then on your head be it, young man. You'll have to explain to your father and Mr. Cummings, not I."

"I'll take full responsibility," Elliot promised.

"Very well." Ralston turned his head and called to the crew, "That's it, men. Don't put up a fight. We're—surrendering." His mouth twisted as if the words tasted bad.

"Thank you, Captain," Roxanne said softly. "I was really hoping I wouldn't have to kill you."

Ralston sneered at her. "I'll just wager you were hoping that—you damned insurrectionist hussy!"

Elliot wanted to spring forward in Roxanne's defense, but he knew he could not do that. In order to make his cover as a Tory stronger than ever, he had to be just as outraged as Ralston was. He stalked over to join the captain, and glared at Roxanne as he did so. "I'm sorry, Ralston," he muttered. "If I had only known."

"Yes," Ralston said bitterly. "If."

"Everyone to the main deck, " Roxanne ordered. "You as well, Elliot."

A few minutes later, the fishing boats hove to alongside the *Carolingian.* Men tossed thick ropes with grappling hooks over the railing of the larger vessel, then scrambled aboard hand over hand. This was the most dangerous phase of the operation, because the *Carolingian*'s crew was armed, and the patriots were momentarily at their mercy. Violence was prevented only by Elliot's order to surrender—and the pistol in Roxanne's hand, which was still trained on Captain Ralston's head.

As soon as the boarders hit the deck of the Markham & Cummings ship, however, the patriots pulled their pistols and covered the crew. The young man in charge of the boarding party called out, "Drop your weapons, gentlemen! I want them all—pistols, cutlasses, daggers, whatever you have. Now, gentlemen!"

Elliot and Roxanne sensed the tension in the air and feared that the crew would ignore the command and a bloody fray would break out on the deck.

Several stubborn crew members caressed the butts of their pistols and the hilts of their daggers, but Ralston growled, "Do as he says," and one by one the sailors surrendered their weapons.

More of the patriots swarmed on board. While some of them kept the crew under the gun, the others gathered the weapons and lashed the sailors' hands behind their backs. Even the officers were subjected to this treatment. The only ones who were spared were Captain Ralston himself . . . and Elliot Markham.

The leader of the rebels was a tall, lean, gray-haired man, who introduced himself as Henry McAdams. His eyes had flicked back and forth between Elliot and Roxanne when he first came aboard, and he had sized up the situation quickly when he saw Elliot standing beside Ralston and Roxanne holding a gun on them.

Roxanne was grateful for McAdams's keen intelligence when the former fisherman said to her, "I see ye got 'em both, Miss Darragh. Good work, says I."

"Thank you, Mr. McAdams," she replied coolly.

"What would you have us do with them? Slit their throats and toss them into the drink?"

For a second, Roxanne was not sure if McAdams was serious or not. But the man's face was turned toward her, and one of his eyelids drooped in a lazy wink. Roxanne made sure her own features remained grim as she said, "No, there's no need for killing unless they give us trouble. We'll take them ashore and leave them there."

"Aye, we'll leave them someplace where it's a long walk to the nearest settlement."

"Good. Perhaps the damned Tories will learn a lesson from the walk."

With the patriots in control, Roxanne put the pistol into her valise. She glanced at Elliot, whose face was an expressionless mask.

She counted on his understanding that her decision to end her pose as his lover in such a dramatic fashion would make certain that never again would she give in to the urges still gripping her. Some distance between them was what she really needed, and today's events provided the opportunity for that. Elliot would return to Boston; as for her, she would have no choice but to stay away, to leave the area as Daniel, Quincy, and Murdoch had done. Maybe she could even find Daniel. . . .

And perhaps the revelation of her activities as a spy would make Sarah Cummings feel differently about what had gone on between Roxanne and Elliot. Sarah might condemn

Elliot for falling victim to Roxanne's charms, but now she would think Roxanne had deliberately seduced him just to get herself on board his father's ship.

Men emerged from the *Carolingian*'s hold and carried crates of guns, casks of powder, and boxes of shot to their own boats. It had not taken long for the raiders to find the munitions hidden behind the trade goods.

As the weapons and ammunition were passed carefully to the fishing boats, Ralston asked stiffly, "What do you intend to do with my ship?"

"Why, we're goin' to scuttle her, of course," McAdams answered. "You didn't expect us to leave her intact so that the British could use her to bring in more guns, did you?"

"You bastard!" Ralston said hoarsely. "You're a seagoing man. Do you know what you're saying?"

"Aye," replied McAdams, a hint of sadness in his voice. "It's a fine vessel, and I'll hate to see her go to the bottom. Too bad she's owned by a bunch of damned Tories who don't mind betraying their fellow colonists."

"You won't get away with this, McAdams," said Elliot, feeling compelled to make a token objection. "This is a private vessel, and you have no right to do this."

"Keep talking, lad," growled McAdams, "and maybe we'll scuttle *you*, too."

Elliot swallowed nervously, looked at Ralston, and shrugged. Surely the captain could see he had done his best, the gesture seemed to say, ineffective though it might have been.

The tied-up crew, along with Elliot and Ralston, were pushed, at gunpoint, aboard a small rowboat. Roxanne, who had grabbed her valise and climbed into one of the patriots' boats, wanted to tell Elliot good-bye, but it was not possible. She had to keep her distance from him, and there was nothing she could do but stand at the railing and watch the captives being rowed to shore, where they were left standing on a rocky beach.

In the cargo hold of the *Carolingian,* sailors carrying axes chopped holes in the vessel's hull, and the sound could be heard from the other boats. When the men reappeared on deck, the vessel was already taking on water. They loosed the lines holding the fishing boats to the *Carolingian* and leapt agilely off the doomed ship.

Elliot watched from the beach and told himself this was a victory. He and Roxanne had done what they set out to do. But he had not expected her to reveal her identity as a patriot agent, creating a barrier between them that might never be toppled.

He saw the flash of her red hair and red cape as she stood on the deck of the fishing boat, and he felt a sickness in his belly. The sickness intensified as he saw the *Carolingian* listing to one side and slipping beneath the cold, gray waves. McAdams was right; it made no sense to leave the vessel intact to be used against the patriots.

The loss of the ship was enough to make Elliot dread what his father was going to say when he got back to Boston. There was nothing he could do about it now, however. The mission was a success. That would have to be enough.

Under the command of Henry McAdams, the smaller crafts turned and headed out to sea, taking Roxanne and the British munitions with them. She was unsure of their ultimate destination but knew they would land somewhere on the Massachusetts coast so the British munitions could be unloaded. She could catch a ride with one of the wagons that would carry the guns away. Either Tallmadge or Townsend, or perhaps both, would be there, and they could help her decide what to do next. The future, Roxanne thought, was as hazy as the skies overhead.

But for the next few minutes she was going to stand at the railing and watch the small group on shore until the mists closed in and there was nothing more to see.

Chapter Thirteen

Murdoch Buchanan hit it off immediately with the Green Mountain Boys, who, like their colonel, sensed that the big frontiersman was a kindred spirit. The fiercely independent Vermonters accepted Quincy into the ranks once the story got around that he had not only participated in the Boston Tea Party but also had been responsible for the destruction of a warehouse full of British munitions.

The acceptance eased Quincy's mind somewhat, but he still spent much of his time worrying about his brother . . . and Cordelia. Quincy and Murdoch had asked around in Bennington, but no one fitting Cordelia's description had shown up in the village during the past few days. Quincy's optimism that Daniel would join them for the attack on the fort was fading.

With Colonel Ethan Allen leading them, the Green Mountain Boys left Bennington the day after Murdoch and Quincy had arrived to join them. Neither Daniel nor Colonel

Arnold's Connecticut Militia had arrived in time to accompany them.

The route of march was due north through the gentle, rolling foothills west of the Green Mountains to the small settlement of Hand's Cove, directly across the lake from Fort Ticonderoga. It was seventy miles to Lake Champlain, according to Colonel Allen, which meant they should arrive in three and a half days. The gently rounded, heavily forested mountains rising to the east hid cores of granite and marble and were alive with new life. Everywhere Quincy looked the colors of spring—violets and pinks, yellows and greens—seemed to vie for his attention. But it all went unappreciated by him.

Under other circumstances, he would have enjoyed this journey. He and Murdoch had left their horses behind in Bennington; the Green Mountain Boys were on foot, and the two newcomers wanted to fit in. But Quincy was apprehensive. Daniel should have arrived in time to come with them, he thought. *Something must have happened to him.*

"Dinna worry about Dan'l," Murdoch advised as they swung along with the soldiers, weapons carried over their shoulders. "Tha's one lad who can take care o' himself."

"I know," Quincy said. "I just wish he were here with us, that's all."

"We'll be seeing him soon enough, I'm thinking."

The Batten Kill River fell behind them the first day, and they passed Equinox Mountain and Dorset Peak the next. For a time they followed the Clarendon River, then stayed with Otter Creek when it merged with the larger stream. During the third day of the march, they passed through the tiny hamlet of Rutland, where many settlers, mostly from Connecticut, had cleared the land for farms.

Their path angled to the northwest, and it was late on the

afternoon of May 9, 1775, when Colonel Ethan Allen paused on a hilltop and leveled an arm toward an expanse of blue that was barely visible in the distance. "There she is, boys!" he called to the volunteer troops following him. "Lake Champlain!"

A cheer went up from the tired men.

"We'll push on to the eastern shore of the lake," Ethan Allen announced. "With luck we'll make it by nightfall."

Twilight was settling over the waters of the long, narrow lake when the soldiers reached it. Calling out his commands softly so the sound would not carry over the water, Ethan Allen said, "No fires, men. We'll have to make a cold camp tonight, I'm afraid. You may use one or two of the oil lamps if you go back into the trees away from the shore. Straight across yonder, unless I miss my guess, is the stronghold of the enemy."

Quincy saw the faint twinkle of lamps and lanterns on the far side of the lake. He could make out the dark shape of the fort, whose stone walls were said to be fifteen to twenty feet thick. All that lay between the patriots and the British post was the narrow but vital waterway, a steep climb up the promontory on which the fort sat, and a long stone tunnel entrance protected by a heavy wooden door.

To the north, Lake Champlain stretched up into Canada. As long as the British held the lake, they could send ships filled with supplies down from their Canadian fortresses. The cannon at Ticonderoga, as well as gun emplacements at Crown Point, several miles farther north on the western shore, would protect the British ships.

But if the colonists were in charge of Fort Ticonderoga and Crown Point, the situation would be entirely different, Quincy thought as he stared across the placid waters of the lake.

A short while later Quincy and Murdoch were resting from their long trek, sitting hunched over a lamp, cleaning their weapons.

A militiaman hurried up to them and announced, "The colonel wants to see you two lads in his tent. Right away, if you please."

"We'll be there in a moment," Murdoch told the messenger. "It would not be good t' go off and leave this job unfinished. Ye should remember that, lad."

The militiaman shrugged. "You've been told. That was all I was instructed to do. But I wouldn't want Colonel Allen angry with me if I could help it."

"Maybe he's right, Murdoch," Quincy said, not wanting to do anything that would cause trouble with the commanding officer.

Unhurriedly, Murdoch finished cleaning his rifle and motioned for Quincy to do the same to his musket. Quincy complied, but impatience gnawed at him. He wondered why Colonel Allen wanted to see them.

A few minutes later, as the frontiersman and the boy made their way through the starlit night to the large tent Colonel Ethan Allen had erected, they saw a stranger conversing with the colonel.

In the light that shone through the open tent flap, Murdoch and Quincy could see that the newcomer was a tall, imposing man wearing high-topped boots, dusty white pants, and a black coat over a white shirt. His tricorn was expensive and decorated with braid and a feather. While he could not be described as handsome, his stance conveyed power and his eyes glittered with anger and impatience.

Ethan Allen was not happy, either. As Murdoch and Quincy approached, he swung toward them and growled, "So there you are. I expected you here sooner."

"We were cleaning our guns, Colonel, and I was brought up never t' leave a task undone."

"That's commendable, Buchanan. But we have quite a dilemma here, and I'm hoping you and young Reed will help me solve it." He inclined his head toward the stranger. "Do either of you know this gentleman?"

Murdoch cuffed his coonskin cap to the back of his head and stared at the thick-set man. So did Quincy. Neither had ever seen the man before.

"There's no reason these men should know me, Colonel," the dark-haired, dark-complected stranger said in a deep, cultured voice. "As I told you, I came here from Cambridge, not Boston."

"Buchanan and Reed have spent some time in Cambridge, haven't you, lads?" Colonel Allen asked.

"Aye," Murdoch said, "but I dinna ken this gentleman."

"I'm afraid I don't know him, either," Quincy added.

With visible effort, the newcomer restrained his temper. "You've seen my papers, Colonel." His light blue eyes flashed at Allen. "They prove that I'm Colonel Benedict Arnold of the Connecticut Militia, and I'm here to take over command of the forces you've gathered to attack Fort Ticonderoga."

Quincy's eyes widened in surprise, and a glance at Murdoch told him the frontiersman was also taken aback by the stranger's brash statement.

"I'm afraid this isn't Connecticut, Colonel Arnold," Ethan Allen said dryly. "This is Vermont, and the Green Mountain Boys are accustomed to taking orders from me, not from some storekeeper playing soldier."

"You can insult me if you wish, Colonel," Arnold said coldly, "but you cannot change the fact that I am your superior officer."

"Seems to me we're both colonels," drawled Allen.

"I'm a colonel in a duly constituted militia!" Arnold snapped. "Not some ragged band of backwoodsmen who are, to use your expression, sir, playing soldier!"

The officers in the vicinity, as well as some Green Mountain Boys standing nearby, heard Benedict Arnold's angry words and glowered at the colonel from Connecticut. One of the militiamen stood up. "Don't matter who ye be or where ye're from, mister. We take our orders from Colonel Allen and nobody else!" he said.

Ethan Allen held up a hand to silence the man. "That'll be enough, Private Soldier Nelson," he snapped. "Colonel Arnold may not be familiar with our ways, but he's still an officer and deserves our respect." Facing Benedict Arnold, Allen went on, "I'm prepared to accept your word as to your identity, sir, even though it would be easier to do if you had the rest of your force with you."

"I told you they're following me and should be here shortly," Arnold said.

"So you said, and as I said, I'm prepared to accept your word anyway. But that does not mean I am going to relinquish command of my men, sir." Allen's voice rose. "The only one who will make me do that is the Grim Reaper himself!"

As the statement resounded in the chill night air, a hushed cheer went up from the Green Mountain Boys, and Murdoch and Quincy joined in. They understood why these fighters for independence felt such fierce devotion to their leader: Colonel Ethan Allen was devoted to them.

Benedict Arnold glared stubbornly at Allen for a moment, then sighed and capitulated. "I suppose I would be a fool to fly in the face of such loyalty," he said. With grudging respect he came to attention and inclined his head toward

Ethan Allen. "Very well, Colonel, I place myself under your command, as well as my men—when they arrive. We are at your disposal."

"Thank you, Colonel. I appreciate your gracious cooperation."

None dared snicker at the ironic words.

"Please come in and have a seat," Allen said. "We'll have a bite to eat, and we can discuss our plans for this engagement. I feel sure we can make use of your insight into the situation, Colonel."

Arnold ducked into the colonel's tent, and before Allen followed him inside, Murdoch stepped up to him and asked, "Would ye be needing us any more, Colonel?"

"No, you and the lad are free to go, Murdoch."

"Thank you, sir."

He and Murdoch saluted, turned from the tent, and headed back to where they had left their gear, while Allen, Arnold, and the officers resumed their planning of the campaign.

Later, as Murdoch was leaning on the butt of his long rifle next to where Quincy was laying out his bed for the night, the Scotsman said, "Thinking about the morrow, lad?"

"I can't help it. I wonder what's going to happen."

"Ye'll do fine, I can tell ye that."

"I know I talked as though I couldn't wait to get here to join the fight, but now I'm—scared. The Boston Tea Party was a lark, but the battle at the munitions warehouse taught me what real war is. While I'm ready to give my life for the cause, I would like to live long enough to see Daniel and our parents again."

It was difficult to admit that to Murdoch, and once again Quincy wished Daniel were here. He was sure his brother would understand.

"Aye, most men are frightened before a battle. But if a man's got the right stuff in him, he can go on, scared or not."

Quincy sat down and looked up. "What about you, Murdoch? Are you afraid?"

A grin split the Scotsman's rough-hewn face. "I said most men, laddie, not old Buchanan."

"I thought so," Quincy said.

"Ah, but consider this," Murdoch said softly, his gaze fixed on the lights of Fort Ticonderoga across the lake. "Sometimes a man is so proud that he'll lie about being afraid. And nobody's got more pride than a Scotsman."

Quincy was unsure what Murdoch was trying to tell him. Whatever it was, it made him feel better. The younger man managed to smile and said, "Cold rations are better than none, I suppose. Let's get something to eat."

"Aye, now tha's the best idea I heard all day, lad."

They settled down under some trees with a group of the Green Mountain Boys and were gnawing on hardtack and cold corn cakes by the light of an oil lantern when one of the scouts approached the camp. He paused beside the cluster of men including Quincy and Murdoch and asked urgently, "Where's the colonel?"

One of the men pointed in the direction of Allen's large tent. "Over there where the faint glow is. What's wrong, Hopkins?"

"I'd better save that news for the colonel," the scout said.

Quincy got to his feet, and, with Murdoch, followed the man. Whatever this development might be, they wanted to know about it.

A sentry outside Colonel Allen's tent stopped the scout and summoned the colonel in response to the woodsman's anxious request. Both Ethan Allen and Benedict Arnold emerged from the tent. The small amount of light that shone through the tent flap allowed the men to see that they had removed their jackets and hats and had been eating supper. Allen still held a piece of corn cake in his hand.

"What is it, Private Soldier Hopkins?" Allen asked, returning the informal salute the scout gave him.

"There's a big body of men coming up from the south, Colonel," the scout replied. "They're making good time, and they're pushing on in the dark like they're bound and determined to make it here."

"Redcoats?" the commander snapped.

"No, sir, I don't think so. I got close enough to hear them talking, and they sounded more like some of our lads."

"My Connecticut Militia!" Benedict Arnold exclaimed. "I'd lay my life on it, Colonel. They've caught up to us at last."

"Could be. We'll send a detail to meet them. If they are indeed Colonel Arnold's militia, our men can lead them back here. If not, the boys can give them the slip without any trouble." Allen's gaze fell on Murdoch and Quincy. "Buchanan and Reed, you'll be part of the detail, along with Hopkins here and four other men."

"Aye, Colonel," Murdoch said. "We'll be glad t' go."

Allen quickly selected the four men to join Quincy, Murdoch, and Hopkins on the seven-man patrol. They checked their weapons and made sure their pistols, rifles, and muskets were primed and loaded. Then, with Hopkins taking the lead, they set out from the camp.

The men moved along the shoreline, staying just inside the forest that reached almost to the water. The thick darkness made Quincy feel as if he were alone in the wilderness, but he knew Murdoch was right behind him. He could sense the big man's presence even if he could not hear his footsteps.

After about ten minutes, Hopkins held up a hand to halt the patrol. Quincy just avoided running into the man in front of him.

Hopkins hissed for quiet, and the patrol stood still, waiting tensely in silence. In addition to the constant sound of the peepers and periodic bellows of the bullfrogs, they heard the footfalls and muffled voices of many men moving through the forest.

Quincy tightened his grip on the flintlock musket he carried. Murdoch laid a big hand on the lad's shoulder and squeezed, and Quincy drew strength from the reassuring touch.

Through the screen of brush in front of them, Quincy could see a small clearing. Shapes entered the clearing from the opposite side. Hopkins said softly, "Stay here," then stepped out to confront the men.

"You're in the land of the Green Mountain Boys," the scout called fearlessly. "Who are you, and what are you doing here?"

The men in the front ranks came to an abrupt halt at the challenge, and the muskets and rifles they carried snapped up to the ready. A voice rang out from the officer in the lead. "Hold your fire!" He faced Hopkins in the faint moonlight and went on, "You're from Colonel Ethan Allen?"

"That's right," Hopkins told him, standing with his musket aimed at the man's chest. "And you haven't answered my question."

"We're the Connecticut Militia," the officer replied. "I'm Captain Norvell Page, in temporary command due to the absence of Colonel Benedict Arnold. Have you seen Colonel Arnold?"

"Aye," said Hopkins, visibly relaxing. The other men lowered their weapons. "He's with Colonel Allen and the rest of our boys, up ahead on the lakeshore."

"Thank God," the captain said. "I was afraid we wouldn't reach you in time."

Hopkins waved the members of his patrol out of the woods.

"We'll escort you to your colonel and ours," Hopkins said. "Best tell your boys to keep as quiet as possible. Don't want the damned lobsterbacks across the lake to hear us."

"I agree completely." Page passed the order for everyone in the ranks to cease talking and proceed as quietly as possible.

Hopkins, Quincy, Murdoch, and the Green Mountain Boys led the Connecticut men through the woods to the shore of the lake and then north to the spot where the rest of the force was camped. Colonels Allen and Arnold were waiting for them when they arrived.

Benedict Arnold returned the salute Captain Page gave him, then said, in a hushed voice, "At ease, Captain. I trusted you to bring the men on, and you seem to have done that in fine order. Any problems along the way?"

"Not really, sir," Page replied.

"No trouble? All the men are accounted for?"

Page took a deep breath and said, "All but ten men, Colonel."

"Ten men?" exclaimed Arnold. "What happened to them?"

"I sent them on a detail—a wild-goose chase, perhaps, but I think not."

"What sort of detail?" Arnold demanded.

"They were to accompany a young man we encountered

who requested our aid in rescuing a woman from her villainous husband."

"My God!" Benedict Arnold blustered, then lowered his voice as he remembered they were trying not to alert the British to their presence. "You mean you committed military forces to help settle some sort of domestic disturbance, Captain?"

"Not exactly, sir," Page said. "You see, this young woman supposedly knew how to find a wagon train carrying British munitions and supplies bound for their forces in New York. The young man—Reed was his name—planned to rescue her, then attack the supply train and capture it for the patriots."

"What a load of balderdash!" Arnold complained. "I'm surprised at you, Captain. I thought you had more sense than to commit any men, even a small number, to such an insane scheme—"

Quincy could not remain quiet any longer. He had to interrupt in order to find out more about Daniel. Ignoring Murdoch's low-pitched warning, he stepped forward and said, "Begging your pardon, Colonel Arnold, but I know something about this, and I think Captain Page is correct."

Both Benedict Arnold and Ethan Allen turned toward Quincy. "No man under my command need fear speaking up, Reed," Colonel Allen said. "What is it?"

Before Quincy could answer, Captain Page exclaimed, "Reed, did you say?"

"That's right," Quincy replied. "Daniel Reed is my brother. Captain Page is right about that British supply train, Colonel Arnold. Murdoch and I know about it. We just didn't know that Daniel was going to try to capture it."

Arnold and Page asked questions at the same time, but Ethan Allen silenced them by holding up his hands. "I think we had best go into my tent and hash all this out. Come along, Reed. You, too, Buchanan, since you seem to know something about this, as well."

"Aye, sir," said Murdoch.

Inside the tent, Quincy and Murdoch stood with Captain Page, while the two colonels sat at the folding table Ethan Allen had brought along. Under the brisk questioning of the officers, Quincy and Murdoch revealed all they knew about the British wagon train, Perry Faulkner's plot to hijack it, and the former wrecker's attempts to silence his wife—permanently, if necessary. Quincy concluded by saying, "After we rescued Cordelia the second time, she snuck off, and Daniel went after her to try to prevent her from warning the British commander at Saratoga. That's all we know. This business about Daniel leading an attack on the wagon train is all new to us."

"I believe you, lad," Ethan Allen said.

"As do I," Benedict Arnold agreed, adding acerbically, "I seriously doubt that anyone could make up such a spectacularly convoluted story."

" 'Tis true, sir, every word o' it," Murdoch assured him.

Ethan Allen leaned back on his three-legged stool. "Well, there seems to be little we can do about it now. Whatever action your brother is involved in, Reed, will be taking place many miles from here, and our own course is clear. We're to take Fort Ticonderoga, and the lack of ten men from the Connecticut Militia will have no effect on that mission."

"I concur, Colonel," Benedict Arnold said. He looked up at his junior officer and went on, "And I believe you showed good judgment in your decision, Captain. A chance to capture such a shipment of British arms was well worth the risk of ten men from our force."

"Thank you, sir," Captain Page said, looking relieved.

"Now, as for tomorrow morning," Colonel Allen said, leaning forward, "I have men out scouring this side of the lake right now, trying to find boats we can use for our crossing. There are several farms along the shoreline, and perhaps Providence will see to it that those families have boats for fishing. Tomorrow at dawn they'll serve another purpose."

"You propose to attack at dawn, then?" Captain Page asked.

"I believe that will give us our best chance of success. It's vital we take the redcoats by surprise."

As Quincy and Murdoch stood and listened, Quincy could not stop thinking about Daniel. He wished they had never split up.

Murdoch was gently pushing him toward the tent's entrance when Colonel Allen told them, "You two had better get some sleep. We'll be moving out early in the morning, well before dawn."

"Aye, Colonel," Murdoch replied. "And 'tis about time, if ye dinna mind me saying so, that we take the fight t' the bloody Britishers."

"I don't mind at all," Ethan Allen replied with a smile, mirroring Murdoch's anticipation of the battle. "And God willing, by this time tomorrow night, gentlemen, Ticonderoga will be ours!"

Quincy had a difficult time falling asleep. In addition to his concerns about the coming battle, he had Daniel's situation to think about. Somehow, when this was all over, he had to find his brother and discover if Daniel was all right.

It seemed that Quincy had just shut his eyes and dozed off when Murdoch shook him awake. He jolted up out of his restless, exhausted slumber.

"Take it easy, lad!" Murdoch said quietly. " 'Tis only me. Ye'd best get up; we'll be pulling out soon."

Quincy rubbed a hand over his eyes and then massaged his temples. He saw that he was still under the tree where he had lain down the night before. The predawn shadows were thick, but he could hear men moving around nearby and knew the Green Mountain Boys, as well as Benedict Arnold's Connecticut militiamen, were preparing to launch the attack on the crumbling old French fort, garrisoned by the British since Lord Jeffery Amherst captured it in 1759.

"The boats?" Quincy asked Murdoch. "Was Colonel Allen able to get enough boats?"

"I dinna ken. The boys found two old scows, but probably not enough t' carry all the troops at the same time, I'd guess."

Quincy stretched to ease the muscles that had stiffened during the cool, damp night. "It could cause trouble if the boats have to make several trips across the lake," he mused.

"Aye. 'Tis the same thing I'm thinking. But I reckon we'll do what the colonel says for us t' do."

An officer walked past their position and alerted them to get ready. Quincy recognized Ira Allen, the colonel's brother, who was part of the inner circle of leaders. "Gather on the shore as soon as you're ready to move out," Ira told them.

"Let's go," Murdoch said. "If there be not enough boats, I want t' be sure t' be in the first one going across the lake."

Slinging his powder horn and shot pouch over his shoulder and carrying his flintlock musket, Quincy hurried after Murdoch, whose long legs took him quickly toward the water.

When they reached the shore, the faint gray light in the eastern sky revealed several dozen men already there, with more arriving all the time. Colonel Allen and his junior officers were standing at the edge of the water, next to the two boats that had been drawn up on the shore.

"Quickly, men," Ethan Allen said. "There's no time for protocol now. Get aboard as fast as you can."

Murdoch and Quincy jumped into the nearest boat, and in minutes the vessels were filled with men armed with muskets and rifles. As Quincy looked around, he noticed that, other than Colonel Arnold himself, none of them seemed to be from Colonel Arnold's Connecticut Militia.

"These are all Green Mountain Boys," he said in a whisper to Murdoch.

Faintly, Quincy could see the answering grin on his friend's face. "Aye, and tha's no surprise. I'd wager Colonel Allen made sure his boys were the first ones t' be roused from sleep this morning. He dinna want the battle t' start without him. 'Twould be perfectly all right with Ethan Allen if the battle was over and Fort Ticonderoga was in his hands even before Benedict Arnold and the Connecticut men rolled out o' their blankets."

Colonel Allen stepped into the boat in which Quincy and Murdoch rode, and without sitting down, called quietly to the men on shore, "Push off, lads, now!"

The boats were shoved out into the lake, and oars were slipped into the oarlocks, which had been covered with cloth to muffle their sound. Smoothly, the boats cut across the water, slicing through the predawn mists toward the faint sparks of light that marked the location of the British fort.

Quincy watched the lights draw near. The mist began to condense on the flintlock of his musket, and he cupped his hand over the frizzen to keep the moisture out. A misfire at a crucial moment was the last thing he needed. Beside him, Murdoch did the same.

In the increasing light Quincy was beginning to make

out individual trees on the far shore, and he judged that the boats were halfway across the lake. The stone walls around the fort were coming into view.

Three-quarters of the way across, Murdoch said softly, "God be with ye, lad."

Quincy was unable to say anything in response. His throat felt clogged, as if a large stone had come to rest there. There was no shame in being afraid, he told himself. The only shame was in letting your fear stop you.

The prows of the boats grated against the rocky shore.

Ethan Allen sprang out, then ordered the oarsmen to stay in the boats. "Go back across and fetch more troops. Quickly, now!" he said.

Eighty-three men stood on the western shore of Lake Champlain, tensely looking toward the fort up a steep hill one hundred yards away. Colonel Allen paced back and forth in front of his men and glowered at the burgeoning radiance in the eastern sky. Already the mist on the lake was shredding and blowing away. Time crept by.

Ethan Allen could stand it no longer. "The element of surprise will be lost if the sun rises before we can attack. I fear I have miscalculated the time required to cross the lake. It is almost light, and the boatloads of patriots are nowhere to be seen. Gentlemen, we must take this fort now! Since this will be a desperate attempt—which none but the bravest of men dare undertake—I shall not urge it on anyone against his will." Drawing his sword, he called out in a ringing voice, "Let every man who will go with me poise his firelock!"

All eighty-three men lifted their weapons and half-cocked the flintlocks. Sweeping his saber forward, Ethan Allen and his men stormed the fort.

At a dead run they thundered up the slope toward the stockade's gate, which, Quincy saw as they drew nearer, stood wide open. For a moment he thought this might be a trap, but he was carried forward by his courage and conviction.

The patriots charged through the fort's entrance.

A sleepy-eyed British sentry let out a cry of alarm as he spotted the dozens of well-armed patriots boiling through the gate. He jerked his musket up and fired a shot in panic, but the ball went wide.

At the sound of the blast, the colonials howled, "No quarter! No quarter!"

The sentry dropped his heavy weapon and ran for his life.

The Green Mountain Boys poured into the fort, and as groggy British troops emerged from their barracks to see what the commotion was, they found themselves staring down the barrels of rifles and muskets wielded by grim-faced men in green and brown uniforms or buckskins and rough homespun. Many of the English soldiers had left their weapons beside their beds, and they were powerless to do anything but lift their hands in surrender.

Quincy and Murdoch followed Ethan Allen as he charged across the compound toward the officers' quarters. A British sentry sprang toward them from the side and jabbed at Allen with his bayonet. Moving with blinding speed, one of the Green Mountain Boys dove between the colonel and the British trooper. The bayonet attached to the muzzle of the Brown Bess slashed across the man's outstretched arm.

"You dog!" cried Allen. He whipped his saber toward the British sentry, and the blade sliced across the man's face. The sentry cried out in pain and dropped his musket. Touching his face, his hands felt the blood well up between his fingers. He stumbled out of the path of the charging colonials.

Ethan Allen stood at the bottom of a sturdy wooden

staircase that led up to the entrance of the officers' quarters. He took the stairs two and three at a time.

A lieutenant appeared in the doorway at the head of the stairs, desperately trying to pull his breeches on before the patriots reached him. Failing that, he staggered back against the gray stone wall of the building.

Colonel Allen lunged toward him, putting the tip of his sword at the lieutenant's throat. "Who might you be, sir?" demanded the colonel.

"Lieutenant Jocelyn Feltham," the British lieutenant replied, his voice showing little fear despite his dangerous, undignified position. He continued, "Assistant commander of His Majesty's garrison."

"And just who is in charge of this post?"

"Captain William Delaplace," Lieutenant Feltham said.

Ethan Allen inclined his head toward the doorway. "He in there?"

"Yes, sir." Feltham's voice quavered with outrage. "By what authority have you entered the king's fort like this?"

Ethan Allen fixed the lieutenant with a murderous glare and bellowed at the top of his lungs, "In the name of the Great Jehovah and the Continental Congress!" Then he turned to the doorway and shouted, "Captain Delaplace! Come out of there, you damned old rat!"

Ashen-faced, his eyes wide with alarm, the British captain appeared in the doorway. He grew paler as he took in the scene before him. Half a dozen colonists stood on the small porch at the head of the stairs, their weapons trained unwaveringly on him as he emerged tentatively from the building. Below, dozens more men were spread out around the compound, holding prisoner the remainder of the garrison.

Quincy held his musket ready to fire, but he hoped the captain would have the good sense to surrender. This attack, if it could be called that, had gone astoundingly well. The patriots were on the verge of capturing Fort Ticonderoga without a single casualty and only one shot fired. But only if Delaplace bowed to the inevitable.

The captain took a deep, ragged breath and said to Ethan Allen, "I believe you have the advantage, sir."

"Indeed I do," Allen replied. "I'm Colonel Ethan Allen, and these are my Green Mountain Boys. I'm calling on you to surrender, Captain. Otherwise—"

"There's no need to threaten, Colonel," Delaplace said, trying to muster up some dignity. "I have eyes in my head. Very well, I surrender. My men will lay down their arms."

"Mite late for that," Murdoch interjected.

"That's enough, Buchanan," Ethan Allen said. But the smile on his face did not waver. He turned back to Delaplace. "Come with me, Captain. I want to inspect the place and see just what we've captured."

It was over, Quincy realized with a surge of relief. The patriots had just won the "battle" of Fort Ticonderoga.

Chapter Fourteen

The Salutation Tavern was busy that evening, as usual. War loomed on the horizon, but people still wanted a mug of ale, a pint of stout, a jot of rum, or a tumbler of whiskey. Old Pheeters, the proprietor, and his serving wenches tirelessly catered to the needs of the tavern's customers.

He was not so preoccupied, however, that he did not notice an occasional visitor unobtrusively making his way to the tavern's back room. On the contrary. He had seen the members of the Committee of Safety's inner circle—those who were still in Boston—slipping back there. Samuel Adams, John Adams, John Hancock, Dr. Joseph Warren, and many other committee members had already surreptitiously left the city when it became clear that war was going to break out.

Something must be going on, Pheeters thought. *Something bloody well important.*

Dr. Benjamin Church, the leading figure in the patriot

cause still left in Boston, was in the tavern's back room, where so much of the strategy that had led to the current situation had been plotted. He looked around at the men and said, "I've had some very interesting news from one of our agents in New Hampshire. It seems that someone—and we're not at all certain *who*—stole a load of British munitions from a private sailing vessel and then sank it."

Excited questions followed Church's announcement. The tall, impressive-looking physician clasped his hands behind his back and let the hubbub run its course. Finally, one of the men asked, "Who owned this vessel?"

"The firm of Markham and Cummings," replied Church. "I'm sure that comes as no surprise to any of us."

"And they were bringing in guns for the British?"

"Evidently the whole affair was supposed to be a secret," Church said. "That's why the Crown used a private ship instead of one from His Majesty's navy. The guns were intended to replace the ones that were lost when our men blew up the warehouse down by the wharves several weeks ago."

Another man slammed a clenched fist on the table. "So Markham and Cummings played along with them, did they? They're nothing more than German George's lapdogs!"

"What did you expect?" Church asked.

"They'll pay for their treason, one of these days," growled another man.

Church nodded and said, "What's important now, I believe, is to discover exactly who planned and carried out this operation. I've been in touch with Samuel Adams and Dr. Warren, in Cambridge, and they insist they know nothing about it."

"What does it matter, as long as whoever wound up with

the guns is on our side?" one of the committee members wanted to know.

"That's just it." Church paced back and forth at the head of the table. "We don't know what's going to happen to those munitions."

"Well, as long as they're out of the hands of the British, that's a help, isn't it?"

"Of course," admitted Church. "But clearly, someone else has set up an intelligence network much like our own, to gather information about the British and strike back at them. Think how much more effective they'll be if their efforts are coordinated with ours."

As the men talked about that possibility Dr. Benjamin Church seethed inside.

He had a meeting scheduled later that evening with Major Alistair Kane, the British intelligence officer who was Church's liaison in his efforts to undermine the cause of freedom. Major Kane would press for answers, answers that Church—irate at having to admit he knew next to nothing—was not prepared to give.

He did have his suspicions, however. He recalled a meeting between Roxanne Darragh, Elliot Markham, and a pair of men called Tallmadge and Townsend. Church knew them to be Daniel Reed's friends, and he remembered the way Roxanne had brushed aside her rendezvous with them as merely social.

Church had a feeling the meeting had been significant. He knew both Roxanne and Elliot had done valuable work for the committee in the past. Were they working for Tallmadge and Townsend now? Church had decided it was highly likely, because the raided ship had been a Markham & Cummings vessel . . . and it was rumored that Elliot and Roxanne had been aboard.

But he had no proof that Tallmadge and Townsend had planned the operation, and that was what he needed now.

Thinking what fools these men were and how easily he was able to manipulate them, Church announced, "I'm going to look into the matter, and with your help, I'm sure I can find out what I need to know."

"Anything we can do to help, you have only to request it of us, Doctor," one of them said as he stood up and gave Church a firm handshake.

"I'll do that," he said, smiling.

And when he had found out everything there was to know about this new spy ring—whoever had organized it—then he would make his move. Such information was going to be very valuable to Major Kane and the British.

Soon, thought Church, soon he would be able to leave this dirty business behind. Let the British and the patriots continue their bloody little squabble. He was going to be a rich man, and that was all that mattered.

Bad news, it seemed, traveled exceedingly fast. Both Benjamin Markham and Theophilus Cummings were standing outside by the front door of the office building when the carriage pulled up and Elliot hopped down from its seat. He glanced at his father and noticed the brick-red flush that suffused Benjamin's face. Theophilus Cummings, on the other hand, was paler and sallower than usual. Both businessmen wore powdered wigs but had not bothered to put on their hats.

Elliot looked at them for a moment as the carriage pulled away, then said, "I didn't expect a welcoming party—"

"Shut up," his father snapped. "Come inside, and keep that mouth of yours closed until we're through with you." He turned on his heel and stalked into the building.

Cummings lifted a skinny finger that shook with anger and pointed it at Elliot. "You are in a great deal of trouble, young man," he said unnecessarily.

Elliot sighed and followed them into the building that housed the offices of Markham & Cummings. They went straight to Benjamin Markham's private chamber. As Elliot eased the door shut behind him, he said in a solemn voice, "I know you're both very upset with me, and you have every right to be—"

"Every right?" echoed Benjamin, who stood behind his large desk. He repeated, "Every right? Every right to have you flogged, that's what we have!"

"Where have you been, Elliot?" Cummings asked coldly. "Captain Ralston came to see us an hour ago and told us what happened."

"I went to the house first. I wanted to freshen up. It was a long, unpleasant journey from New Hampshire."

The flush on Benjamin's face darkened. "You help some rebel whore sink one of our ships and all you're concerned about is changing your clothes?" His voice cracked with fury.

Elliot kept a taut rein on his temper. It was not easy to hear his father talking about Roxanne like that, but he had to remember the role he was playing. In a surly voice, he said, "I had no idea what she was doing. It's not my fault, Father."

"Then whose fault is it?" demanded Benjamin.

Before Elliot could answer, Cummings said, "She played you for a fool, young man. Surely you can see that."

With a shamefaced nod, Elliot said, "She tricked me. I'll admit that. But I still say it's not my fault."

"It's *all* your fault," Benjamin said heavily. "My God, I never dreamed I could raise a son so stupid!"

Elliot said nothing. For the next few minutes Benjamin

Markham berated him for his part in the taking of the *Carolingian,* and Elliot endured the tirade in silence.

Theophilus Cummings was content to stand back and allow his partner to administer the primary tongue-lashing, but when Benjamin was finished, Cummings confronted Elliot and said harshly, "Sit down, boy. I have a few things to say to you, too."

Elliot sank into one of the chairs in front of the desk. His father's ire had been expressed in loud, blustering tones, but Cummings's voice was calm, steady, and as cold as ice. It raked Elliot like a whip.

"You've not only dealt a blow to the business your father and I have worked so hard to establish," Cummings said, "but your lust for that redheaded doxy has led you to near treason—if not treason itself! Sarah has already informed me that Avery saw Roxanne Darragh talking to Benjamin Church, and everyone in the colony knows he's deeply involved with the damned rebels. Are you part of this conspiracy, Elliot? As angry as I am about that, young man, I'm angrier that you hurt my daughter, hurt her very badly, and neither she nor I will ever forgive you for it."

A painful twinge of guilt passed through Elliot. He was well aware of the unhappiness he had brought Sarah; it was his biggest regret.

"Sarah's engagement to you is over, as you know, and she's well rid of you," Cummings continued. "Thank God for Avery Wallingford! He's been wonderful, the way he sprang to Sarah's side in her time of need. From now on, however, Elliot, I forbid you to speak to my daughter ever again. So if you're harboring any thoughts of winning back her affection, you can dismiss them from your mind this very instant! If you even come near her, I'll have you horsewhipped!"

"And I'll stand by and watch," Benjamin Markham

added. He crossed his arms over his chest and glowered at his son.

Elliot's face was hot, and he wanted to rage at this pair of self-righteous old men. They knew nothing of what he had gone through, nothing! They cared not a whit for the sacrifice Roxanne had made for the cause in which she believed so ardently. All they cared about, he knew, was the ship and the cargo they had lost, and the fear that the Crown might expect them to make recompense for the stolen munitions.

Slowly, Elliot rose to his feet. "Is that all?" he asked.

"No, it's not," his father said. He glared again at Elliot, then went on, "I came very close to disinheriting you and telling you to leave my house. Your mother, who is sometimes too softhearted for her own good, insisted that I not do that, and for her sake and her sake alone, I agreed. But she has no say in my business affairs, and I hereby declare that you will have nothing more to do with the firm of Markham and Cummings!"

"I heartily agree," Theophilus Cummings said, sneering.

Elliot drew a deep breath. He had never liked working in the offices of the shipping firm, but—

"What about my salary?" he asked.

Benjamin Markham laughed, but it was a thoroughly unpleasant sound. "That ended when your position with the firm did."

"What am I supposed to do for money?"

"That's no longer any of my concern," Benjamin answered. "You shall have a roof over your head and food to eat, because your mother wants it so. But other than that, you'll get naught from me, ever again!"

Elliot swallowed hard. He looked at Cummings and wanted to knock the smirk down his throat. As for his father—they had never been close, but Elliot knew him all too well. The man was unyielding. The barrier between them would never fall.

"All right," Elliot said in a whisper. "If that's what you want, sir, that's the way it will be."

"Damned right," Benjamin said.

"For what it's worth . . . I am sorry."

With that, Elliot turned and walked out of the office. Neither of the men tried to stop him.

Irreversible choices had been made—by Roxanne, by his father, by him.

Despite being dismissed from his position at Markham & Cummings, Elliot still had some money of his own. He had never been one to save much, but he had a few coins put aside. For the rest of the afternoon, the night, and the following day, he put his funds to the best possible use. He got drunk.

Filled with anger, depression, and uncertainty, he visited each of his favorite taverns and grog shops in Boston, and when, on the evening of the second night, his money ran out, he was walking down a street in the city's business district. His head was pounding, his stomach was queasy, and his mouth tasted like he imagined the mops used to swab the decks on his father's ships must have. He was unshaven, and his clothes were disheveled. He knew he looked like a common drunkard as he made his way unsteadily along the street.

This is just how I'm supposed to look and act, Elliot told himself. *Everyone takes me for a wastrel anyway—a n'er-do-well filled with self-pity and petulance, because he has been revealed to be a fool, the dupe of some pretty rebel spy. Going on a binge is what everyone expects from me. And I haven't let them down.*

Shaking his head and starting a fresh set of hammers pounding inside his skull, he concentrated on finding his destination. A few minutes later he located what he was looking for. A sign over the door read WM. DARRAGH—PRINTER AND PUBLISHER.

It came as no surprise to Elliot that a light shone through the front window. Roxanne had mentioned her father's tendency to put in long hours at his printing shop. Elliot hesitated only a second, then squared his shoulders and went to the door. He reached down and tried it, but it was locked. He rapped on the door, but there was no response, so after a moment he knocked on the window. When that did not bring anyone, he clenched his fist and pounded on the door.

Through the window Elliot could see a gray-haired man of medium height wearing a canvas apron smudged with black marks. The man hurried to the door, unlocked it, and opened it a few inches.

"What the devil do you want?" he demanded.

Elliot tried to look as respectable as he could and asked solemnly, "William Darragh?"

"That's right. Who are you?"

"My name is Elliot Markham."

For an instant, Elliot thought the man was going to fling the door open all the way, leap upon him, and try to throttle the life out of him. That was the intent he read in William Darragh's eyes. But the printer merely growled, "What do *you* want?"

"Just to talk with you for a few moments, if I might."

Darragh's jaw worked, clenching and unclenching. Finally he said, "All right. Though I'm damned if I know why I'd be willing to listen to the likes of you."

"May I come in? I came after dark so no one would see me paying this visit to you."

"And am I supposed to be thankful for that?" Without waiting for an answer, Darragh swung the door open. "Come on in. But be quick about whatever you've got to say. I have work to do."

Elliot stepped in, and Darragh slammed the door behind him. It was a large room filled with unfamiliar equipment, and Elliot assumed the huge iron contraption was a printing press. To him, its array of arms and levers and plates held a vaguely ominous aspect.

Darragh turned to face him. "Speak your piece, then get out of my shop."

"I just wanted to tell you that Roxanne is all right. I don't know where she is, but I'm certain she's safe."

Darragh just stared at him, then snorted. "We know that. Her mother and I have heard from her. We know where she is."

Elliot blinked in surprise. He wanted to leap forward, grab the printer by the shoulders, and shake out what he wanted to know. *"Where?"*

"You don't think I'm going to tell *you,* do you?"

The pounding in Elliot's head increased. He took a deep breath to try to calm his raging emotions. "How could you have heard from her?"

"You ought to know better than most that there are ways of getting messages in and out of Boston."

"I don't understand," Elliot said.

"I know you and Roxanne were working together to steal those guns from the British," Darragh said in a low voice. "She's told me enough for me to know that you're on the side of the patriots, no matter what face you display in public." He grimaced. "I'm the same way. I stay neutral, as far as most people know, but I want the colonies to be free, too. That's the only reason I'm doing you the favor of talking to you right now, Markham." His voice sank lower. "I'm just as glad as you are that those guns won't wind up in British hands. But did you have to ruin my daughter's reputation and make her into a fugitive in order to get what you wanted?"

Slowly, Elliot said, "It was Roxanne's own choice to reveal that she was working against the British. I didn't like it, either."

Darragh clenched his ink-stained hands. "But the whole town already knew she was your slut, Markham. Maybe it was all an act, maybe it wasn't. I don't really want to know. Either way, she's ruined."

"No," Elliot insisted. "When the British are gone, she can come back. I'll tell everyone what really happened—"

"You're assuming one hell of a lot," Darragh said. "I want you to stay away from my daughter, mister. If you ever come near her again—assuming she ever gets to come home—I'll kill you. Now get out of here before I forget that I'm a tired old man and we're supposed to be on the same side. Get out before I throw you out!"

Elliot turned away. The last thing he wanted was a fight with Roxanne's father. He had brought enough grief to the Darragh family already, though none of it had been intentional.

William Darragh was right, Elliot realized now. It was better for him not to know where Roxanne was. It was enough to be reassured that she was all right, that she had come to no harm in the aftermath of the raid on the *Carolingian.*

He left the printing shop without looking back. A bleak smile tugged at his mouth for a moment as he realized

William Darragh had said almost the same thing as Theophilus Cummings the day before. What was it about him, Elliot wondered, that made fathers warn him to stay away from their daughters?

Elliot shook his head and walked away into the night.

Chapter Fifteen

"They'll be coming along that trail right beside the crick," said the scout called Asa, pointing a knobby finger down the hill toward the stream that ran through the valley. "Be here in about fifteen minutes, I'd say."

He and Jasper had just returned from taking a look at the British wagon train that was following a winding trail through the heavily wooded hills. The path below, beside the creek, was the only straight stretch of trail in the area.

"Good," Daniel said. "This is the place to take them."

"I agree," Asa said.

"Plenty of cover up here," Jasper added. "We'll hit them like the Indians would. Fire and move, and keep moving." A grin creased his leathery face. "Chances are they won't know there's only eleven of us."

"Could you tell how many men the wagons have with them?" Daniel asked.

Asa and Jasper considered the question as they rubbed

their jaws. Finally Asa ventured, "Nigh a dozen on horseback. They're the ones we'll need to take care of first."

"And another twenty with the wagons," Jasper put in.

"So we're going to be outnumbered almost three to one," Daniel mused grimly.

"We got surprise on our side," Asa said. "That's worth a heap."

The members of the Connecticut Militia had been standing close by, leaning on their rifles and listening to the scouts' report. If any of them were worried about the impending attack on a much larger force, their faces did not show it.

"I can't believe I'm doing this," Cordelia said, walking back and forth hugging herself. "Helping to set up an ambush on the king's men . . . "

"You're helping men who saved your life," Daniel reminded her. During the day and a half it had taken them to get there, Cordelia had suffered several fits of conscience.

She sighed. "I know. And you're right. I never thought much about politics and government. All I knew was what my father said. And when I married, I adopted Perry's opinions. But I'm starting to understand." She met Daniel's eyes. "You rebels aren't all wild-eyed madmen."

"Thanks," Daniel said dryly. "Now, you'd better get well back in the trees. There'll be quite a lot of lead flying around here soon."

"All right. Be careful, Daniel."

He saw no trace of mockery on her face. She seemed to mean what she had said.

"I will be," he promised her.

Daniel preferred to keep his men together, even though the thought of catching the British in a cross fire was appealing. If they did as Jasper had suggested and moved from tree to tree with each shot, reloading on the run, eleven men might be able to convey the impression that there were many more of them.

Acting on advice from the two scouts, Daniel spread his men along the slope. Firing downhill would be tricky, but it would be even more difficult for the redcoats who would have to shoot uphill to return the patriots' fire. If he and his men made every shot count, they would have a chance, even with the odds against them.

As he waited, crouched behind the trunk of a pine, Daniel listened intently. The creaking of wagon wheels came to his ears, and at first he thought he was imagining the sound because he was so anxious for the supply train to arrive. Then, as the noise grew louder and was joined by the voices of men and the thudding of hooves on the trail, he knew the British had arrived. Now all he had to do was wait for the right moment to spring the trap.

Cordelia drew back at least a hundred yards from the spot where Daniel and the others waited for the wagons. Her mouth was dry, and she swallowed nervously as she hid in a small cluster of boulders that protruded from the side of the hill. The rocks would protect her in the unlikely event that the musket balls happened to carry that far.

She settled down on the ground, grimacing as a small, sharp stone dug into the soft flesh of her hip. Peering down the hill, she realized she could not see the attack from this position. She would be able to hear the fighting, but she would not know the outcome of the battle until it was over.

Then she heard the scrape of a bootheel behind her and abruptly turned her head. A man lunged at her, and in the second before his hand closed over her mouth and stifled her scream, she recognized her husband. Perry Faulkner's hat was gone, his clothes were disheveled, and he was unshaven. Wrapped around his upper left arm was a crude, bloodstained bandage. But it was unmistakably he, and panic surged through Cordelia as she tried to writhe away.

His grip was too strong. His one arm looped around her and jerked her against him as his hand clamped over her mouth. His fingers dug cruelly into her jaw.

"Not a sound, you witch!" he hissed in her ear. "I'll break your neck if you utter so much as a whisper."

Held in his iron grip, Cordelia managed to bob her head. Faulkner took his hand away from her mouth but shifted it instantly to her throat. She was glad she gasped for air while she could, because he held her so tightly that she couldn't breathe.

"You're going to be quiet," he said, his own voice low and rasping with hatred and pain. She smelled something rotten and realized the wound in his arm was already beginning to putrefy.

"Where's Reed?" he asked. "Tell me the truth, Cordelia! I've no further use for you, and I'd love to watch you die slowly and painfully right now."

He relaxed the grip on her throat enough for her to gulp down another breath, then say hoarsely, "I'll tell you nothing! I don't care if you kill me!"

Blood pounded in Cordelia's head. Regardless of what it would mean to her, she could not betray Daniel and the other men. There had been a time when she could have done that easily, but no longer.

Faulkner laughed, and she knew from the sound of it that he was insane. "It doesn't matter. I know where they are. I've been following you ever since you left the inn. I know what you're up to, Cordelia. You want those British guns for yourself."

"No, Perry, the patriots are going to have them."

"Patriots?" He stared at her in disbelief. "My God, Cordelia, have they won you over? I'd never have believed it."

Neither would she, Cordelia thought. But that appeared to be the case.

Suddenly she remembered all the pain and degradation she had suffered at the hands of his men as he looked on, that horrible, arrogant smile on his face. A fiercer rage than she had ever known made her lash out. She bent her fingers like hooked claws and reached desperately for his eyes. Faulkner cursed and jerked his head to one side, but her fingernails tore into his cheek, his flesh rending beneath them. Blood trickled down his face.

Then Faulkner hit her.

His fist caught her squarely on the jaw and sent her sprawling onto the rocks. Cordelia barely felt the impact as she landed on the hard, stony ground. Her face was numb, and consciousness was fading rapidly as she heard him growl, "I'll come back and deal with you later, when I'm finished with that bastard Reed and the others."

How appropriate, she thought, and then there was nothing but darkness around her. Blessed, silent darkness.

Daniel peered past the tree trunk until he could see down into the valley. He counted the wagons as they rounded the bend in the trail that led into the straight stretch beside the creek. There were nine of them, he saw, flanked on both sides by redcoated outriders. As Asa had said, it was imperative they take care of the horsemen first. The soldiers with the heavy, slow-moving wagons would be easier targets.

He glanced to right and left. The other men, concealed

behind trees and bushes, were waiting for his signal to launch the attack. The first shot was his.

He lifted the long-barreled flintlock rifle to his shoulder and put the weapon at full cock. The sight at the front of the muzzle settled on the redcoated breast of the lead rider. The man was casually walking his horse, unaware that death lurked above him.

Daniel pressed the trigger.

The rifle boomed and bucked against his shoulder. All along the slope, shots rang out, an entire volley in the next few seconds. Squinting through the haze of powder smoke that filled the air, Daniel saw his man toppling from the British military saddle. There were several more empty saddles up and down the wagon train, and the riderless horses plunged and reared in fear as gunfire rang out like thunder.

Instantly Daniel moved to his next cover, another pine tree twenty feet away. As he dashed toward it, he began the cumbersome process of reloading the rifle. He poured powder into the muzzle, slammed ball, patch, and wadding down the barrel with the ramrod, charged the firing pan with powder, and snapped the frizzen closed over the pan. Long hours of practice enabled him to complete the task before he reached the second tree. Still clenching the cork from the powder horn between his teeth, he let the horn fall back to his side and lifted the rifle to aim his next shot.

Men darted from bush to tree, from tree to rocks, as the colonists poured fire down on the wagon train. The wagons had been hauled to a stop, and the British soldiers used them for cover. Musket balls whined through the trees, clipping off small branches and thudding into tree trunks, as the British troopers mounted a defense.

Daniel fired again and again, the explosions blending together in his battle-numbed brain. The acrid smell of burned powder stung his nose, and clouds of smoke burned his eyes. His hands were blistered from the heat of his gun. Twice more he saw men fall under his shots, and the accurate fire of the militiamen was taking its toll as well. All the British outriders were down, a few writhing in pain from their wounds but most lying on the ground in the stillness of death.

Ten minutes after the battle had begun, it ended. The surviving redcoats stumbled out from behind the wagons, threw down their guns, and lifted their hands high in the air in surrender.

It was over, Daniel realized. They had won.

He caught the eye of Asa and Jasper and waved them down the hill. The scouts led the way, keeping their rifles trained on the defeated redcoats as they hurried down the hill at the head of the militiamen. Daniel stepped out from behind the tree he had been using as a shield. He leaned on his empty rifle and watched his men noisily gathering up the redcoats' weapons.

A stone rattled somewhere behind him. Before he could turn around, something slammed into his side and knocked him to the ground. He was so stunned by the impact that his brain barely registered the fact that he had heard a pistol crack. But as he tried to push himself into a sitting position, he felt a warm, sticky wetness on his side and understood that he had been shot.

"Now it's time to settle the score between us, Reed." Perry Faulkner tucked away the empty pistol he held in his hand and pulled a second gun from his belt. "This one will finish you off, my young friend. Then I'll deal with Cordelia."

The shots would draw the attention of the militiamen below him, and they would come running, Daniel knew.

Faulkner's minutes were numbered. Help would not arrive in time to save Daniel, but Cordelia would still have a chance.

He tried to reach for his pistol, but the muscles of his arm stubbornly resisted him. He gasped as a fresh wave of pain radiated out from his side. If he could get his hand on the gun, he might be able to take Faulkner with him.

Faulkner stopped ten feet away and laughed. He lifted the pistol in his hand. "Good-bye, Reed," he said.

Before Faulkner had a chance to pull the trigger, Cordelia lunged out of the woods behind him and leapt onto his back. He cursed as she crooked one arm around his neck and reached for his gun with the other. Pulling her off him, he slammed a savage backhand across her face.

Daniel's strength was ebbing, but he managed to touch the butt of his pistol.

Faulkner hit Cordelia in the stomach. He caught her blond hair and yanked cruelly on it, making her stumble to the side. He kept battering her, but Cordelia refused to give up. Again and again she sprang at him, like a wild animal that had turned on its tormentor.

The barrel of Faulkner's pistol cracked against the side of her head. Cordelia moaned and crumpled unconscious to the ground. Sweating and breathing hard, his hair hanging over his eyes, Perry Faulkner turned back to Daniel—and found himself facing the muzzle of the young man's pistol.

Faulkner tried to aim his gun, but before he could, fire and smoke belched from the barrel of Daniel's weapon. The ball drove into Faulkner's chest. Convulsively, his finger pulled the trigger as a grisly blood-red flower bloomed on the front of his shirt. The ball went harmlessly into the ground, and Faulkner fell to his knees, life fading from his crazed eyes. He pitched forward to lie still on the carpet of pine needles.

The pistol slipped from Daniel's fingers, and he, too, slumped to the ground. He heard footsteps pounding up to him and heard Jasper exclaim, "Good Lord! It's that Faulkner fella!"

Asa dropped to a knee beside Daniel. "You're hit," he said unnecessarily, "but we'll take care of you."

"Cordelia," whispered Daniel. "See about . . . Cordelia."

"Aye, don't worry."

"The guns?"

"We got them," Jasper said. "And soon the redcoats'll be gettin' a dose of their own medicine."

A fresh spasm of pain hit him, and he gasped, "Roxanne!"

There could be worse things than to die with the name of the woman you loved on your lips.

Epilogue

Daniel stepped out onto the porch of Gresham Howard's house in Saratoga. He moved somewhat awkwardly due to the bandages wrapped around his torso. Cordelia stayed close beside him, but he made it to the wicker chair without any trouble and sank down in it to enjoy the afternoon sunshine.

Cordelia's father came out of the house and sat in a chair across from Daniel. Gresham Howard was a burly man, just below medium height, with grayish-brown, thinning hair. He held a long-stemmed pipe in one hand, and as he sat down, he put it in his mouth and puffed on it.

"It's a lovely day," Howard said as he looked out at the streets of Saratoga.

"Indeed," Daniel said. *Every day is lovely after one discovers himself to be alive instead of dead.*

The ball from Faulkner's pistol had plowed a shallow furrow across his side, underneath his left arm. The injury had bled freely, causing him to pass out, but otherwise it had not done much damage. Asa had cleaned it with some good Connecticut whiskey, then packed it with moss to stop the bleeding. Along with Cordelia, the two scouts had brought Daniel to Saratoga, to the house of Cordelia's father. The rest of the militiamen had headed for Lake Champlain to deliver the captured British munitions to Benedict Arnold.

Already the news had reached Saratoga: Ethan Allen and the Green Mountain Boys had taken Fort Ticonderoga, capturing the British stronghold without loss of life. Then Benedict Arnold and the Connecticut Militia had captured Crown Point, north of the fort. The patriots now controlled the lake, and the British could not use it to cut the colonies in half and resupply their forces from Canada.

It was only a beginning, Daniel knew, but it was a good one.

Frowning through the smoke from his pipe, Gresham Howard mused, "I still can't believe Perry was such a scoundrel. From what you've told me, the lad would have double-crossed me sooner or later. And may he burn in hell for what he did to you, my poor daughter!"

"I'm sure that's exactly what he's doing, Father," Cordelia assured him.

Howard looked at Daniel and went on, "And you've certainly changed my mind about this war, young man. I can see now I've been blind in more ways than one."

"I'm glad to hear that, Mr. Howard. After everything you've done for me the past few days, I'd hate to think I was beholden to a Tory."

Howard snorted and pointed the stem of his pipe at Daniel. "There's not much danger of that. I'm still not certain that armed rebellion is the answer to all the problems with the Crown, but I agree that something has to be done."

Cordelia stood behind Daniel's chair with her hands resting companionably on his shoulders. Except for some fading bruises, she had recovered from the beating by Faulkner. Daniel had thought that he and Cordelia would never be friends, but saving each other's life had changed that.

Suddenly, her grip tightened on his shoulder. "Look down the street!" she exclaimed.

Daniel got up from his chair as he saw the two figures riding toward the house. One of the men was tall and broad shouldered, dressed in buckskins and a coonskin cap; the other was smaller and leaner.

"Quincy!" Daniel yelled. "Murdoch!"

The two riders reined in their mounts and swung down quickly from the saddles. Quincy took the porch steps in a single bound and threw his arms around Daniel in a fierce hug. Daniel gasped and said, "Hold on there, brother! There are bandages under this shirt."

"Oh, no!" Quincy cried out as he hurriedly released Daniel. "I forgot you were hurt!"

Murdoch stepped up onto the porch and shook hands with Daniel. "Those boys with the wagons full o' British guns told us what happened. Ye're sure Faulkner's really dead this time?"

"He's dead all right. And I don't think we ever need to talk about him again."

"Aye, tha's the truth," agreed Murdoch.

Cordelia went to Quincy and hugged him, causing the usual blush, and while they were greeting each other, Daniel asked Murdoch, "Did the wagons reach Lake Champlain all right?"

"No trouble," the big frontiersman confirmed. "Colonel Allen and Colonel Arnold took charge o' the firearms, and I know they'll put them t' good use. When he heard that you'd been hurt, Colonel Allen did'na mind musterin' out a couple o' temporary recruits."

Daniel slapped Murdoch on the arm. "You'll have to tell me all about the battle, such as it was," he said. "From what I've heard, I'll wager you were a little disappointed."

"Aye. There were no more than forty troops in the fort. 'Twas no fight at all."

Gresham Howard cleared his throat. He was standing nearby, waiting to be introduced to the newcomers. Daniel took care of that, and as Howard shook hands with Quincy and Murdoch, he said, "You'll be staying on, of course, gentlemen?"

"If we will'na be abusing your hospitality."

"I insist. I have the best cook in New York, and I'm sure she'll be glad to feed two extra mouths."

"Ah, a home-cooked meal," Murdoch said. " 'Twill be a delight after all these weeks o' eating on the trail."

At supper the Scotsman put away enough food for three men, and Gresham Howard poured brandy for everyone, even Quincy.

"What did you young men have in mind to do now?" the wagon builder asked as he sat down again at the head of the table and leaned back in his chair.

Daniel sipped his brandy, then said, "I hadn't given it much thought other than recuperating from this wound. I suppose when I'm able to travel again—and that should be soon, the way I'm being taken care of around here—I'll be heading back to Massachusetts. I'll have to get in touch with the Committee of Safety and report on the Ticonderoga campaign once Quincy and Murdoch fill me in on the details."

"Boston again?" Murdoch asked. "Not me, lad. I've had enough o' civilization. I'm ready for the open spaces o' the frontier."

Daniel felt a twinge of regret. He hated the thought of splitting up once more. But Murdoch's decision fit right in with an idea he had had earlier.

"The frontier . . ." repeated Gresham Howard. "I like the sound of that, young man. I'm thinking about heading west myself."

"You are?" Cordelia exclaimed. "This is the first I've heard about it, Father."

"Well, with everything that's happened, my eyes have been opened to some harsh realities, sweetheart. There's going to be a great deal of bloodshed before this conflict is over, and I think you and I should avoid it if we can."

"Run away, you mean?" she snapped back at him.

Daniel spoke up. "Don't think about it like that," he told her. "You've done your part, Cordelia. Without you, those guns would still be in British hands."

"Then you think I should go, too?"

"I do," Daniel replied solemnly.

Howard turned to Murdoch. "Perhaps you'd like to accompany us, Mr. Buchanan? I don't mind telling you, I'd like to have an experienced guide along with us."

" 'Tis an idea," Murdoch allowed.

"I'm going to close up this house," Howard went on, warming to the subject now, "and load up a couple of good wagons from my wagon yard. We should be able to travel in comparative comfort. What do you say?"

"I'll do it," Murdoch declared. "Ye have yourself a guide, Mr. Howard."

"And I'm sure there will be room for four instead of three on this journey," Daniel said.

Quincy's eyes widened in surprise. "Oh, no, Daniel," he said. "I know what you're thinking, but I'm going back to Boston with you."

"There's no way of knowing what I'll find there or what sort of mission I'll be sent on next. It would ease my mind a great deal if you'd go with Murdoch and Cordelia and Mr. Howard, Quincy."

"But we're brothers, blast it! We should be together!"

Daniel had expected this argument from Quincy, and he was not sure what to do about it. Quincy was sixteen, almost a grown man, and Daniel did not want to have to give him a direct order.

Cordelia reached across the table and took Quincy's hand. "Please, Quincy," she said. "I'm still not sure about this—it's all so sudden—but if I have to go west, I'd feel better about things if I had a good friend like you along with me."

Quincy beamed for a moment, and Daniel knew that his brother's decision was a foregone conclusion. He was very grateful to Cordelia for this gesture.

"All right," Quincy said proudly. "If it'll make you feel better, Cordelia, I'll be glad to go."

Daniel leaned back in his chair, satisfied for the moment. He was not as sure as Howard seemed to be that the frontier would be that much safer than the more populated areas in the days to come. Daniel was certain the war would spread through the colonies now that hostilities had broken out.

At the moment all he wanted was to hold Roxanne Darragh in his arms and taste the sweetness of her lips, but he knew any reunion they had would be a short one.

War—and the cause of liberty—would be waiting.

Author's Note

Writing a series such as PATRIOTS requires a great deal of research, and I want to take this opportunity to thank Judy Whitt, librarian, and the entire staff of the Azle Public Library, Azle, Texas, for their assistance in this area.

Thanks also to Bill Crider, for his friendship and professionalism, and to L.J. Washburn, who was right all along, as usual.

Finally, this book is dedicated to the memory of Patches, a one-of-a-kind cat who managed to leave this world, as he did everything else, with impeccable timing. We still miss you, old son, and we always will.

ABOUT THE AUTHOR

"ADAM RUTLEDGE" is one of the pseudonyms of veteran author James M. Reasoner, who has written over sixty books ranging from historical sagas and Westerns to mysteries and adventure novels. Reasoner considers himself first and foremost a storyteller and enjoys spinning yarns based on the history of the United States, from colonial days to the passing of the era known as the Old West. He lives in Azle, Texas, with his wife, Livia, and daughters Shayna and Joanna.

PATRIOTS—*Volume III*

THE TURNCOAT

by

Adam Rutledge

The bloodless Battle of Fort Ticonderoga forces brothers Daniel and Quincy Reed to go their separate ways.

At great risk, Daniel returns to Boston to report to the Committee of Safety—and to find Roxanne Darragh, the beautiful redheaded spy with whom he is in love.

Quincy, along with Murdoch Buchanan, Cordelia Faulkner, and her father, travels to the western reaches of New York Colony, where he finds adventure and intimacy.

In Boston, Elliot Markham works feverishly devising an ingenious scheme to unmask a traitor—but can he do it before he himself is betrayed?

At the same time, British commander Thomas Gage is joined by generals Burgoyne, Clinton, and Howe. Burgoyne's careless talk sets the scene for the bloodiest fighting of 1775—the Battle of Bunker Hill.

Turn the page for a preview of *The Turncoat*, Volume III in the PATRIOTS series, on sale January 1993 wherever Bantam paperbacks are sold.

Daniel could have ridden at the head of the column of militiamen with Captain Aaron Webster and the other officers, but after the warm welcome he received from volunteers Thad Garner, George Cummings, Benjamin Hobbs, and Fred Dary, he preferred to stay with his newfound friends. He led his horse and walked alongside Thad as they marched toward Cambridge.

In the following three days Daniel learned that Thad and the others were farmers from the Stockbridge area and were very curious about the battles at Lexington, Concord, and Fort Ticonderoga. The men regarded Daniel as a hero and would not let go of that notion, no matter how modestly he downplayed his part in the events.

On the afternoon of the third day, they arrived in Cambridge, and when the militiamen reached the Harvard College Yard, they found troops gathered in front of Holden Chapel, Hollis Hall, Harvard Hall, Stoughton Hall, and Massachusetts Hall. Daniel looked up at the impressive four-story brick buildings and remembered the hours he had spent in each of them, listening to his professors' lectures on law, philosophy, and the natural sciences. Those days seemed so simple—and so far in the past.

"Look at that," Thad Garner said, awestruck. "Did you ever see such a place."

"As a matter of fact, I spent a year here reading for the law," Daniel told the young farmer.

"Go on with you. Is there anything you *haven't* done, Daniel Reed?"

"Plenty," he replied, thinking of Roxanne.

He tore his thoughts away from the lovely, redheaded

young woman and went on, "Captain Webster's motioning for us to keep marching."

When Daniel and the men reached a large open area near the Charles River, they saw a scattering of tents that appeared to be a military camp. Webster rode up to the largest one, swung down from his horse, and spoke to a blue-coated officer who had just stepped out of the canvas tent. Behind Webster, his troops came to a halt.

A man with thinning white hair and a slender frame also emerged, and he was followed by an elderly, white-haired officer, who seemed to Daniel to be more robust than his companion. The men spoke with Aaron Webster for several minutes, and then the burly captain turned to his followers and bellowed, "Look sharp, laddies, and listen close. These are your new commanding officers, General Artemas Ward and General Israel Putnam!"

General Ward stepped forward and said in a thin voice, "Welcome to Cambridge and the Massachusetts Provincial Army, men." He paused momentarily as he was seized by a bout of coughing, and Daniel realized that General Ward was ill.

"As you may know," he continued, "At this very moment the Second Continental Congress is meeting in Philadelphia, and we await their pleasure. Until such time as we receive instructions from them, Major General Putnam and I, as well as our fellow officers, will do our best to train you men into an efficient fighting force. The British are going to be bloody well sorry they started this fight, gentlemen!"

Though they were voiced in weak tones, the words spoken by General Ward drew a cheer from Daniel and the men. Ward stepped back then and deferred to Major General Israel Putnam. Daniel had heard of the man, known affectionately to his troops as "Old Put." He was a veteran of the French and Indian Wars, and now, around the age of sixty, looked and sounded vital enough to saddle up and ride into battle.

Putnam put his hand on the hilt of his saber and said, "I

hope you men have come to work and fight, because you'll be obliged to do both before this war is over. That's all I've got to say."

The men gave another cheer, and Captain Webster ordered them to fall out. "Camp where you will," he bellowed, "but any man who abuses the hospitality of the citizens of Cambridge will answer to me, do you understand? Report to Harvard College Yard in the morning, and we'll begin our drills. Dismissed!"

Daniel turned to Thad and the others and said, "Why don't you fellows come with me? I have an apartment not far from the college, and while it may be a bit crowded with all five of us staying there, it'll be better than camping."

"Sounds good to me, and mighty generous of you to offer it," Thad replied. "Come along, boys."

They walked quickly to the side street near Harvard, to the apartment over the stationer's shop where Daniel and Quincy had stayed in more peaceful times. The rent on the flat had been paid through the end of the year, and though it seemed to Daniel that he had been away for years, mere months had passed since he and his brother had fled from Cambridge.

Daniel walked into the shop, and when the landlord looked up, he stared in disbelief at Daniel. "Is that you, Mr. Reed?" he asked after a moment.

"It is indeed," Daniel told him. "Is my apartment still empty, Mr. Gidden? The rent *was* paid up, you know."

"Aye, the rooms are vacant, and all your belongings are still there." The landlord frowned darkly at Daniel. "The way you disappeared like that, son, I would've been justified in selling off your possessions and renting the apartment to someone else."

Daniel did not want to explain why he had been forced to leave Cambridge so abruptly a few months earlier, so he said simply, "I'm glad you didn't, sir. My friends and I have come to join the Provincial Army, and we need a place to stay."

"Well, why didn't you say so? You're welcome to the apartment, lads, for as long as you need it." Mr. Gidden grinned. "Which probably won't be for long. It won't be any time at all until the army's run those damned lobsterbacks out of Boston. Then you can stay in a fine house in the city."

Daniel didn't respond to the landlord's confident claim. He was worried that too many supporters of the patriot cause felt the same way—that the war with England would be a short and victorious one.

But Daniel knew from experience that the British would not give up easily. As General Putnam had said, the next few weeks would bring more than their share of both work and battle.

The days turned into weeks, and Captain Aaron Webster, new to the military, drilled his men unmercifully on Harvard Yard. Prior to leading the militia, he had been a farmer like the others—albeit wealthier and with more extensive holdings—and many of the men still called him Squire Webster. General Ward assigned an experienced lieutenant to Webster's command, and with the help of the junior officer, the squire turned the men into a disciplined fighting force. It didn't matter that only the officers had uniforms, the important thing was that the ragtag army was feeling and acting like a unit.

Daniel had never officially joined either the militia or the Massachusetts Provincial Army, but that did not matter under circumstances like these. All that counted was whether a man was willing to fight and die for the cause in which he believed.

Not all of Daniel's time was spent in training, and soon after he arrived in Cambridge, he rode to Charlestown Neck and across the narrow strip of land to the heights of Bunker Hill, where he could gaze across the Charles at the city of Boston. Several lookouts were posted at the top of the hill, and as Daniel swung down from his saddle, one of them called out to him, "Have you come to relieve one of us, matey?"

"I'm afraid not," Daniel said. "I was just wondering about the British patrols on the river."

"Thinking about trying to slip across into town?" asked one of the men. He laughed harshly before Daniel could answer. "I'd forget that idea if I were you, lad. That's a quick way to get killed. The damned British aren't letting as much as a gnat across the Charles."

The claim had been made before, but Paul Revere had used a small boat to slip across unchallenged at night, and Daniel thought he could do the same thing.

His intent must have been plain to see because one of the sentries said, "Don't try it, my friend, even on the darkest night. Our officers have studied the waterfront through their spyglasses, and the British have guard posts set up every hundred yards or so. And they have patrol boats tacking back and forth from this side of the peninsula all the way 'round to the other. You'd wind up getting shot—or hung, if the British feel like a more elaborate entertainment."

Daniel shivered. Pinned down as they were on the Shawmut Peninsula, surely the British felt as if their backs were against the wall, and he had no doubt they would execute anyone they believed was a spy.

He thought about his cousin Elliot Markham, somewhere in the city, and he hoped he was being very careful if he was still working with the Committee of Safety.

"What about Boston Neck?" asked Daniel.

"What about it? It's barricaded, closed off just like the rest of the city." The guard who had answered Daniel's question looked at him suspiciously. "Why are you so curious about getting into Boston, boy? Could it be that you're a redcoat trying to get some information to them about our forces?"

"Not likely," Daniel said grimly. The opposite was true,

in fact, but he did not want to tell that to these men. "You see, there's a girl over there. . . ."

One of the men snorted in disbelief as Daniel's voice trailed off. Holding their rifles tightly, the sentries closed in around him. "If he *was* a redcoat spy, he'd lie about it, now wouldn't he?" one said.

"Aye, he would," responded another. "Mayhap we better try to beat the truth out of him. We'll find out why he's so damned curious!"

Daniel glanced around. They had cut him off from his horse, so he would have to fight if he wanted to get away from there; outnumbered or not, the last thing he wanted was to get into a brawl with his fellow patriots.

"What's going on here?" a stern voice asked sharply as a tall man on horseback topped the hill.

Daniel looked up at the handsome, well-built rider and felt a surge of relief as he recognized Dr. Joseph Warren, one of the members of the committee's inner circle.

"Hello, Doctor," Daniel said. "It's good to see you again."

"Daniel Reed? Is that really you?" Dr. Warren leaned down from his horse and shook hands with Daniel. "I thought so when I caught a glimpse of you riding across Charlestown Neck, but I followed you to make sure. When did you get back in the area?"

Before Daniel could answer, one of the sentries demanded, "Do you know this man, Dr. Warren?"

"Indeed I do," he replied. "And I'll vouch for him unequivocally—no matter what the trouble is."

"No trouble," Daniel said. "Just a simple misunderstanding."

"Well, get your horse and come along," Warren said with a look that made the guards turn around and hurry back to their posts. "We have a great deal to talk about."

Daniel swung up into the saddle and trotted his mount down the hill alongside Dr. Warren's horse. "I arrived in

Cambridge a few days ago with a group of militiamen from western Massachusetts."

"Ah, yes, Captain Webster's group. Good sturdy yeomen all, from the looks of them." Warren lowered his voice, even though there was no one nearby to hear them. "How went your mission to New York?"

"Quite well, though not exactly what we'd planned," Daniel replied. "It's fortunate you came along when you did, Dr. Warren. Not only did you save my neck from the guards, but you can help me figure out a way into the city so I can deliver my report to the committee."

Warren sighed. "I'm afraid that's not going to be possible for a while," he said. "No one goes in or out of Boston anymore. The only reason I'm not there is that I was in Cambridge on business when the British slammed all the doors. But I hope to be back soon, once we've retaken the city."

Despite the bold words, Dr. Warren did not sound confident. Daniel twisted in his saddle and peered past the hill and the river. He could faintly see the roofs of the buildings in Boston.

"Did you happen to speak to Miss Darragh when you were in the city?" Daniel asked, keeping his tone impassive.

"Not for several weeks," replied Warren. For an instant, the physician seemed to be on the verge of saying something else, but he fell silent, and when he spoke again, he said, "I believe Roxanne may not be in the city, but as to her whereabouts, I really couldn't say."

Daniel stared at him in surprise. "Not in the city?" he repeated. "But where else could she be? I know she planned to return there."

"And she did. Dr. Church brought her back to Boston, in fact, and she was working with your cousin, young Markham, gathering intelligence for us. But then . . ." Warren shook his head. "She seems to have disappeared. For all I know, the British have captured her. I hate to be the bearer of this news, Daniel, but I believe you have a right to know the truth."

He felt as if someone had plunged a knife into his belly and cruelly twisted the blade. Roxanne . . . gone? Disappeared? Perhaps in the hands of the British?

"I have to get over there," he said raggedly.

"It's impossible," Warren told him again. "General Ward has issued strict orders that no one is to attempt to sneak into Boston. When the fighting begins, we're going to need every man we have, Daniel. If Roxanne *is* in trouble, you can do her more good by staying here and helping us."

Daniel knew Dr. Warren was right, but every instinct cried out for him to rush to Roxanne's side—wherever she was. He sighed heavily. "So what do I do in the meantime?"

"The same as the rest of us. You get ready to give the bloody British the fight of their lives!"

The training went well, and by the middle of June, the Provincial Army had begun to look like a bona fide military force, even if it could not march as crisply as the British regulars it would oppose. Morale was high, but so was impatience. The men had not left their farms and families to march around Harvard Yard; they had come to fight redcoats, and the time for that was drawing nigh.

Anticipation dominated the encampment in Cambridge, and generals Artemas Ward and Israel Putnam were well aware of it as they sat in Ward's tent and sipped glasses of sack. Ward was propped up on his bunk, and from time to time, he was racked by coughing that the sherry did little to ease.

"I thought certain we would have received word from the Congress by now," he complained as he leaned against the pillows stuffed behind his back. "Orders of some sort should have been forthcoming. What the devil are they *doing* down there in Philadelphia?"

Putnam felt sympathy for his ailing colleague Ward, and he thought the man should have been in bed in his own house, recovering from his illness rather than leading an army. Although he was older than Ward, Israel Putnam was still ambitious enough—and honest enough—to feel that command would be better off in his hands rather than Ward's.

"I'm afraid you're going to have to do *something,* Artemas," said Putnam. "With every day we wait, the men grow more restless. Besides, we're just giving the British a chance to strengthen their own positions."

"I know. But I've always been a cautious man, Israel—"

"Caution can be dangerous at the wrong time," Putnam ventured, daring to speak up in the privacy of Ward's tent.

Ward shrugged his narrow shoulders, then coughed again. He was still struggling with the spasm when the entrance flap of the tent was thrust back and an officer entered, snapped to attention, and saluted the two generals.

"I hate to barge in here like this, sirs, but we've just received an important dispatch from one of our agents in the city," he said.

"That . . . that's quite all right, Colonel Prescott," Ward answered, holding out his hand for the paper held by the colonel. "Let me see it."

Colonel William Prescott, the regiment commander of the Massachusetts Provincial Army, gave the dispatch to Ward, who read it and handed it to Putnam.

"So the British are planning to cross the Charles, eh?" Ward mused. "Their objective must be Bunker Hill and Breed's Hill."

"Undoubtedly," agreed Putnam. "Whoever controls those hills controls Boston. Cannon emplacements there could bombard the city and bring it to its knees." Putnam had recommended just such a tactic some time ago, but General Ward had not acted on the suggestion.

Colonel Prescott took off his black tricorn and said, "If I may be so bold, General Ward. If you will give me a thousand men to take across Charlestown Neck, sir, I'll fortify those heights and occupy them this very night. The

British will get quite a welcome if they try to take the hills!"

"I concur, General Ward," agreed Putnam.

"Very well," Ward said, looking gaunt and tired. "You will have your thousand men, Colonel Prescott. And may God be with us all!"

Roxanne was in the farmhouse cook room, helping Lottie Parsons with supper, when they heard hoofbeats in the yard outside. The women looked at each other and frowned. Lottie wiped her hands quickly on a cloth and said to Roxanne, "You go fetch Lem. I'll see who our visitor is."

Roxanne ran out the back door of the house, and as she approached the barn, she saw a musket leaning against the open door. Lemuel did his chores with the weapon close by now. He was not expecting trouble, he said whenever Lottie asked him if it was necessary, but a man was a fool not to be cautious in times like these.

Lemuel came out of the barn as Roxanne hurried up. "Someone just rode into the yard," she told him. "Lottie went to see who it is."

Lemuel snatched up the musket and said anxiously, "She shouldn't have done that. Come on!"

As she followed him, she was glad the children were inside studying the lessons Lottie had given them earlier. She hoped they stayed there.

Lemuel relaxed when he rounded the corner of the house and saw Lottie talking to a man on horseback. The visitor wore rough work clothes, similar to Lemuel's, and had a battered tricorn pushed to the back of his head. A lock of brown hair hung over his forehead.

"Howdy, Lem," he called.

"Evenin', Chris. What brings you here?"

"The British are going to attack Cambridge tomorrow."

"No!" exclaimed Lottie. "Are you sure?"

"Sure as sure can be, Lottie, and I'll be heading there first thing in the morning to join the militia."

Lemuel reached up and shook hands with Gannett. "Thanks for bringing the news, Chris."

"What about you, Lem?" the farmer asked bluntly. "Are you going to be there?"

Lemuel glanced at his wife, hesitated, then said firmly, "Ayuh. I'll be there."

Gannett grinned, waved, wheeled his horse, and rode out of the farmyard.

"Are you sure about this, Lem?" Lottie asked, breaking the tense silence.

"I don't see that I have much choice," he said, his lean face solemn. "It's my duty as a militiaman and a patriot."

"But you've already done your part! You fought at Lexington and Concord." It was the same argument she had used effectively before to keep him at home.

Roxanne understood how Lottie felt. She knew from experience what it was like to watch a loved one go off into danger, not knowing if he would return or not. She had worried about Daniel for months now.

"This war's a long way from over. I can't let the other fellows do all the fighting," Lemuel said stubbornly. "Roxanne knows what I mean, don't you?"

"Indeed I do," she replied.

"Roxanne doesn't have children who are depending on her," Lottie said sharply. Instantly she looked contrite. "I didn't mean any offense, my dear."

"I know that," Roxanne assured her. "And you're right, I don't know what it's like to leave a home and a family behind me . . . other than my parents, of course. They're still back in Boston."

"I'm sure they're probably fine," Lemuel said. "Your father's the best printer in the whole town. The blasted redcoats'll leave him alone as long as he stays neutral."

"That's a choice you and I no longer have left to us,"

Roxanne said softly.

"Aye. That's why I'll be going to Cambridge in the morning."

Lottie caught her bottom lip between her teeth but did not say anything, sensing it would not do any good to protest. Lemuel's mind was made up.

So was Roxanne's. "I'll be going with you when you leave," she said.

"What?" Lemuel and Lottie asked the question in unison.

"I'm going to Cambridge, too. Maybe Daniel is there with the militia."

Lemuel looked dubious. "That's not likely. Besides, you heard what Chris said. There's going to be fighting."

"That's why I'm going," Roxanne insisted. "There are bound to be injured men, and volunteers will be needed to tend to them."

"You've never done any nursing, Roxanne," Lottie pointed out.

"Then it's time I learned." Suddenly the anxiety was too much for her, and she paced back and forth. "Don't you see? I've been on this farm for weeks, not knowing if Daniel, Quincy, and Murdoch are alive or dead, not knowing how Elliot is, not knowing anything! I've got to become involved in this war again. You understand, don't you, Lemuel?"

"Aye, dear girl," he said quietly. "Indeed I do."

"Well, I don't," Lottie said, a faint trace of bitterness tingeing her voice. "But I know I could talk until I'm hoarse and not change the mind of either one of you! I wish this war would just go away and let us live our lives in peace!"

"It's not going to happen unless we make it happen," Lemuel told her, taking her into his arms and patting her on the back. "But I'll be safe, Lottie. You have my word on that." He looked at Roxanne. "There's not going to be any talking you out of this, is there?"

"No, I'm afraid not."

The farmer sighed. "All right. You can go with me to

Cambridge, but you'll have to ride horseback because I want to leave the wagon here for Lottie and the children."

"I've ridden a horse before," Roxanne said with a faint smile.

"What you do once we get to Cambridge is your own business. I'll be too busy to look out for you."

"I wouldn't have it any other way," Roxanne assured him.

"So it's settled." Lemuel glanced at his wife. "Isn't it, Lottie?"

She nodded sadly. "I wish it could be some other way, but I know it can't. You'll do what you have to do, Lemuel, just as all the rest of us will in these dark and bloody times."

"Aye." Lemuel hugged her tightly, then looked at Roxanne and forced a smile. "I hope you find Daniel and bring him back here when the fighting is over. He's a fine young man."

"Yes, he is," Roxanne agreed softly. But would Daniel feel the same if he found out about what had happened between Elliot and her? There would be time to worry about that, Roxanne told herself sternly, *after* the battle.

OFFICIAL PRIZE LIST

LL-SBB

GRAND PRIZE: *$25,000.00 CASH!*

FIRST PRIZE: FISHER HOME ENTERTAINMENT CENTER

Including complete integrated audio/video system with 130-watt amplifier, AM/FM stereo tuner, dual cassette deck, CD player, Surround Sound speakers and universal remote control unit.

SECOND PRIZE: TOSHIBA VCR *5 winners!*

Featuring full-function, high-quality 4-Head performance, with 8-event/365-day timer, wireless remote control, and more.

THIRD PRIZE: CONCORD 35MM CAMERA OUTFIT *35 winners!*

Featuring focus-free precision lens, built-in automatic film loading, advance and rewind.

FOURTH PRIZE: BOOK LIGHT *1,000 winners!*

A model of convenience, with a flexible neck that bends in any direction, and a steady clip that holds sure on any surface.

OFFICIAL RULES AND REGULATIONS

No purchase necessary. To enter the sweepstakes follow instructions found elsewhere in this offer. You can also enter the sweepstakes by hand printing your name, address, city, state and zip code on a 3" x 5" piece of paper and mailing it to: Winners Classic Sweepstakes, P.O. Box 785, Gibbstown, NJ 08027. Mail each entry separately. Sweepstakes begins 12/1/91. Entries must be received by 6/1/93. Some presentations of this sweepstakes may feature a deadline for the Early Bird prize. If the offer you receive does, then to be eligible for the Early Bird prize your entry must be received according to the Early Bird date specified. Not responsible for lost, damaged, misdirected, illegible or postage due mail. Mechanically reproduced entries are not eligible. All entries become property of the sponsor and will not be returned.

Prize Selection/Validations: Winners will be selected in random drawings on or about 7/30/93, by Ventura Associates, Inc., an independent judging organization whose decisions are final. Odds of winning are determined by total number of entries received. Circulation of this sweepstakes is estimated not to exceed 200 million. Entrants need not be present to win. All prizes are guaranteed to be awarded and delivered to winners. Winners will be notified by mail and may be required to complete an affidavit of eligibility and release of liability which must be returned within 14 days of date on notification or alternate winners will be selected. Any guest of a trip winner will also be required to execute a release of liability. Any prize notification letter or any prize returned to a participating sponsor, Bantam Doubleday Dell Publishing Group, Inc. its participating divisions or subsidiaries or VENTURA ASSOCIATES, INC. as undeliverable will be awarded to an alternate winner. Prizes are not transferable. No multiple prize winners except for Early Bird Prize, which may be awarded in addition to another prize. No substitution for prizes except as may be necessary due to unavailability in which case a prize of equal or greater value will be awarded. Prizes will be awarded approximately 90 days after the drawing. All taxes, automobile license and registration fees, if applicable, are the sole responsibility of the winners. Entry constitutes permission (except where prohibited) to use winners names and likenesses for publicity purposes without further or other compensation.

Participation: This sweepstakes is open to residents of the United States and Canada, except for the province of Quebec. This sweepstakes is sponsored by Bantam Doubleday Dell Publishing Group, Inc. (BDD), 666 Fifth Avenue, New York, NY 10103. Versions of this sweepstakes with different graphics will be offered in conjunction with various solicitations or promotions by different subsidiaries and divisions of BDD. Employees and their familiies of BDD, its division, subsidiaries, advertising agencies, and VENTURA ASSOCIATES, INC. are not eligible.

Canadian residents, in order to win, must first correctly answer a time limited arithmetical skill testing question. Void in Quebec and wherever prohibited or restricted by law. Subject to all federal, state, local and provincial laws and regulations.

Prizes: The following values for prizes are determined by the manufacturers' suggested retail prices or by what these items are currently known to be selling for at the time this offer was published. Approximate retail values include handling and delivery of prizes. Estimated maximum retail value of prizes: 1 Grand Prize ($27,500 if merchandise or $25,000 Cash); 1 First Prize ($3,000); 5 Second Prizes ($400 ea); 35 Third Prizes ($100 ea); 1,000 Fourth Prizes ($9.00 ea); 1 Early Bird Prize ($5,000); Total approximate maximum retail value is $50,000. Winners will have the option of selecting any prize offered at level won. Automobile winner must have a valid driver's license at the time the car is awarded. Trips are subject to space and departure availability. Certain black-out dates may apply. Travel must be completed within one year from the time the prize is awarded. Minors must be accompanied by an adult. Prizes won by minors will be awarded in the name of parent or legal guardian.

For a list of Major Prize Winners (available after 7/30/93): send a self-addressed, stamped envelope entirely separate from your entry to Winners Classic Sweepstakes Winners, P.O. Box 825, Gibbstown, NJ 08027. Requests must be received by 6/1/93. DO NOT SEND ANY OTHER CORRESPONDENCE TO THIS P.O. BOX.